HIGH CRIMES ON THE MAGICAL PLANE

A Samantha Brennan and

Annabelle Haggerty Mystery

HIGH CRIMES ON THE MAGICAL PLANE

A Samantha Brennan and

Annabelle Haggerty Mystery

Kris Neri

Red Coyote Press
Phoenix, Arizona

HIGH CRIMES ON THE MAGICAL PLANE

Copyright © by Kris Neri 2009

This novel is a work of fiction. All the characters, places and events portrayed are either fictitious or are used fictitiously.

Cover by Jack Hillman/Hillman Design Group
Cover photos: Girl in Purple Dress: © iStockphoto.com/Chris Fourie
City on Fire: © iStockphoto.com/Dane Wirtzfeld

ISBN-13: 978-0-9766733-5-4
ISBN-10: 0-9766733-5-5
Library of Congress Control Number: 2009928082

Published by
Red Coyote Press, LLC
P.O. Box 60582
Phoenix, Arizona 85082
www.redcoyotepress.com

For Sedona's readers and writers, who offered us and our bookstore,
The Well Red Coyote, the warmest of welcomes.

CHAPTER ONE
Samantha

When the clown car burst from the underground garage of the tony *Bonne Chance* tower, my only thought was whether I could scoot from its path fast enough to avoid being sent on to my Final Reckoning. I felt no inkling of the dark force that vehicle carried. Nor the hellish turn my life had already taken.

What can I say? I am not clairvoyant. Really not. I am so lacking in prescient powers that, if I were about to be hit on the head by a two-by-four, my premonition of pain wouldn't kick in until the headache wore off. Not such a startling admission perhaps—except when you take into account that I garner the lion's share of my totally inadequate income by making predictions about the future for anyone gullible enough to believe me. Consistency is overrated in my opinion.

I'd been hoofing my way up Wilshire Boulevard in the Westwood section of Los Angeles, to the poshest joint in that corridor of high-rise, high-priced dumps, where I had an appointment with an occasional client, Dodi Drake. You know Dodi, of course. She's the widow of Manfred Drake, the conservative vice president from a few administrations back. A man so inflexible that, in a poll taken during his lone term, the majority of Americans chose him as the politician most likely to be hiding a broom up his ass.

Prior to today, I'd always driven Lady Stang, my oxidized blue 1966 Mustang convertible, up to the door so the valet attendant could stow it in the building's garage. Only the last time I came, the valet informed me the *Bonne Chance's* management would rather I park it elsewhere. Okay, maybe ol' Stangie leaked more oil than the Valdez left in the Gulf of Alaska, and the cough of smoke she blew out her exhaust pipe when I gunned her did cause people for miles around to question whether a nuclear power plant had exploded. Was that any reason to turn my poor baby away? Rich folks—they just don't appreciate a classic.

Having parked blocks away, and being in lousy shape, I was

moving kinda slowly when I crossed the *Bonne Chance* driveway. And that was why the clown car nearly made me into a permanent driveway stain, which I bet they wouldn't have liked darkening their doorway any better than my car.

I leaned against a lamppost to catch my breath. And it was only then that the oddity I'd witnessed tickled my curiosity.

That was a car full of *clowns,* for chrissakes. Black SUV, the size of a moving van, to be precise. But clowns. Now I wasn't using that word as a colorful euphemism for your usual L.A. jokers—Westside lawyers, drug dealers posing as indie producers, show biz agents and such, who hurl their Mercedes sedans into traffic without regard for riff-raff like me. I'm talking actual Bozos, with painted faces, frizzy wigs and big red noses. There weren't a million of them stuffed into that land boat, circus-style, but there must have been at least four. Hard to say for sure, since the windows had been tinted pretty darkly.

That wasn't a sight you see every day, even in a city as reality-impaired as Los Angeles. I looked off in both directions for anyone I could share my observation with. Only L.A. wasn't a city of walkers, either, unless you count the getting-nowhere-but-getting-there-fast treks people take on their electric treadmills. I was the only pedestrian for as far as I could see.

So I had only myself to confer with, my favorite conversationalist anyway. Clowns...? Suddenly, that bizarre event seemed a lot more interesting. Even before my mind made a conscious link, my gaze traveled up the *Bonne Chance* tower to a floor higher than the one Dodi occupied. And I flashed on a connection.

Movie star Molly Claire, the sweet and sexy eternal ingénue, with her quirky, chopped blonde hairdo and her beguiling grin, was not only America's cinema sweetheart, she was Hollywood's biggest box office draw. Dodi told me that Molly had quietly moved into the *Bonne Chance's* penthouse after the collection of weirdos who had been stalking her were acquitted at their celebrated trial.

Around here, the whack-jobs who stalk prominent folks can usually count on a fast trip to the Big House. At their trials, it was invariably obvious to the jury that: a) the celeb was genuinely frightened, and b), the alleged stalker was not rowing with every possible oar. But Molly Claire wasn't as fortunate as most of her colleagues. Not when Eddie Plotnik, the most outspoken of the little group of nerds who idolized Molly from afar, if not far enough, made an impassioned plea at their trial. "Can't a clown gaze at a queen," he'd cried, "without meaning her harm?"

The press took to calling the four defendants "Molly's Clowns." And thanks to the nightly rerunning of Eddie's moving speech at the televised trial, the derogatory term took on noble proportions. Eddie's testimony was said to be so stirring, there wasn't a dry eye in the courtroom that day. Including those of the jury members, who let him and his cohorts go free.

Unfortunately, Molly's Clowns took their acquittal as a license to harass the object of their desire more than ever. That was said to be why, using an alias, she gave up her Beverly Hills home the Clowns had broken into on a regular basis, for the *Bonne Chance's* more secure penthouse condo.

That penthouse far up in the tower above me, I thought, as I squinted at its smoky-colored windows. The penthouse in a building that an SUV full of men dressed as actual clowns had raced away from.

As the toes of my scuffed black boots kicked my long skirt out of their way again-and-again, while I paced on the sidewalk, my mind shifted into overdrive. I never had much patience for math, but even I knew when one and one could add up to a big payoff for me. Everyone, except for the bird-brained members of that jury, knew that Molly's Clowns really were stalking her. And stalkers often escalate to more serious crimes. If those Bozos had just abducted Molly Claire, this could finally be my big break, even if it wasn't such a hot one for Ms. Claire.

I had to admit I wasn't doing well at all financially, which was really surprising when you consider all the creativity I bring to the job as my clients' spiritual advisor. And I wasn't a kid anymore. When I hit the twenty-eight and three-quarters mark, just five days back, I knew I had to get on the stick soon if I was going to make something of my life.

Maybe this was my chance. Though countless cars had driven past the building, I had to be the only person who'd seen the odd occupants of that SUV and put together what it meant. If I timed it right, I could appear to predict what had happened here before anyone else knew. If only one reporter said on the nightly news,

"Psychic Samantha Brennan is helping the authorities with the case," even I could predict that I'd be on my way to Easy Street.

Still, I'd have to be sure about this, or I'd look like a flake. More of a flake than usual, that is. And I had to be quick, before Molly's Clowns contacted the cops themselves. Prior grabs at the brass ring had taught me that a prediction after the fact serves no purpose at all.

Somehow I had to get into Molly's condo to scope out whether she was indeed gone, and if something violent had happened there. And I still had to make enough time to see Dodi, since I needed the bucks she'd throw my way today to make ends meet until my big score hit.

I gave the little drawstring purse that dangled from my wrist a shake, as I started toward the entrance to the *Bonne Chance* at a trot. I felt a grin tugging at my cheeks, the one I wear when I feel especially clever. I might not know a psychic vision from an enema, but nobody can sniff out opportunity like me. Before pushing through the smoked-glass door to the lobby, I took one last glance at the brilliant, cloudless sky above me, serene in my good fortune.

I know I said I wasn't psychic, but even I should have seen that bad moon hovering overhead.

CHAPTER TWO

Hurrying through the voluminous lobby, it occurred to me the *Bonne Chance* probably *could* look a smidge colder—but only if they hooked it up to refrigerator coils. The whole place was a study in icy grays. From the pearl gray marble floor underfoot, to the dove gray leather couches clustered about the lobby, to the charcoal granite check-in desk—the impression greeting a guest was as steely as armor. Even the chick behind the front desk, whose mouse-brown hair was as sleek and straight as chain mail, wore a gray shantung silk jacket, on which the words *Bonne Chance* had been discreetly stitched over the breast pocket.

Bonne Chance. Good luck, right? They obviously meant the inhabitants of those pricey digs had it. Weren't they afraid they were tempting fate, throwing those words around? Like maybe Someone, Somewhere, would decide they'd had enough good fortune for one lifetime?

Not that I believed in fate. That was just a word I fed to the suckers who paid me to tell them what hadn't happened yet, but would, now that I gave them directions. A circular trap for the credulous. It was just that, sometimes, life would hurl something at me with all the force of that clown car. By the time I diverted it, I found myself in a different place from where I expected to be, and I wondered...

But, as you've probably noticed, I digress.

The check-in chick was new. Ooh! Not good news. I had counted on finding my friend, Doreen, behind that desk, and making her the centerpiece of my little scam. Doreen wasn't the brightest bulb in the marquee, so she was easy to lead astray. Probably why they fired her in favor of someone with all the warmth of canned tuna. As if this chick's pale lips weren't thin enough, she sucked at them until they disappeared into her face. She also blinked her small murky eyes about twice as often as normal. Creepy. Now how was I going to pull this off?

I'd have predicted that nothing would faze this babe, making her a perfect choice for the gatekeeper role in this palace. She fooled me, though. When I swept up to the check-in desk, her narrow eyes widened to the size of golf balls, and they stopped blinking.

Who could blame her? The shiny surface of the soot-colored granite slab, attached to the wall behind her, mirrored my appearance right back to me. Man, what a sight I was! Long blonde hair curling wildly in every direction, crowned with a wreath of battered silk flowers held together with Christmas tree garland. Makeup by Crayola. And that dress I wore—half Renaissance ball gown in bright blue satin and lace, half soothsayer garb with its filmy organdy layers, half jester suit. Too many halves, I know, but it was quite a dress.

I marched right up to the desk and, with a confident air, proclaimed, "Madame Samantha Brennan for Dodi Drake."

Then the floodgates opened and all the eyelid blinking she'd held back when her eyes bulged, rushed out at once. I wondered if she could see through all that eyelid flickering, or was it like the ineffectual sweep of windshield wipers during a downpour? I took another gander at my reflection on the granite. Maybe she didn't *want* to see.

"*You* want to visit Dodi Drake?" she asked through the blinks.

No, what I wanted was to check out Molly Claire's place, but I could hardly say that. My client, Dodi, was my only way past this babe. But I didn't care for the way she emphasized *you*. Like my seeing Dodi was the craziest idea in the world.

"Mrs. Drake has requested an appointment with *me*," I said. "And she won't be happy if you hold me up. If you don't believe me, call upstairs to check."

She would have anyway; announcing guests was her job. I thought that by suggesting it, I showed how honest I was. I spent nearly as much of my time finding ways to act like I had nothing to hide, as I did hiding things.

Fun as it was, today I had no time for this dance. I had to get up there now.

She took her time finding Dodi's extension and tapping it in to her computer-phone. While she waited for an answer, she eyed me through those fluttering lashes, as if I were some unknown creature. Hadn't she ever seen a psychic before? Did she think they dressed just like everyone else?

When someone answered and apparently gave her the go-ahead to send me up, she sputtered, "You're sure? Blonde...hair? Samantha Brennan? *Madame?*" The sarcasm she poured into that word could fill the Coliseum.

I smiled broadly when she hung up. "Told you to hurry it up, didn't she?"

Her lack of response was answer enough.

She pulled a guest electronic keycard from the slot behind the desk, as those check-in gals always did. But then Ms. Blinks surprised me. With another series of glances my way, ranging from speculation to disapproval, she popped a small gray-and-black sign on the desk, which advised visitors that she'd return in five minutes.

"Come on," she said with a smug set to her thin lips. "I'll take you up there."

So she didn't trust me, huh? Wise move, considering. I glanced away, seemingly unconcerned, even if I was about to bust a gut. But not before I saw her slip the guest card into her jacket pocket. Yes! Trust me or not, this babe was going to provide what I needed.

Security in the *Bonne Chance* was as tight as last year's jeans. The elevators required keycards to operate, and the residents' cards were programmed with just the communal floors, like the ones where the gym and the screening rooms were located, and the floors of their individual condos. But there was a flaw in the system. I'd learned from Doreen that the guest cards could access all the floors, and even all the units themselves, something the management didn't want anyone to know.

Miss Prim and I rode the elevator to Dodi's twelfth floor condo in silence. But when the doors opened, and she stepped from the car, I pretended to trip. Not too suspicious, considering my gown dragged on the floor. I grabbed onto her as if to keep myself from falling. And while she helped me to regain my footing before the elevator doors closed on me, I palmed the guest keycard she'd put into her blazer pocket and slipped it into the blue drawstring bag that dangled from my wrist.

Sometimes it's just too easy.

But it's never fast enough, dammit. She dawdled her way

down the hall ahead of me toward Dodi's corner unit, with as little regard for time as I usually displayed.

Dodi didn't live in L.A. most of the time. She was from Minnesota or Michigan—one of those M-states, or maybe it was an N. I could never keep track of them all. She kept what she called a *pied-a-terre* here for whenever she came to town for meetings related to the biopic some cable TV network was making of her life.

I had to admit Dodi was a cut—or twenty—above my usual client. Who was I kidding? Before she became my client, I had never crossed the threshold of a joint like the *Bonne Chance*. But when she came to town, Dodi always had her hair done by Ramon at the Tousled Salon in Beverly Hills. Ramon and I had had something going, or so I thought—until the bastard robbed the eight hundred bucks I was saving for a move to Sedona, so he could pay for the headshots his new actress girlfriend wanted. I'd hounded Ramon relentlessly for the money he stole, even threatening to stand outside the salon telling all his customers that he secretly used drugstore shampoo on them, until he agreed to repay me with this referral.

I still hadn't made up the eight hundred smackers, though, so I was no closer to making my move to Sedona. Sedona, now there's a town where they appreciate psychics like me. Unlike Southern California, where the cynicism wafts off people like that wavy gas that rises from asphalt in the summer. And, no, I didn't mean fake psychics. Trust me on this, all psychics are fake. If I believed that any of the crap I tossed around could really exist, it would turn my entire universe on its ear.

The chick from the lobby deposited me outside Dodi's door, where one of the Secret Service agents assigned to her detail, Gus Nagy, stood at attention. Law-enforcement types and I rarely see eye-to-eye, since they invariably find some point to those corners I always cut. But Gus was one I could tolerate, since he possessed a modicum of a sense of humor, not to mention being kinda cute in the overly buff way I like.

I knew there were other Secret Service agents on Dodi's detail. And occasionally I caught sight of servants or a secretary. But mostly she kept me away from her entourage, apart from the one agent who vetted all her callers. You'd almost think she was ashamed of me. Weird, huh?

"*This* is the woman you meant for me to send up?" the

blinker asked, her voice reeking of disapproval.

With the slightest of winks at me, Gus said, "That's the one. Madame Samantha is Mrs. Drake's psychic." He threw another glance my way. "And even a Celtic Goddess, I believe."

Yeah, I was adding the goddess-bit to my repertoire now. As intense as the competition is among spiritual advisors, you gotta be kicking it up all the time. And who better than me to claim that distinction? I was four-fifths Irish, or something like that. Besides, I'd flunked every test they gave us on Greek and Roman Gods when I was a kid, but I'd read an article about Celtic mythology a few months back and a few of those facts had stuck.

Ms. Blinks sniffed. "A Goddess, huh? Calling yourself a psychic wasn't ridiculous enough?"

I wrinkled my nose at her, as if she'd farted in a confined space.

She threw her palm out before me. "Why don't you tell me what the future holds for me?"

As if that was how I did my readings. Still, I took hold of her dry palm and said, "You've already suffered a great loss, you just don't know it yet." I meant the keycard I stole, of course. "The *Bonne Chance* will also prove to be a less than congenial place of employment for you, so I suggest you look for another job." Soon, before they figured out I swiped the card. I tossed her hand away.

Without a word, but no less than a dozen blinks, she turned and headed back down the hall, her straight, mousy hair swinging as she shook her head in disbelief.

Gus bent his thick neck my way. "Things might go easier for you, Samantha, if you dressed a bit more conventionally."

"Gus, without the gown, no one would take me seriously," I insisted. "Don't announce me yet, huh? There's something I gotta do before I see Dodi."

With a sigh, he said, "She's in a hurry today, Samantha."

"Five minutes, I swear, that's all I need."

Despite my begging, Gus just kept shaking his closely shorn head. "We've learned how little time means to you, Samantha. You ought to consider wearing a watch."

Wear a watch, lose the gown—like anyone would trust a spiritual advisor who looked like that.

"Samantha, you really don't want to make her mad," Gus

said with rare candor.

Right. Dodi's underlying nastiness was as legendary as her superficial charm. Gus swung Dodi's oak door open for me. With the weight of time pressing on my shoulders, I trudged through.

Given Manfred Drake's status as the most tight-assed of recent veeps, it wasn't surprising that Dodi ranked among the most conventional of political wives. Throughout her husband's career, she had always looked the same: a slim woman, though not so well-endowed as to stop traffic, who wore dowdy knit suits in muted tones. Her only flamboyant touch was the discreet blonde highlighting that brightened her ash brown hair.

She still wore those unfashionable suits, and hid whatever private thoughts she might have behind correct, if vapid, smiles. But her life had undergone a few changes since the old man kicked it. The blonde streaks had given way to—purple. No kidding. Bright, screaming, neon purple streaks on the head of that otherwise totally predictable woman.

She might have also had a few nips-and-tucks done, since Dodi looked way too young for the years she spent on the campaign trail. Younger even than my mom, who was such a girlish fifty, she often claimed we were sisters. But my mom was another story. If not a full book.

Since I didn't see Dodi often, those purple streaks always gave me a jolt. I kept telling myself that I should applaud her for kicking over the traces. Yet that color still looked so jarring—when compared to the rest of her, I mean. That was my only problem with the purple streaks, I swear. It had nothing to do with the fact that people keep making it harder for me to stand out.

Gus handed me off to Dodi in the condo entry, and she led me in. The place was as conventionally appointed as Dodi herself. More, even, since nothing there was purple. And though the condo wasn't small, it appeared so, since she'd crammed it with furnishings and knick-knacks. Every time Dodi returned from her permanent home, she brought more memorabilia associated with Fred-Man, as I thought of Manfred, the departed V.P.

When I sank into the beige-on-cream striped satin sofa, I noticed a new picture of Dodi's hubby as a young man had been added to the crowded mantle. On this photo, Manfred had inscribed,

"To Snooks, from her Man." I nearly hurled right there.

Dodi pressed herself next to me on the couch. "So, Madame Samantha, what do you and your fellow gods hold for me now? Is Manny still...okay with things?" Dodi lowered her eyes.

There was one other tiny addition to Dodi's life since Fred-Man departed. Or maybe not so tiny. Jason. He was a young guy of twenty-five or so, whom Dodi alternatively introduced as either her assistant or her protégé. Both terms were accurate—as long as you spelled them b-o-y-t-o-y. That's right. Conventional, correct Dodi Drake was getting it on with a hunky kid. Maybe that explained the particularly vapid nature of her smile these days. Yet she worried that her late husband might disapprove.

Usually I made a real production of going into my trance. Today I reminded myself: Molly Claire, clowns. And then that trance came on real quick.

"Manfred is happy for you, Mrs. Drake. Happy that you're happy." Get it—he's happy; how many more ways could I say it?

"You're sure?" she asked.

Through the crack in my closed eyes, I looked at the photo she'd added to the mantle. "Mrs. Drake, he's saying, 'Snooks, your Man is glad that you have the boy looking out for you.'" See, observance was just one of the skills demanded in my job. And people say I don't earn my dough—no one was more observant than me.

Dodi flushed. "Snooks? Why he hasn't called me that since before his first mistress."

That was why I failed to understand Dodi's reluctance over Jason. He might have been a stiff old fart, but ol' Fred-Man had swung a wild sword in his time. And it had all been his time.

To my surprise, Dodi always seemed disappointed by the message I conveyed, that he didn't judge her harshly. Maybe she just couldn't overcome her guilt.

Since Dodi was pressed for time, and I sure was, I popped right out of my trance. While Dodi went to the antique mahogany desk in the corner for the envelope she always had ready for me, I walked to the window. Instead of looking at the commanding view of the city, I directed my gaze down at the street below.

"Mrs. Drake, is Molly Claire still living here?" I asked, oh-so casually.

"As far as I know."

"How 'bout Molly's Clowns. Ever spot those guys hanging around?"

"Several times. And I'm not here often, you know. They're still obsessed with that poor woman." Dodi handed me the ivory envelope.

"Ever see them dressed as...you know, real clowns?"

Despite the political-wife mask she wore, spite surfaced in her sharp blue eyes. "That was just an expression, dear. No one meant those men stalking Ms. Claire actually dressed like clowns."

Really? Maybe next time I came, she could teach me to suck eggs.

We set an appointment for two days later, when I could deliver the same message at greater length. Then I made my escape. Once out in the hall, I lifted my skirt and raced to the elevator.

While waiting for the car to arrive, I looked into the envelope and counted the stack of bills. It was always the same, dammit. Exactly what I'd asked her for the first time I came. It was a hefty amount, too, since I knew she could afford it. But no tip. I'd heard women in her bracket often tip their psychics. What was I doing wrong?

When the elevator finally arrived. I jumped in and fished the purloined keycard from my drawstring bag. The card worked as well as I expected when it whisked me up to the thirtieth floor. The doors opened to reveal the oak entry of Molly Claire's penthouse condo, the only unit on the floor, dead ahead.

The real test would be whether I had the balls to use the key to open those doors. I mean, Molly Claire was a prominent, powerful person. And I was proposing to break into the place she moved into so she could feel more secure. If those clowns had come just for some kiddy party, I was gonna be wading hip-deep in dog doo.

With a shrug I stepped from the elevator. *In for a penny*—the story of my life.

I slipped the keycard into the small brass slot in the door, and when I heard the click, I opened it just a few inches.

"Yoo-hoo, Miss Claire. Anybody home?" I called. Real friendly-like.

When no one yelled back, or stuck a shotgun in my face, I slipped inside and took a gander around the sprawling living room.

The décor of the place proved that even someone with Molly Claire's bucks could get taken by a decorator. I wasn't sure how you would describe the style. Asian maybe, or African. The plush black velvet couch, which rested low on the floor, looked like a barge the slaves might carry to the Nile.

It was probably a good thing then that someone had totally trashed the place. Most of the furniture had been overturned, and a small glass-and-brass table was smashed. Excuse me, that was glass-and-*gold*. How do you get to be that rich? But the table was still shattered.

Yes, I was right. There had been a struggle here. And Molly Claire, who never left her home, was missing. Even more telling was the sight of red acrylic fingernails that had been broken from someone's hand and tossed on the plush rug, and the spray of blood on the white wall.

Blood? Was she...dead? My gaze traveled slowly around the wrecked room. I also spotted a small bloodstain soaking the white carpet outside a closet off the living room.

I galloped to the closet and yanked the door open. A man in work clothes, still clutching a hammer in his tightened fist, tumbled to the floor before my feet, dead as a doornail. Someone had made him that way by leaving a small bullet hole roughly in the center of his forehead.

I think I might have shrieked at that point. And started thinking crazy thoughts, like if he had to be dead, how doornail-dead was the way to do it, considering his job.

Suddenly the idea of my big score drifted away, replaced by a vision of steel bars before my face. What had I gotten myself into? Consequence isn't a concept I normally take too seriously. Knowing I can pretty much talk my way out of anything, I don't bother to check to see if the pool is filled with water before diving in. But I'm also good at getting myself *into* trouble. If the cops walked in right now, they'd find I'd broken into this place and was now cozying up to a carpenter who was rapidly becoming as stiff as a piece of his own lumber.

I took a deep breath. This was no time to panic. I could still pull it off if I hurried. My prediction might be even better now.

I looked at the carpenter and felt guilty about my self-serving attitude. Poor slob. He had probably been trying to protect Molly

13

when her Clowns popped him. Chivalry was now officially dead. I thought about poor Molly, too, and what she might be enduring. But no one was better than me at rationalization. I convinced myself that as soon as I predicted Molly's dire situation, the sooner someone could rescue her.

Though it was icky to touch him, I put the workman back into the closet so he could be found where they had stuffed him. I whispered, "I'll send help." Just not right away.

Then, using my skirt, I wiped any place I had touched, and I hightailed it out of there. I took the elevator down to the garage this time, so I didn't have to pass Miss Prim in the lobby. And I sprinted all the way to the street.

As I trudged back to Lady Stang, I found myself thinking about the carpenter. Had he just been in the wrong place at the wrong time? Or was it possible that his death on this day really was his destiny? If so, had he just passed that destiny off onto me?

No! I thought, shaking my shirt for emphasis. This baby charters her own fate. And as I stepped up my pace, I figured, I was going out to meet it.

Nothing, I felt sure, from this point on, could possibly go wrong.

CHAPTER THREE

I had raced through Dodi's reading, scoped out Molly's pad in record time, considering my little tête-à-tête with the carpenter, and forced Stangie to break the land speed record in the short distance between her parking spot and the Federal Building on Wilshire—only to find myself cooling my heels in some waiting room at the FBI Field Office, which is where I decided to spin my tale, instead of the local cop shop.

Worse yet was the company I found myself keeping. On one side of me sat a man who had covered his balding pate with some well-used aluminum foil—so he could receive transmissions from Saturn directly into his brain, he bragged. While the guy on the other side, surely a first runner-up in the Charles Manson look-alike contest, had a fake knife sticking out from his chest, and on his shirt, a trail of what seemed like cherry Jell-O. Nutjobs were always trying to help the cops and fibbies, but why had I been lumped with them?

I tell you, if I weren't staring down the barrel of adulthood, at twenty-eight and three-quarters, I might question the direction of my life.

I had to admit I had no one but myself to blame for the company. Logic just isn't my strong suite. I was always zipping so fast from A-to-Z that I often failed to connect some of those letters in between. Until one of those forgotten letters rose up and bit me in the ass. I'd counted on using my connection to Dodi to grease my way to someone high up in this outfit—that's why I came down on the side of the feds, instead of the local cops. Now I realized if I wanted them to buy my act, I had to hope my association with Dodi never surfaced. Nobody was going to believe my psychic vision if they knew I had scammed my way into Molly's lair to see it for real. I had no choice but to make my approach with the rest of the nuts.

Making me more nervous still was the fact that everyone there kept racing around like a swarm of ants on a sugar cube. Had they learned about Molly? Was that the cause of the furor? I stopped a clerk and asked.

15

"We're all busy with the exhibit, of course," the stout clerk snapped, as if the cause of that furor should have been apparent even to an idiot like me. *"The Power of the Pyramid* show, you know? We're charged with doing the background checks on the foreign dignitaries who'll be attending."

I should have felt better when the woman brushed past me, since I had now confirmed the cause of the bustle in the fibbie hive had nothing to do with the scoop I held in my hot little head. With the opening of *The Power of the Pyramid* show little more than a week away, naturally, the exhibit would be creating lots of work for them. Some diplomatic soul had convinced all the nations of the world that held ancient Egyptian treasures to pool them into one show that would tour the great museums around the globe. And it would debut at our new Museum of the Antiquities, which recently opened in the mid-Wilshire area of L.A.

I should have felt better, but strangely, I didn't. As time passed, I began to feel guilty about whatever Molly Claire must be suffering at that moment. How could I sit there waiting to spin this tale out for my own benefit, wasting time Molly might not have? What kind of person does that?

Obviously, one who needed to get clear on precisely how much conscience she could afford to be burdened with in her line of work. Yet I couldn't stop thoughts of Molly and the carpenter from whirling around in my head until I thought I would scream out what I knew to the next person I saw.

As luck would have it, that was precisely when the FBI finally decided to recognize the existence of the flakes filling their waiting room, so I was able to avoid the good-citizen bit and stick to my plan.

Taken together, the two agents who came to clear us proved the FBI attracted a wider range of personalities than I would have suspected. The unsmiling, twenty-something woman, with her copper-colored hair pulled back into a severe knot and her steel gray skirt suit, was strictly standard-issue stuff. She'd present a challenge, but at least I had her pegged from the get-go.

The man, on the other hand, broke the mold. He was a short guy in his fifties, as wide as he was tall, in a battered brown suit that looked like it came from a Goodwill thrift shop. With a head as round as a bowling ball, an impression he'd reinforced by sticking three bands of graying clumps across his scalp with hair goo, he looked like he should be sitting with us flakes, not vetting us.

They just stood there, eyeballing the three of us. The guy at least offered us weirdos a smile. His sparkly little raisin eyes beamed out good cheer from within folds of flesh. He didn't mean it, of course, but he was trying to make nice. Predictably, the deep blue eyes that peered from below the woman's thick dark lashes didn't hide a bit of her contempt for us loonies.

They were clearly dividing us up. I concentrated really hard and sent the man a silent message to pick me. Okay, I'll admit it—I carried a few more pounds than I needed to. Who was I kidding? I had long ago raised the white flag in my battle of the bulge. You see, in my work, I have to eat on the run. Of course, I didn't have to eat and eat and eat while running. Still, even though squeezing myself into junior sizes had now become nothing more than a test of will, I could always count on my bod having a favorable effect on men. It was my big rack that did it. Besides, as fat as this guy was himself, he'd probably consider me as skinny as a stick. I knew I had a better chance of selling my story to him.

Pick me, pick me, I said mentally to him again and again.

The woman pointed in my direction and said, "I'll take her, Billy. You get rid of the others."

"You got it, kiddo," Agent Billy cheerfully agreed.

So much for ESP. I clutched my skirt in my fists and followed along behind her. She led me to a tiny windowless office, which scarcely had enough room for the desk, guest chair and file cabinet that filled it to overflowing. The stark little space was totally devoid of personal touches. No photos of the hubby, the kids or the dog. No faded little drink umbrella saved from the Hawaiian getaway. No champagne corks from celebrating cases she'd broken. Zilch. How was I going to get a read on this chick if she refused to display anything in her office that revealed something about her character? Well, nothing but a small silver bowl filled with such vibrant-looking Red Delicious apples they seemed to throb with vitality. What significance could apples have?

The nameplate on the front of her faux-walnut desk identified her as Special Agent Annabelle Haggerty. She seemed like a new fibbie, close to my own twenty-eight and three-quarters in age. Not good for my purposes. That meant she wasn't anywhere near the inner-circle there, so she wasn't in a position to offer me much help. Even worse, she wore her skepticism like armor.

Despite the severity of her look, she was really quite attractive. Her jaw was a little too firm, but she had great cheekbones and beautifully translucent skin. Way skinnier than me, too. But there couldn't be much joy in her regimented existence, nor any secrets buried beneath her steel-suited exterior. To think, only moments before I'd questioned the wisdom of my chosen path. Now, the mere idea of living a life anything like this woman's gave me the creeps. Besides, what would I do with myself if I weren't a fake psychic and scam deity?

Special Agent Haggerty sent a scowl my way. "I don't recognize your getup, so maybe you better tell me what you are. And make it good—I haven't had many laughs lately."

I gave her my name. Then, with a flip of my lilac organdy shawl, which sent my drawstring bag swinging, I said, "I'm a direct descendant of the ancient Celtic goddess, Abnoba, the goddess of the hunt. She defied her parents and married the mortal, Froach. Though I'm part human, I retain all of my heavenly powers."

Haggerty's full lips twitched with amusement. "You don't say? Funny, I seem to remember from my college mythology course that it was the goddess, Findabar, who married the mortal, Froach. But who's keeping score?"

Obviously, she was. No matter how I tried, I couldn't keep that goddess crap straight. Just my luck to run into the one person who could.

"I'm so many generations removed, I get confused," I explained, before going into my usual patter. "Gods and goddesses do walk among us, you know. They take human form as camouflage." Pure bunk, of course, but I had to insist on that. How else could I explain this goddess scam?

"Do they now?" Her blue eyes bore into me. "What do you want with us, Your Worship?"

"I had a vision this morning," I said. And I swayed a bit to emphasize it.

Haggerty tented her fingers and pressed them to her nose, obscuring her face, but not so much that I couldn't read her cynical sneer. Let's face it—on some level, we were the same, both too real world for this hocus-pocus, even if I had to hide my take on it.

I drew my slouching spine up and said with as much dignity as I could muster while wearing that dress, "In my vision, I saw actress Molly Claire taken by force by the men described as Molly's Clowns, who were dressed as—well, clowns."

Haggerty's face went pale and the tented fingers fell away. "Clowns? You saw actual clowns?"

Why? Did Agent Haggerty know something about that? No, how could she?

"It might just have been their metaphysical personae," I said with great solemnity. Huh? What the hell did that mean? I remembered the carpenter. "And there was someone else involved." I squinted into the distance. "I'm seeing a man in work clothes, and I sense his time in our realm is limited. Now I don't know when this will happen, but I swear to you—"

"Shut up a minute, will you?" Haggerty snapped. She rubbed her temples briefly with her fingertips. Though her fair skin looked pasty, tension had tightened her full lips so much, they seemed a match for the thin lips of that door-dragon at the *Bonne Chance*. "Let's cut to the chase," she said at last. "You're a total fraud, right?"

I can't explain what came over me then. Rather than deny it, I flashed her a conspiratorial smile. And I pressed my finger to my lips and said, "Shush."

Was I shooting myself in the head? To my surprise, Haggerty just sent a speculative look my way.

Then at last she said, "Get out."

So much for my ability to read people. I thought I was winning her over.

"To the reception room," she added with an impatient sigh. "Stay there until I check something out, okay?"

Confused, I merely nodded. I returned to the waiting area, where I sat alone now, since the other flakes must still have been with Agent Billy. Five minutes, ten. What was she doing? Usually when non-believers want to throw me out, they don't make such a production of it.

When I was about to leave on my own, Haggerty emerged from her office. She had put a taupe trench coat on over her suit. She gestured toward the door. Unsure of what that meant, I just stood there.

"Come on, Madame Samantha, you're coming with me,"

Haggerty said.

"Where?" I asked, without moving.

Haggerty took hold of my wrist and squeezed so hard, my head ached. She gave me a tug.

"To see if your future and mine are going to overlap."

As if that could happen.

Haggerty led me to a black Ford Taurus parked in the staff area of the Federal Building lot. Bureau-issued, I discovered, when I saw the Taurus had been outfitted with one of those police radios in the dash, rather than the cool CD changer I had been hoping to play with. Agent Haggerty didn't speak at all during our drive. We didn't drive far—just back to the *Bonne Chance*. That meant, when she kicked me out of her office, she checked with someone, probably the LAPD. It also meant whatever happened in Molly's condo had already been discovered. Another great coup bit the dust.

Any doubts I might have had of that were erased when I saw the crowd at the base of the *Bonne Chance* tower. The building's circular drive had been commandeered by the cops, as had two lanes of Wilshire. Haggerty pulled her car behind a crime scene van. Before stepping out, she yanked a placard from behind her seat, which identified the car as belonging to the Bureau, and popped it onto the dashboard. With a jerk of her head, she indicated that I should follow her.

Haggerty flashed her ID for the rookie cop guarding the yellow crime scene tape stretched across the driveway.

"So I was right," I said, ducking under the tape.

She just gave me a look that ended in an incredulous quivering of her head. Before she turned away, I saw that her features were rigid with anxiety. I was the one whose schedule was being held up. What did she have to worry about?

She led me through the lobby, flashing her ID at the various points. Nervous, nosy residents filled the place, but they were being kept off to the side in edgy little clusters. I feared the front desk chick would scream, "There she is!" when I passed through, but it was so packed with people that I didn't even see her.

One of the cops on crowd control escorted us into the elevator and whisked us up to the penthouse. When the doors opened, facing us was a gurney being pushed by a crew from the Medical

Examiner's office. On it rested a black body bag. While I couldn't afford to show any sign that I'd been there before, I gave the poor carpenter a tip of my head as he moved past.

Strangely enough, Haggerty also acknowledged him, in a way. She hesitated beside the gurney. As if she were taking note of it, though she never looked that way. She also allowed her fingertips to brush the surface of the bag covering the carpenter's remains. Ever-so casually, like it was an accident. Who accidentally touches a dead guy? I only alluded to the carpenter when I told her about Molly; I never mentioned him directly. Yet I got the craziest sense that she was confirming something she already knew. Was I the *second* person to report on Molly? How else could Haggerty have known?

Our escort introduced Haggerty to the man in charge, Detective Jake Azar. Everyone ignored me, as if I were just Haggerty's appendage, like her purse or something, only less valuable.

"Great," Jake said. "My first day in Homicide, and I not only catch a messy, high-profile murder, now I have to investigate it with a fed looking over my shoulder."

Haggerty assured him she was only there to check on something peripheral to his case. I noticed her fair cheeks flushed when she spoke, like Jake might have pushed her buttons.

I guess he was kinda cute, in a soldier of fortune-sorta way. Both dashing and dissolute. Not my type, though. He was a smallish, wiry man, with swarthy skin and a craggy nose, who radiated tremendous intensity. He had a thick shock of dark brown hair, which, while unusually shiny, seemed to grow in little cowlicks that made him look like he had permanent pillow hair. Then again, given his five o'clock shadow, his worn boots and jeans, and his scuffed black leather jacket, all of which appeared to have been slept-in, maybe he had just woken up.

The penthouse looked pretty much as it had when I saw it last, minus the carpenter, and plus a whole lotta cops. Same Lady of the East furnishings, tossed every which way. For the first time, I took a look at the stuff hanging on the walls. Strictly Ego Central. Larger-than life photos covered every surface. Glamour shots of Molly fought for space with behind-the-scenes candid pics.

My gaze landed on one shot showing Molly clowning around with what I gathered was her stand-in, since their respective canvas director chairs were labeled *star* and *stand-in*. I realized stand-ins were chosen for the physical similarity to the stars they represented, but this chick was bucking for clone. She and Molly shared the same small builds and sculpted arms, as well as identical choppy blonde haircuts. Hell, even the bright white teeth in the stand-in's big smile looked so much like Molly's, I figured they'd had their veneers done by the same dentist.

How could I have missed all those pictures? They were so big, so overbearing, my retinas practically burned with the sight of them now. Just shows what a strong sense of purpose—and a dead carpenter—will do to your focus.

Haggerty had apparently assuaged the detective, because she finally got around to introducing me.

"Psychic, huh? You believe in that stuff, Agent Haggerty?" He took me in, from my boots to my wild hair, with one dismissive sweep of his dark eyes. "Wouldn't you think a goddess would be in better shape?"

"We don't have that much room for working out on Valhalla," I said with a defensive sniff.

"Tir na n'Og," Haggerty murmured. "Celtic gods go to *Tir na n'Og."*

Her superior knowledge was starting to piss me off.

Haggerty gave me a nudge. "Why don't you tell Detective Azar what you told me, Samantha?"

She said that with a straight face yet. Since I had more-or-less admitted I was a con, why was she still playing the game? Did she think she could embarrass me? Hah! She should know I have the hide of a rhino.

Still, I repeated my tale of Molly's abduction for the detective.

When he again directed his black eyes my way, they weren't quite so dismissive. "Abducted, huh? That's the first we've heard about that."

"So what do you think happened here?" I asked. "That Molly Claire wrecked her own place and killed some guy who was working for her, and put him—" I broke off abruptly. I'd almost added the dead guy had been stuffed into the closet, till I remembered I wasn't supposed to know that. Someday my lack of impulse control will be the death of me.

With a shrug, the detective said, "Coulda happened that way. All we know is she told her assistant to meet her here, and when he showed up, he found Molly gone and the place looking like this. You know anything else, Madame Samantha, you might want to tell us now."

"What do you say, Samantha?" Haggerty threw her arm across my shoulder, in a surprising show of familiarity. "Any more visions? Are you getting any feelings now?"

Yeah, one feeling—that I wanted outta there. Normally, I can spin out that goddess-speak without plugging my brain in. Yet something happened to me now. A thick gray sludge came to cover my mind's eye, which nothing seemed to penetrate.

Until some unexpected words floated in. "Check the answering machine," I blurted out. I felt as if someone else had spoken through me.

He called to his men. "Anyone see an answering machine?"

"No, but look at this, Jake," a younger detective, with a shiny shaved head, said. He pointed to where a telephone had fallen on the floor beneath an upset end table. "She had voice mail on speed dial."

Jake crouched before the phone. He put the phone on speaker and hit the speed dial button. After a few rings, Molly Claire's voice mail came on and indicated she had one new message, which had come in right after I'd left there. Jake hit a button to play the message.

A mechanical voice said, "We have Molly. Don't try to find us. She is ours now." The remarks were followed by hysterical canned laughter.

When the voice mail menu voice came on with instructions for saving or deleting the message, Jake saved it. Then he ordered the bald egghead to get a copy from the phone company. Jake seemed awfully subdued now. So did Haggerty. The law enforcement types couldn't seem to handle this. My guess was that hostages were always taken for a reason—for ransom, to serve as cover. They weren't taken just to keep, like something you store on a bookshelf.

After a moment, from where he still crouched before the phone, Jake looked up at me. "How'd you know that? Lucky guess, huh?"

Sure, that was what it had to be, right? *Wrong*. I had known what that message would be like before it played. I'd sensed the voice would be tinny-sounding. And I knew the caller would claim ownership of Molly. No joke, I swear. No bragging, either. Despite the bilge I feed my clients, I never wanted knowledge of the future. I liked being surprised by life.

For the first time in my cynical little existence, I was scared out of my wits. I fervently wished I had never broken into that joint, never met any of those people. But mostly I wished I could shake the uneasy sense that my life had already taken a detour from which I'd never return.

CHAPTER FOUR
Haggerty

For Special Agent Annabelle Haggerty, the hours since the discovery of Molly Claire's bizarre abduction were a nightmare, and they crawled past at an agonizing pace. Finally, desperate for a break, she seized at the pretext of checking on their material witness, Samantha Brennan. Haggerty needed to escape from her boss's marathon brainstorming session into the quiet of her office. Once she slipped behind her desk, she closed her eyes and massaged her temples with her fingertips.

She'd awoken that morning with a raging headache—and that was before Samantha steam-rolled into her life. While Haggerty suspected Samantha of scattering headaches wherever she went, she couldn't blame this one on the flaky girl. Haggerty knew what it meant when this particular pain struck behind her eyes. And because of that, she had to keep Samantha close at hand. No matter how much it irked her personally.

And it did irk her. She resented people like Samantha, who floated through life without a care, except for how they could turn someone else's misfortune to their own advantage. By skirting the forces of darkness, and disguising them with her charm, the pseudo-goddess made that murky world more acceptable to those with shaky judgment. That made the battle to which Haggerty had devoted her life so much harder.

That was one reason why she couldn't stand Samantha. That and—a quiet little voice deep inside of her admitted—that she envied Samantha the unburdened ease with which she could live her life.

With a sigh, Haggerty held her throbbing head in her hands. What an ungrateful woman she was. With all the gifts bestowed on her, how could she envy anyone's life? It was just that sometimes the responsibilities that came with those gifts weighed so heavily on her. Responsibilities that someone like Samantha never had to face.

Haggerty reminded herself it wouldn't do to let her resentment of Samantha get out of control. She needed the girl, for a variety of reasons. For one thing, it was Samantha who brought the case to the Bureau.

Haggerty had been honest with Detective Azar when she burst into his crime scene. She had a reason for checking out Samantha's story, but she wasn't there to horn in on his case. Once it became clear that Molly Claire had been abducted, the crime became more the province of the FBI than the LAPD. After a flurry of calls to their respective superiors, a joint agency taskforce had been formed, to which both of them were assigned.

Haggerty thought the LAPD would have put up more of a jurisdictional struggle, except work on the opening of *The Power of the Pyramid* exhibit had left both teams too strapped not to join forces. Everyone in the L.A. Field Office of the FBI was working overtime clearing dignitaries for the opening, and the LAPD was stretched to its limit over the security plans.

Samantha had been declared a material witness, so her dubious services were available to them as well. Ironically, Samantha alone took her designation seriously, actually trying to solve the case herself. Haggerty remembered what happened in the car.

Driving back to the Federal Building in Haggerty's Bureau vehicle, Haggerty and Jake tested boundaries and chatted about their regular functions. Coincidentally, both were experienced in gang-related activities. Haggerty normally served on a team working to bring RICO charges against some of the area's more powerful gangs; she had only been assigned to the Molly Claire taskforce because she'd brought the case in. Jake, before his recent promotion to Homicide, had been assigned to the LAPD gang-detail, working one-on-one with gang-members on the street. He claimed to have a good record for getting those kids off the streets and into jobs.

"I've had some successes," Jake said. "I got one kid a good job as a records clerk in the office of some dentist to the stars in Beverly Hills." He shook his head. "But for every success, there are countless failures. Some of these kids, if you let 'em, they'll break your heart."

Haggerty nodded knowingly. "I don't work with them in that way. I try to put their leaders away. But my boss does volunteer work with at-risk kids. He says the same thing."

"First homicide I've worked since I got bumped from the

gang unit," Jake had said, "and it's gotta be such a high-profile case. Just my luck to catch something like this." With a sigh, he ran his hand through his thick dark hair.

"Me too," Haggerty had commiserated. Only she meant it literally. Given the way the headaches were coming on now, it really was lucky that she caught this case. Lucky for everyone involved, even if the Bureau didn't know it.

All at once, Samantha, who had been sitting quietly in the backseat, suddenly smacked the back of Haggerty's seat and cried, "Molly Claire—the exhibit."

Haggerty jerked in surprise. Unfortunately, in that instant, the car's tires hit an oil slick on the road. The car went into a spin that Haggerty struggled to control.

Once she had, Haggerty vented her anger. "What were you thinking, Samantha, shouting like that? You almost made me crash the car."

Apparently unconcerned, Samantha continued shouting, "Molly Claire—isn't she the chair of *The Power of the Pyramid* project?"

Haggerty stifled a gasp. "The ceremonial chair, at least. Still, she did seem to be actively involved." She glanced at Jake. "Connected, do you think?"

Jake pressed his hand to his hair, flattening those cowlicks for a moment. "Hard to say. It could mean Molly's Clowns aren't the only suspects to consider."

Their eyes met one more time, and Haggerty felt sure she and Jake had shared the same incredulous thought. The amateur had made the link, the flaky amateur.

Back in her office, remembering the exchange, Haggerty admitted to herself how tightly-strung the headaches always made her. Samantha had shouted quite loudly and without warning. But losing control of the wheel was a bit much.

At the other extreme was Jake's reaction. He scarcely flicked an eyelash during Samantha's outburst. For a man who displayed such obvious tension, he sure kept his nerves under control. Something Haggerty had better emulate if she was going to make it through what promised to be a bumpy stretch of road ahead.

There was no denying how aware she was of his reactions.

Why *now?* Why did she have to meet a guy now who awakened the feelings she thought she had closed off? Or ever, for that matter? Relationships didn't work for her. She carried too much baggage for any man to accept.

As if he'd been reading her mind, Jake appeared in the doorway. "You okay?" Concern corrugated his brow.

Haggerty rose and smoothed out her gray silk skirt. "Sure. Just needed to take a Tylenol for a headache." As if medication would tame these headaches.

"Your boss will do that to anyone. He sure likes to hear himself talk. Is he always like that?"

When Haggerty nodded, they shared a short conspiratorial laugh. Their eyes held a moment too long, before both quickly looked away.

Jake absently tapped his fists together. "Me, I have to jump in, take action. Talk makes me restless."

Haggerty could tell. Energy radiated out from him.

"Listening to that gasbag, I doodled on everything in sight. After I filled a pad on the table, I doodled on all the business cards in my wallet." While chuckling to himself, Jake glanced around her small office. "Hey, where's our seer? Rusler wants to meet her."

Haggerty came around the desk. "I stashed her in an interview room. Come on, I'll show you."

She led Jake toward the room where she'd left Samantha. Yet she stopped in her approach when she saw that someone had opened the door she had left closed. She ran into the interview room, whipping her head in both directions. The room was small, with just a table and three chairs, and no place to hide. It was empty now.

"Samantha? Samantha!" She turned to Jake. "She's gone."

"So what?" he said. "We'll find her again if we need her. What's your problem?"

"We need her now," Haggerty said through tightly clenched teeth. She started running toward the elevator.

"You don't really believe she actually sees things, do you? Psychically, I mean?" Jake called after her.

She knew damn well that Samantha didn't see anything, not in the mystical sense, not even what was right before her nose. Haggerty also knew she couldn't crack this case without her.

CHAPTER FIVE
Samantha

The hours since we discovered Molly Claire's abduction—well, since Jake and Haggerty did, as I already knew—passed at a snail's pace. I wasn't good at cooling my heels. I mean, what can you do when you're waiting, except—well, wait? Too boring for me.

Haggerty had stashed me in a room by myself and told me to stay there. I think she even alluded to some punishment I'd suffer if I left. I couldn't say for sure, since I wasn't listening. My mind wanders. Selectively. Mostly when other people are talking. I never mean for it to happen, and I swear I'm really not as self-involved as it sounds. I always start out listening, only something catches my attention and leads it away. When I return to the conversation, the speaker is invariably in a totally different place, often with a question I'm expected to answer. At that point I'm faced with the choice of faking my way through, or admitting the truth and confirming for the speaker what she invariably suspected, that my intelligence had all the value of dryer lint. Naturally, I always chose the former and ended up proving the latter.

So while Haggerty railed on about the fate I'd suffer if I left—I kept thinking about what would happen to me if I didn't. Leave, I mean. Let's face it, this scenario wasn't playing out as I planned. When the clown car nearly sent me to the hereafter that morning, I thought I'd struck gold. I figured I'd regale an adoring public with my role in the operation, and they'd throw fistfuls of bucks at me. Only my part seemed to be limited to warming a chair in an interrogation room, and even that was being kept secret.

No question—I had to bust outta that joint.

The trick to doing anything, I've discovered, is simply to act as if you have that right. It's the indecision, checking to see if they've spotted you, that trips you up every time. I figured making my escape would be a slam-dunk, provided Haggerty hadn't locked me in there. Fortunately, the knob turned easily in my hand. Boy, I could tell she really wasn't used to dealing with people like me.

I strolled through the reception area and punched the down button on the elevator.

The gal on the front desk noticed me then. "Hey there, Agent Haggerty said—"

I produced an innocent expression before turning around. "The vending machine on this floor was out of soda. Agent Haggerty said I could go as far as the building's coffee shop."

I didn't even know if that floor had a vending machine, or the building a coffee shop. But like I said, observation is a job requirement in my line, and I'd already taken a read on this chick. I pegged her as thirty-something, and there she was, still a flunky for people making something of their lives. She had her nose stuck in a law book, like a student would. I figured between work and school, and trying to get somewhere at last, she was far too busy to focus on banalities like where they kept the vending machines.

A line formed between her brows. Had I underestimated her dedication to her job? I turned back to the elevator to await the verdict.

"Oh," she said at last. Out of the corner of my eye, I saw her shrug. "As long as you cleared it." Her nose returned to the book propped up before her, just as the elevator doors opened.

I thought with a sigh, once the elevator doors closed behind me, I sometimes wished it were more of a challenge.

During the ride to the lobby, I decided I should skedaddle fast. In case anyone noticed I was gone. Grab Lady Stang and rush to the nearest TV station so I could get a little mileage out of this before the Molly Claire story broke.

When I reached the ground floor, I saw that once again opportunity had come to me. The Federal Building plaza was a popular spot among the citizenry of Los Angeles for staging protests. A demonstration was being mounted there against *The Power of the Pyramid* exhibit. *Stop the rape of antiquity,* the signs read.

It seemed to me that barn door had already been bolted shut, while the horse had raced far into the next county. I mean, *The Power of the Pyramid* wasn't causing anything to be dug up from the ruins of ancient Egypt, it was just gathering stuff that had already been ripped-off. Who was I to tell those lost souls what hopeless cause to waste their time on?

Though there probably weren't more than twenty-five

people clamoring their disapproval, and no more than a dozen dissenters encouraging the exhibit to go forward, news crews had set up to interview them. It's all a matter of angles; a good cameraman can make three stragglers look like a crowd.

What a lucky break. All I had to do was cut in line, something I do well anyway, and I would become part of a story that would doubtless lead on tonight's eleven o'clock news. I found a segment producer grabbing a smoke in the cab of one of the news vans. By talking a lot, without really saying anything—another specialty of mine—and sticking my chest out, I convinced him to give me a shot, while never exactly revealing what I knew. In a heartbeat I found myself standing before the background they'd chosen, waiting for the reporter to conclude her interview with the spokesman for the protestors.

Man, it had worked out exactly as I'd planned. I watched as the reporter ended her interview, and when the producer prepped her on me. Then she approached my side, gave an intro, and stuck the microphone in my face.

But *that* was when Haggerty flew from the building and put the kibosh on the whole thing. I thought she'd make like a storm trooper and cancel the interview. But she took a more creative approach.

"Step away from her!" Haggerty gave every appearance of blocking the camera with her body by sheer chance, but I knew better. "She's highly contagious. Unless you've been inoculated for the...Rascal Virus, you shouldn't be near this woman."

Faces paled all around me. *En masse* they tripped over wires and equipment, over each other, even their own feet, to get away. If I'd known the members of the Fourth Estate were so gullible, I'd have tried running a con on them before this. In an instant Haggerty and I were alone together. With that accomplished, she clamped her hand on my arm and dragged me away.

So close and yet so far—the story of my not-so-young life.

When Haggerty threw me into the elevator car for the ride back to her office, the only question was which of us was more furious at the other.

Countless recriminations flooded my brain. Yet when I finally burst into indignant speech, the only thing that came out was,

"The Rascal Virus?"

I thought she'd revel in her petty witticism. But she was still too angry for that. She pushed me against the back wall of the elevator car, and tapped her index finger against my chest, so hard she created a sore spot. "You little fool. You think I just wrecked things for you, but I may have saved your life."

"Oh, yeah? Listen to me—"

"No, *you* listen. Some people out there abducted a woman who was prominent enough to warrant a relentless search, and they killed a man who just happened to be in the way. If they believe there's a chance you can determine their identities, by any means, they're going to have to take you out. Got it?"

Man, she thought through that awfully fast. My mouth opened to protest her reasoning, only nothing came out.

"What's the matter, Samantha? Don't tell me you're speechless."

For the first time in twenty-eight and three-quarters years, I was. I'd always thought it would be so cool to be a real psychic, and a goddess, the ultimate. Assuming such things could exist. Hah! Never before had I imagined there being a downside. Now I saw that if someone were what I claimed to be, there could be some very good reasons for keeping it secret.

Haggerty dragged me back upstairs, but apparently my isolation had ended. Instead of putting me in a more escape-proof room like I figured she would, she brought me directly to where the taskforce had set up. Their command post centered around a long wooden table, surrounded by a cluster of small computer cubicles. Weary law enforcement-types filled most of the chairs at the table and before the terminals. Of the dozen or so assembled there, the only one I recognized was Special Agent Billy, the guy who helped Haggerty sort through the nut brigade. At the sight of me, his thin, wide lips curved into a greeting, while above it, his chubby apple cheeks quivered with amusement. Hey, the amusement was mutual, pal.

In addition to Haggerty, and now me, there was only one other female on the team. A young woman in a coral twin set, to whom I gave high marks to for individuality—until she met my introduction with a demand that I tell her fortune. Snotty bitch.

Jake joined us after a moment, hooking his cell phone onto

his belt as he walked.

After a distinctive rat-tat-tat of footsteps, taking his place at the head of the rectangular table was a man in his forties who was introduced to me as the SAC, Special Agent in Charge, Kale Rusler. There was no question that he was the boss.

"So, Annabelle, this is the little lady who's going to tell us how it all ends, eh?" Rusler said.

Patronizing ass. When he smiled, his lower lip dropped as if on a hinge, displaying thick, square teeth. What was doubtlessly meant to disarm looked menacing to me. I half expected him to growl.

Rusler wasn't good at hiding his vulnerabilities, though. Despite the wedding ring he wore, he couldn't keep his eyes off Haggerty. When she rose at one point to get a drink from the water cooler that stood between two cubicles, Rusler's gaze followed her so intently, it reduced his speech to mumbling. And while he addressed the others as "agent" or "detective," he consistently called Haggerty by her first name. Was this chick taking the mattress route to career advancement? Nah. When she returned to her chair, she stole a glance at Jake, not the SAC. Rusler's feelings weren't reciprocated. *Attagirl.*

Across the table, Agent Billy's small eyes met mine with a brief flash of amusement. Was he a kindred spirit? Another person who went through life in search of naked emperors to snicker at? I anticipated the chance to share silent yuks across the table, only his cell phone rang. With one last glance in my direction, he rose and went somewhere to talk in private.

Apparently, the investigation was making progress. Representatives from the LAPD and the DA's office had transferred the files of the investigation into Molly's Clowns and their trial. And other special agents and cops were out somewhere running down leads that had come up in those files.

Molly's assistant—a guy who looked so much like Muscle Ken that I half expected Stairmaster Barbie to follow him through the door—dropped off a box of the negative mail fans had sent.

Ol' Ken was a tasty-looking nugget, if you like 'em fair and built as I do. Although, he seemed remarkably plodding, even dense, when questioned. Was he what Molly Claire's taste ran to?

On second thought, Ken was probably too tame for Molly.

What kind of man would have appealed to her? Doubtless someone in the business—how many opportunities does a movie star get to meet a regular Joe? Could Molly simply have gotten involved with the wrong man?

I reminded myself that not every woman pulled what Dodi Drake did, making her assistant into a concubine. But if the tabloids were right, Molly had slipped the rails after her actor husband dumped her for a newer model a couple of years back. While typed as a perennial ingénue, she was nearing forty now, and the strain of projecting permanent, plucky youth had started to show. As the hairdos got progressively trendier, her quirky expressions became more like desperate caricatures of the cutesy, though appealing, looks that were her onscreen trademark. Molly was also moving into my bailiwick, claiming to be a psychic, exploring past lives, and all that stuff.

Despite all the avenues the investigators pursued, the greatest hope of the people gathered around that table was that the abductors would call and make some demand. Molly's telephone line was now routed there for tracing. Yet that line remained silent. No one called. So many hours had passed, and no one had called.

Haggerty rose again for another sip from the water cooler. I was getting the idea that she wasn't really that thirsty, just too restless to sit. For a moment, the slim form beneath her gray suit slumped against the water cooler. I knew she was plenty strong—I discovered that when she threw me into the elevator. Yet now she looked so frail. Dark smudges had formed beneath her eyes. And a slick sheen of sweat covered her face, even though it wasn't hot. Maybe she was getting sick.

Or just anxious. This investigation had to be an opportunity for her. Why was it okay for her to score a career coup, but not me?

Haggerty walked back to her chair, a trifle unsteadily. Instead of taking her seat, she stood behind me and began massaging my shoulders.

"You're so tense, Samantha. You're not used to this pressure like we are," she muttered.

Tension wasn't an affliction I had ever suffered from, though some insisted I was a carrier. But the massage felt so good, I didn't argue.

As I stared off into the distance, lulled by the relaxing rub, an image drifted into my mind. A serene picture of a mountain lake that was as calm as glass. A few boulders studding the small inlet in the foreground made it even more picturesque. My mind's eye stayed on that picture before slowly shifting to a cabin a short way up the hill. How pretty it all looked. It didn't occur to me to question why I was imagining a place a city girl like me had never seen.

"Doing okay, Samantha?" Haggerty asked, still moving her thumbs across my shoulders.

"Great," I said.

I spoke too soon. The sound of screams, echoing against the hills surrounding the lake, were added to the picture. And I felt myself filled with a level of fear that was totally foreign to me. Then suddenly, as if I were standing before it, I saw the cabin's rough wooden door. It flew open, and I felt as if I were being hurled through the open doorway.

I shifted in my seat, restless, afraid. Haggerty's hands bore down harder on my shoulders.

My surroundings in the Field Office blurred, as my mental perception of that cabin claimed all my senses. I could feel the cabin's wooden floor beneath my butt, and I looked up at its roughhewn walls. The moldy odor of that unused space filled my nostrils. Then a person came into view. A tall man—dressed as a clown. My vision widened to include three more men, all clowns.

I screamed, as my fear spiked. Tears sprang from my eyes. "I see them—clowns."

"No shit," Jake said in a shocked whisper.

Then the position of those men shifted. But their posture made no sense to me.

Rusler, standing at the head of the table, made an irritated sound with his nose, like a bull's snort. "Annabelle, we've humored this nonsense long enough."

Haggerty ignored him. "Where, Samantha?"

"Lake," I said. When confused faces stared back at me, I shouted, "Lake, lake, lake."

The female agent in the sweater set was seated now at one of those computer carrels, and in her hands she held a *Thomas Guide*. "There are Lake Streets in Pasadena, Glendale, Burbank—"

"Water," I said with difficulty. "Not...street."

The feelings in that cabin attacked me so fiercely, I couldn't bear them. Neither could I shift back to reality. Everything became so hard, it was like trying to swim through rubber cement.

Although I hadn't seen him come back, Agent Billy must have returned from taking his call. He stood before me now. "I think she means *a* lake." He focused his beady little eyes on me with intense scrutiny, "Where?"

"Can't...do it." I started to cry.

Haggerty leaned closer to me and spoke softly into my ear. "Try, Madame Samantha," she said, less derisively than usual.

Unable to resist the power of her appeal, I let my mind return to that place. It drifted to a sign at the entrance to the lake. "Big Bear Lake," I read aloud in a monotone. That was a mountain recreation area east of Los Angeles. I now knew for sure that I had never seen that place in real life. Slowly, I told them about the boulders studding the inlet, the cabin I saw, the screams I heard.

Rusler paced in the small space at the head of the table, his hard-soled shoes beating that peculiar rat-tat-tat. "We have to know where that cabin is, dammit," he insisted.

I shook my head. It ached when I moved it.

"Just a little more now," Haggerty said. "You can do it." Her massage of my shoulders had become frantic.

Thoroughly spent, I stopped resisting. I allowed my mind's eye to focus on the street signs of the roads that climbed the hill, right to that cabin. Lastly, I read the numbers on its mailbox.

Haggerty finally released me. I slumped over the table, sobbing with a level of emotion I'd never experienced before. Haggerty gave my hair a gentle stroke.

"And the guys in the clown suits?" Jake demanded, his voice a tad shaky.

"They're at the cabin," I muttered, though I couldn't say how I knew. And the way I'd seen them—I still couldn't explain that.

"Now?" Rusler asked.

"Now," I insisted.

CHAPTER SIX

The team mobilized quickly. Jake placed a call, as did a few others. Haggerty used that time to change into dark pants and a sweater, over which she placed a navy windbreaker that identified her, in large yellow letters across the back, as *FBI*.

I had to give Rusler credit. Once I told him I saw clowns in that cabin, he immediately gave the order to send part of the taskforce there. I knew he thought I was leading them around like wild geese. It was evident from the scorn that kept his hinged lips firmly shut. He just couldn't risk ignoring my warning on the tiny chance that I was right.

At one point during the rushed preparations, I found myself alone with him, and he confirmed my suspicions. "I warn you, if I send those people out there and something happens to Miss Claire closer to home, I swear I'll see you prosecuted to the full extent of the law." He displayed those blocky teeth, in what I took to be a threat.

But his warning didn't trouble me. For once in my sorry life, I hadn't done anything wrong; I just reported what I saw. How I had come to see those images rattled me more than Rusler's pesky legal concerns.

What a day! Having had some idea of the call left on Molly Claire's voice mail was bad enough. To be able to see those men in that cabin, to feel it as vividly as if I were there—nothing like that had ever happened to me. And I passionately hoped it never did again. During all the times I'd thought it might be cool to be a genuine psychic, I had no idea what effect a vision would have on the recipient. I hadn't known that emotions could come with such brutal force and leave their victim feeling so bruised and battered.

After issuing his warning, Rusler stalked away. I noticed that he walked with a slight limp, which had to be responsible for the peculiar sound of his steps. Good. That meant I could outrun him. After that, I hovered near Haggerty. When she began moving out, I marched in step behind her. Well, as much as woman in a gown billowed out by several petticoats could.

Jake stopped in his tracks. "Whoa, Princess. Where do you think you're going?"

"Please, you gotta let me go," I said. I had to see this for myself. It could change my entire life.

"This ain't the amateur hour, Ms. Brennan. These people are dangerous." Jake leaned into my face, causing me to step back.

Haggerty slipped between us. "Jake, we might need her."

Jake? So those two had already jumped to first names. *Way to go, girl.*

"We'll definitely need her," Rusler snapped, as he rat-tat-tatted up the rear.

I guess Rusler meant to punish me when my prediction was proved wrong.

After flashing a scowl that darkened his face, Jake acquiesced with a tight nod. Together we three made our way to Haggerty's car, while the rest of the taskforce members went to other vehicles.

We set out at rush hour, when wrestling the exodus from the city usually made tangling with a bear seem like a kid's pastime. But Rusler had pulled all the stops. A helicopter overhead radioed traffic warnings. And the California Highway Patrol made frequent traffic breaks, to clear the way for us. No wonder the SAC had vowed to make me pay if this all proved unnecessary.

Since I tend to live more in the moment and not worry about consequence, the trip should have been a cool experience for me. Not only was I traveling through territory I'd never seen before, even though I was an L.A. native, the escort screamed of our importance. Jake and Haggerty, lost in their own thoughts, weren't even distracting me with conversation.

But I still couldn't throw off what had happened to me. I felt empty now, vacated. As if something vital to my life was missing. Mind you, I didn't want it to return. I wished I could turn back time, to erase my encounter with that clown car outside of the *Bonne Chance*. So I could go on living my life in a cloud of ignorance, which I hadn't been wise enough to cherish before.

Once again, I wondered about fate. Was I living out my own dark destiny—or just suffering the result of the bad choices I'd made? Was there a difference?

The local law, along with a pair of ambulances, met us at the turnoff to Big Bear Lake. Our car followed Rusler's up the hill. The cabin that had appeared in my vision came into view, precisely as I'd seen it in my mind's eye. I braced myself for a return of the emotional turmoil I'd felt earlier. But it didn't happen. While the whole place looked weirdly familiar, it produced no reaction in me at all.

The caravan of cars stopped a short distance away from the cabin. Before stepping from the vehicle, Jake turned to me. "Stay here, Ms. Brennan. No matter what happens. Got it?"

I nodded, before making brief eye contact with Haggerty. She looked stronger now than when she'd leaned against that water cooler.

Agent Billy stayed with me. Ostensibly, he'd been left behind to protect me, though I suspected he'd been given that assignment because no one believed, with his weight, that he could make the climb. Why was he there at all? Or part of the team, for that matter?

Since Billy inspired absolutely no confidence, when they began their approach of the cabin, I dropped to my knees in the backseat of the car, ready to shield myself. I peeked out from between the front seat's head restraints. Dusk was approaching, and it was hard to see. I could only just make out all the figures in dark clothing and jackets that bore the words *LAPD* and *FBI*, as they fanned around the small house.

I watched as one man kicked the front door open. And I heard the sound the backdoor made when it received similar treatment. The dark figures stormed the cabin all at once. I held my breath, ready to duck. But nothing happened. Nothing—no shots, no noise.

I wasn't sure if what I felt was letdown or relief. I couldn't identify anything I experienced anymore. Except for nosiness—I still knew that. And I had to know what had happened up in that little house. I leaped from the car and started up the hill.

Behind me, Billy shouted, "Ms. Brennan, no."

I ignored him. He could never move fast enough to stop me anyway. My dress caught on some bush along the way, but I just gave it a yank to free it and kept running up the dirt road. I didn't even hesitate at the open cabin door—I just burst through.

I jerked to a halt behind a few FBI agents who blocked my view. To my surprise, big ol' Billy bumped into me. He'd actually kept pace. Go figure. The guy gave new meaning to the phrase, *light on his feet*. I took a moment to stare at the wall to my left—it was the identical roughhewn wood that I'd seen in my vision. Same jagged texture, same muddy tone. I wiggled through the folks standing before me and followed their glances to the distressed wood floor that looked exactly like the surface I'd fallen on in that vision.

Four men, of different heights and weights, but all made up like clowns, were laid out on the floor, one next to the other. I gasped and covered my mouth with my hand. That image was precisely the same as the last vision I'd had of those men. I hadn't understood it then. With the wooden floor behind them, so similar to the walls, I believed they were standing. I wondered about their lax posture and the fact that they were lined up in a row, so close together. It hadn't occurred to me that they were lying on the floor. Or, I thought, as a chill rippled through me, that they'd been *placed* there.

Bloody patches marked all of their multi-colored clown suits. Where they'd been shot, I realized. Yet there was little blood evident on the wooden floor, except for a small pool beside the man farthest from me.

I expected Jake, the experienced street cop, to take charge. But he just stood there. It was Haggerty who knelt down beside them and rubbed at one clown's makeup.

"Anybody got a cloth or something?" she demanded.

I reached into my drawstring bag and pulled out one of the Handi Wipe packets I always carried, which I extended to her. She ripped open the package, and wiped at the makeup with the moist paper towel.

"Is it them, Molly's Clowns?" one of the fibbies asked.

"Looks like it," she confirmed, though she hadn't yet removed that much makeup.

My own voice came out in a squeak. "Are they—dead?"

Haggerty had been going down the line of them, wiping away makeup and checking for pulses. When she cleared the clown whiteface from the final body, I realized it was Plotnik, the one who had addressed the jury in their stalking trial. Jake finally jumped in and pressed his fingers to that body's neck.

"This one's circling the drain, but he still has a beat. Get those EMTs up here. Now," he shouted.

The paramedics rushed in and began working on Plotnik.

"The other three, they're—" I started to ask.

Haggerty's eyes found mine. "Dead as doornails," she said.

Like the carpenter. Funny how she would use that expression, huh? A noise came from me that sounded like half a giggle, half a whimper. I didn't understand anything anymore.

The paramedics stabilized Plotnik for the journey to the hospital. In a stupor, I watched as they rushed him from the cabin on a gurney.

Finally, something in my mushy brain fired again. "Molly Claire," I exclaimed. "Is Molly here?"

Someone pointed to the cabin wall on the right. On it someone had written in block red letters, *Now WE have Molly.*

"What does that mean?" I demanded. "That someone else abducted the victim from the abductors, and *killed* them?" When nobody bothered to respond, I shrieked "Who?"

CHAPTER SEVEN

While part of the taskforce remained at the cabin to process the crime scene, the rest of us accompanied Plotnik to a local hospital. Once the doctors there stabilized him, he was airlifted to a hospital in L.A. We were told he went straight into surgery, but his chances were iffy.

It was fairly late by the time we headed home. We must have hit less traffic on the return trip, although I couldn't say because the whole drive passed in a blur. I knew Haggerty and Jake talked more, as they batted theories around, but I scarcely remembered a word they exchanged. My brain was just too numb to process anything.

Haggerty dropped Jake off at the West L.A. station. He left with no more than a taut nod to both of us. Then Haggerty drove on to the Federal Building. After she parked her car and led me toward the rear lobby entrance, it occurred to me that I was passing close to where I'd parked Lady Stang. If I wanted to, I could leave right now. Yet I followed along behind Haggerty as if I'd been tied to her with a string.

Back upstairs, she left me alone in her office when she went off to change again. I plopped into the guest chair and slouched down till I was more or less sitting on my neck, staring at myself. My beautiful gown had torn and gotten grimy. I'd bought that dress in a costume shop, and I paid more for it than you'd think, considering the miniscule demand for Renaissance gowns. But it would have required more effort than I was capable of to mourn the loss.

After a while, I sensed Haggerty had been gone too long. I wandered back to the bullpen. The night relief taskforce members worked there now—making calls, poring through files. Haggerty was nowhere around.

I finally found her with Rusler in his corner office. Not wanting them to see me, I stood down the hall at an angle where I could peer in without being noticed. They didn't seem to be having a comfortable chat. Haggerty perched anxiously on the edge of one of Rusler's gray tweed guest chairs, her back rigidly erect. Her right hand remained locked in a fist that she kept bringing down on the front of his large mahogany desk.

Despite Rusler's feelings for her, there was starch in his posture, too. He didn't sit as she had, but stood behind the desk, looking down at her. And he kept shaking his head. He was pulling rank, I sensed. But Haggerty wasn't backing down from her position.

Not surprisingly, Rusler had claimed the suite's primo corner office position; during daylight hours, the window facing the ocean must have given him quite a view. His furnishings were also a cut above the government-issue stuff around the rest of the place. It looked more like a CEO's office.

He'd crammed his office with his ego-memorabilia, as over-the-top as Molly's place. I couldn't make out the stuff on the far wall, but closer to me, I spotted a commendation from the Bureau director, as well as some souvenir shots of Rusler posing with various dignitaries. A number of other pictures depicted his volunteer work among gang members, which Haggerty had mentioned earlier.

Whenever anyone refers to gang-bangers, I always think of young boys who get seduced by the street. But lots of those gangsters were grown men, with arms covered in prison art. In some of the posed shots, with Rusler displaying his hinged smile for the camera, and the gang members showing their scary choppers, I couldn't help but wonder, for all the toughness he displayed here, whether Rusler was any match for those bad boys. Was he using them, or were they using him?

As interesting as my speculation was, though, after a while I got bored with the unchanging scene. I decided to risk drawing closer to hear something. The first sound that came my way, when I was only close enough to catch an occasional word, was "Samantha Brennan."

Crap. Why were they talking about me? Rusler couldn't want to throw me in the clink, could he? I delivered exactly what I told them I would. I wished I'd run to my car when I had the chance. I wanted to be someplace else. I wanted to sleep in my own bed, and soon. I wanted to get so far from those people that I would never see any of them again.

When I noticed Haggerty rising, I zipped away, but not before I saw that a smile of some satisfaction had settled on her weary face. She must have won whatever concession she'd wanted from him. Still, there was none of the gloating I usually display when

I worm something from someone. If anything, I thought I saw resignation in the twist of her full lips.

I made it back to her office just an instant before she walked in. She called the hospital to check on Plotnik. She absently reported that he'd made it through surgery, though they'd taken four slugs out of him. He was in ICU now, in critical condition, under the watchful eye of an LAPD officer.

"You must feel disappointed about not finding Molly in that cabin," I said.

"I'll live," she snapped, while gathering her purse and briefcase. "I just hope Miss Claire does, too. Given the shape we found her Clowns in, it doesn't look good."

I was so tired, I spoke without thinking. Even less than usual for me. "I'd pack it in at this point."

Haggerty slammed her purse against the desk. "And what? Leave her to die? That's the difference between you and me, *Madame* Samantha—I don't quit when things get tough."

That *was* the difference—I did, and I wasn't ashamed to admit it. I wished I'd quit sooner.

"Look, Haggerty, I'm sorry for how that sounded. I know you'll find Molly. And I bet it will be in time."

Haggerty's lips twitched with amusement. "Not *me,* Samantha—*us.* I just confirmed with Rusler that you're going to be put on our payroll as a consultant. You're in for the long haul."

"No freakin' way!" That was the first time I'd ever refused money, but nothing could change my mind. I sank back into one of her chairs and covered my eyes with my hands. "Look, Haggerty, you don't understand. What I experienced before, with me seeing the cabin and all—was the first and only time that ever happened to me. It'll probably never happen again."

She perched on the corner of the desk, just a foot or so away from me. "Oh, I think it will," she said, seemingly unconcerned.

I groaned, but I let the idea carry me along. "Maybe I've been the real thing all this time, but I camouflaged myself as a scam artist to protect myself from the effect of my own powers."

"That must be it," Haggerty said neutrally. "So it will happen again."

"Man, I hope not," I blurted. "It was brutally intense. I thought it would be cool to be—you know, what I claimed to be. But it was dreadful. I never want to experience anything like it again. I can't do it."

"You can, Samantha, and you will." She took my wrist and squeezed it, hard.

Another image floated into my mind, that of a woman, beautiful beyond description, with soft white skin, deep blue eyes and long, flowing red hair. She drifted in a cloud of sorts. I understood somehow that she really was one of the goddesses I professed to have come from. Her gown was the green of a grassy hillside, and it seemed to circle her, not cling, because it wasn't made of fabric, but ether. All at once, her flawless face seemed to change, from maiden, to mother, to wise old crone, the three forms the Celtic goddesses were said to take. Then the woman assumed all three forms at once, in a way that was impossible to describe in any words we humans could understand.

I felt weak from an overwhelming rush of emotions, and looked at Haggerty to see if she had any idea what I was experiencing. She watched me with a peculiar concentration. A knowing look came into her blue eyes that gave her an aura of wisdom far greater than usually seen on anyone her age, or mine. Then I saw it—the similarity. The color of her eyes, the shape of her jaw, her milky white skin and her copper-red hair—she shared all of those features and more with the goddess.

With an amused twinkle in her eyes, she released my wrist. The image of the goddess instantly vanished from my mind and understanding flooded me instead. During the times when every vision came to me—Haggerty had always been touching me.

"You," I gasped. *"You're* the real thing. You're a *goddess."*

She offered me the first genuine smile I'd seen in the hours I'd known her. Then, suppressing a laugh, she put her finger to her lips and said, "Shush."

CHAPTER EIGHT

"Oh, God," I moaned, before downing my drink.

Haggerty and I had walked the few blocks from the Federal Building to a restaurant in Westwood Village, where I now slumped across the bar, crying into my beer. Only it wasn't beer. I had just knocked back my second tequila shooter, while I noticed she had scarcely touched her glass of white wine.

Incapable of originality at this point, I said again, "Oh, God." I glanced at her. "Not you, that is. I mean—" I shook my head. "No offense intended."

In the mirror behind the bar, I saw her suited shoulder flex in a shrug. "None taken."

While Haggerty took such a ladylike sip of wine, I questioned whether it had even wet her tongue, I held up my empty glass to signal to the bartender that I was ready for a refill.

"I don't know why you're so upset, Samantha," Haggerty pointed out. "You said you didn't really want the gifts you claimed to have, and you don't have them. You should be thrilled."

I shook my head too fast and the room began to spin. "You don't understand. I always believed the only things going bump in the night were people who walked into the coffee table in the dark. If all that woo-woo stuff is just hocus-pocus, and the only psychics are fake psychics—then as long as I was a good fake psychic, I was a success. Now that you've shown me what's possible, I know I can't be anything but a failure in my chosen work."

Haggerty raised one of her well-arched auburn brows. "And you're just getting this now? How old are you?"

My twenty-eight and three-quarter years weighed heavily on me. "None of your business," I snapped.

With a sigh, I stretched my arm across the bar again and rested my head on it, viewing the scene through the small glass of tequila the bartender placed before me. The booze began to mend the savage tear Haggerty's revelation had made in my worldview.

So did the music. From somewhere in the adjoining restaurant, someone was playing a harp of all things. Normally, I don't go for lounge acts, even those less lame than harp solos. Tonight the lilting tones of the folk songs the harpist played soothed me. As they did everyone else, from the relaxed smiles I saw on the faces reflected in the mirror. Hardly anyone was drinking. With dreamy expressions, they just stared off into space.

Now that was going too far. I loved those lyrical sounds, too, but nothing was stopping me from getting wasted tonight.

Haggerty seemed to notice the music as well, only it didn't affect her like everyone else. When she directed an ear toward the sound, a puzzled look came over her face.

With a sigh, I pressed my chin against the polished wooden surface of the bar and stared at her in the mirror. With no one close and the bartender busy at the other end of the bar, I seized the chance to ask the questions—whose answers I really didn't want to know.

"What exactly are you?" I asked.

Haggerty shrugged. "Precisely what you claim to be."

"A Celtic goddess?"

She nodded.

"So what you're saying is…there's a magical plane right here on Earth." I'd always insisted as much to my clients. I even knew the metaphysical crowd spelled it *magykal* with a *y* and a *k*, instead of the usual letters. But that looked too strange to me. I just never expected that plane to be real. I *certainly* never expected to go splat on it. "For all I know, there could be millions of creatures like you milling around out here. Maybe the whole space is one big spiritual realm. How did *I* get stuck on it?"

"You stuck yourself there, Samantha."

She sure was good at assigning blame. Fortunately, I was a whiz at weaseling out of it.

"Haggerty…?" I hadn't even questioned why I called her by her last name. It just seemed to fit. Or maybe I wanted to distance myself from someone who still seemed like an uptight law-enforcement-type. Now that I thought about what she was, it seemed presumptuous. "If it's okay to call you that? Would you like me to…?"

"It hasn't worried you until now," she said. "Call me whatever you want."

She might be doing a bit of distancing herself. Without budging my chin, I drew a sip off the top of my drink. "You're psychic?"

Haggerty tilted her head. "I see things. Get visions, impressions, feelings. Occasionally, I hear people's thoughts. Sometimes I even get a glimpse of the future. It's not a videophone, though. I don't have much control over it."

"Still, you have it. You were the one who saw that cabin and knew what had happened to those men."

With a sad sigh, she stared into her wine glass. "Not soon enough."

I refused to get waylaid by her private worry. Instead, I thought of some of the other words I typically throw around in the course of my job. "Do you see auras?"

"Usually." Haggerty reached for a bowl of popcorn the bartender had left a couple of stools down. She placed it before me. "Maybe you should eat something, Samantha."

Then again, maybe I should just get drunk enough to forget this day ever happened. But since I never turn down food, I grabbed a fistful and stuffed it into my mouth.

"I hear melodies, too," Haggerty went on to say.

Struggling to swallow the popcorn, I said, "That's the harp you hear."

"No, I hear melodies coming off of people. Like the auras some see." She took a moment to listen again to the music; a question wrinkled her forehead.

"Melodies? I never heard of anything like that."

"Why should you, Samantha? You're mortal."

"And proud of it," the booze said stupidly. "So…what's my melody like?"

"It's very happy, carefree." She smiled at me. "But really simple and childlike."

I snorted. "Hah! And you claim to be sensitive. *I* could have predicted that."

I grabbed another handful of popcorn. Absently, Haggerty reached out and plucked a few kernels, too, which she slowly munched on. I moved the bowl so it rested between us.

"Do you have powers?" I asked. "You know, can you do other-worldly-type stuff?"

After a moment, Haggerty gave a reluctant nod. She started to say something else, but after considering it, she just clamped her mouth shut.

"Man, if I had magical powers, I'd be using them all the time. Predicting the Lotto numbers would be my first move."

Haggerty scowled into the mirror. "That's another difference between you and me, Samantha. I'd consider that wrong."

I frowned right back at her. "You know, Haggerty, you're awfully judgmental for a person whose family photos are displayed in the dictionary next to the word *debauchery.*"

Haggerty's lips thinned with disapproval. "Are you like everyone in your family?"

"Yeah. Why do you think I turned out like this?" I finished my shooter.

"Well, I'm not," she spat.

I held up my empty glass to the bartender, but Haggerty pushed my arm down. "You've had enough." She signaled the bartender for the check and threw a credit card on the bar. "Here's another difference between us, Samantha. I know there's a price for everything. Sometimes the price of using my gifts becomes too high. I can move things, change their form, yet it often makes me weak. In my line of work, without the strength to defend myself, I'd be too vulnerable during a clash with a suspect."

I sucked out the last of the liquid in my glass. If I wasn't getting any more tequila, I was at least getting it all. "You mean, you can die? What would happen to you if you were to die?"

"I'd be called home, to Avalon."

"Avalon! Celtic gods retire to Catalina?"

Haggerty rolled her big blue eyes. "Not very educated, are you? I don't mean the city of Avalon on Catalina Island. The original Avalon. In our language it's called *Tir na n'Og*. It's an island west of Ireland."

I swayed unsteadily on the bar stool, but I wasn't sure whether to blame the tequila. "In the ocean?"

"Not...precisely."

Definitely not the tequila. I suffered from TMI. Too much information. "You mean...Heaven."

She shrugged. "If that's the way you understand it."

I munched more popcorn. "I think that'd be cool. Gotta be

49

better than Earth anyway." As if I'd know. I'd never seriously considered the idea that there might be someplace else.

Haggerty looked down at the bill the bartender placed before her. "I can think of worse places. I'm in no hurry to leave."

While she signed the check, I leaned against the bar as I listened to the piece of music the harpist played. I realized I didn't care about having my tequila cut off anymore, maybe because I had drastically reduced the world's supply of it, yet I was sorry to be leaving that music. Just then the harpist announced that he was taking a break.

A moment later, the most beautiful man I'd ever seen entered the bar from the restaurant. When a beam of light from a ceiling fixture landed on his skin, his prominent cheekbones glinted like pure gold. The hair that fell to his broad shoulders in silky waves was the color of sunlight on a brilliantly clear day. And his to-die-for bod looked like the statues I remembered from a field trip my high school class took to a museum. When that gorgeous creature greeted the bartender, his luminescent smile lit up that sad, shadowy room. The harpist? If so, this guy could make beautiful music with me anytime.

My heart gave a little flutter when I thought he would be walking right past us. And it beat like a bongo when the love of my life came to a stop right behind Haggerty.

"Hello, Annabelle, luv," the hunk said in a soft Scottish burr.

Haggerty spun around. "Angus? I thought that sounded like your music."

"Your mum has been monitoring your situation, and she figured you might need my help," he said.

She groaned softly. "Why you?"

He gave a cheerfully unoffended shrug with his buff shoulders. "No idea. But this space is always good for a laugh. You know your mum has a soft spot for me." Sparkling blue eyes flecked with silver glints turned my way. "And who is this charming creature?"

Haggerty gave him my name, and said to me, "Samantha, this is my...cousin, Angus."

Angus took my hand in his and actually bent over to kiss it. With his lips still pressed to my fingers, his gaze traveled up my body. "Delighted," he said at last. "And what a fetching figure you have, dear girl. So few women in your century do."

"My *century?*" I looked from him to Haggerty.

"Don't ask," she said to me. She took a step away from the bar. Over her shoulder she said to the man of my dreams, "If I need you, Angus, I'll find you." Her tone decidedly conveyed that he'd be the last person she'd call.

With a crick of her finger, she told me to follow her. She took a few steps, but then stopped and swayed. Swayed worse than me even.

I rushed to her side. "Haggerty, what...?"

She collapsed against me. "Molly," she said in a soft, breathy tone. "I see—" She broke off, her face pinched with pain.

From the corner of my eye, I watched Angus give us a jaunty little salute before sauntering off. Haggerty was writhing in pain, and he was leaving? Part of me wanted to run after him, to beg him to look at me again with his strange blue-and-silver eyes. But I couldn't leave her in that condition. She would fall to the floor if I let go of her.

"You see Molly?" I whispered.

She started to shake her head, but it must have hurt too much to move. She pressed her fists to her forehead. "I don't see her, I see *through* her—what she sees. But I can feel it's her."

"What does she see?" I demanded.

"She's tied up in a basement."

"In L.A.? How is that possible?" There were virtually no basements here in the Southland, as we locals called it; this was earthquake country.

Despite her pain, Haggerty took an instant to glare at me. "Do you want to hear this or not, Samantha?"

Meekly, I nodded.

"The basement floor is dirt, and it's cold. And there's a broken pipe that's been leaking down one stone wall, where algae have spread into a dark green sludge that smells vile."

"Don't hit me now, but...where is that basement?" I said, breaking in at last. "It really can't be here."

With a sigh, Haggerty's head fell back, as the vision must have released her from its grip. "I don't know," she said with weary resignation. "I don't have a clue where she could be. Just that wherever it is, it's...agony."

CHAPTER NINE

Haggerty laid two bombshells on me during our return to the Federal Building. The first one I could have predicted if I hadn't had all those shooters—but if I hadn't had all those shooters, it wouldn't have been a factor. She insisted I was not fit to drive, and I had to leave poor Stangie in the parking lot. Then she told me I wasn't even going home.

"That's what I discussed with Rusler before we left. He wanted you placed in protective custody in a hotel, but I argued that I would be responsible for you. We're going to my place."

I stomped one of my boots against the sidewalk. "Huh? Unless you run a room service kitchen at all hours, you made the wrong choice. Why did you nix the hotel stay? Do you know how rarely I get to live like that?"

Haggerty grabbed my arm and yanked me forward. "Trust me, the Bureau's accommodations don't run to much luxury."

Any luxury at all was more than I usually enjoyed. Still, with just a bit more grumbling, I agreed, mostly because I was too tired to make enough use of room service anyway. I was also nosy, and I wanted to check out where she lived.

"We have to swing by my place first. You gotta let me pack a few things." I swished the skirt of my torn gown to show what a mess it was.

"Samantha, I'll loan you whatever you need. Please understand, I need to get home now." Haggerty squeezed her eyes closed for an instant.

She could keep her powers if that's what they did to her. She looked so weary, she seemed more wasted than I was. Maybe I'd be the better driver after all.

Once we reached the Federal Building's parking lot, Haggerty led me to, not the government-issue Taurus we'd used earlier, but to her personal car, a newish Honda Accord in silver. Pretty, I had to admit, though it lacked Lady Stang's character. Then again, its contoured black leather seats had it all over my car's busted springs.

We didn't talk during the drive. I won a bet with myself when she headed north on the 405 Freeway toward the San Fernando Valley. The Valley is strictly middle-class, and nowhere near as cool as the guesthouse I rent in Santa Monica. Yet it fit her.

That made no sense to me. Most people start life with their noses firmly pressed to the grindstone, and they only search for some spirituality when the quest for success has worn them down. Lucky for me, my family gave that whole achievement-route a pass. There was something to be said for coming from a long line of carnie queens. But Haggerty was an oddity, too. She started out with a built-in level of spirituality many people eventually come to crave, yet she did everything possible to make herself into an ordinary grind.

I knew, no matter what I said, despite the price she seemed to be paying for it, that I would give anything to live her life. Man, would I make better use of it.

She exited the freeway in Sherman Oaks and drove along surface streets north of Ventura Boulevard. The Boulevard is the dividing line between the pricier houses to the south of it in the hills, and the family bungalows in the flatlands. Once again, I predicted to myself that Haggerty would turn north. Do I know people, or what?

She eventually pulled into the driveway of a tidy little house, painted gray with white trim, the front yard surrounded by an old-fashioned picket fence. This chick wasn't just trying to be plain ol' mortal, she was bucking for a '50s time warp. Two apple trees, planted in grassy patches on either side of the sidewalk dividing the front yard, were heavy with fruit. The only tacky touch about the tasteful home was one of those garish lawn gnomes stuck in the wide flower border along the path that led to the front porch.

Tipsy and tired as I was, I made a silly face at the gnome. He turned his head and made one back at me. I swear! I was seeing things. I must have been drunker than I thought. I blinked my eyes hard. Now the gnome looked still as a statue—as, of course, it always had been. To anyone sober at least. Still, when we cut behind the gnome, along the path that led from the driveway to the door, I refused to look at him. It.

Haggerty unlocked the door and led me into a small foyer, with a Mexican tile floor between a pair of redwood planter boxes. Like the yard outside, the boxes were planted with a lush variety of colorful flowers.

While Haggerty paused at the entrance to the front room, I stared at the flowers. Once again something weird happened. While I looked at them, the flowers appeared to blur, as if the very surface and color of their petals were moving.

"Uh, Haggerty, these flowers are...alive."

With a knowing smirk, she turned to me. "All plants are."

"But they're—I saw—" I felt my face pinch together, almost as if I were about to cry.

Haggerty took pity on me. "You saw the coloration of the petals appear to move, right? Those are the flower fairies."

I tightened my arms to my side, so as not to touch anything.

"Relax, Samantha. You've seen them thousands of times. Flower fairies tend to all the flowers around the world. You don't notice them often because they always take the color of the flower they're working on. How else do you think flowers bloom in the right colors and produce their scents, and attract the insects necessary for pollination? Fairies see to all that."

"Yeah?" I said. "Then why haven't I ever seen them before?"

With a kindly smile, Haggerty said, "Maybe you never wanted to."

"And that gnome out in yard," I asked. "Did he...?"

Haggerty's tired eyes widened in surprise. "There was a gnome in my yard?"

I stuffed my fingers in my ears. I didn't remove them until I'd followed Haggerty away from those little flower creatures. If I could have followed her with my eyes closed, I would have.

The interior of the house surprised me. Not only was it bigger than it appeared from outside, with large rooms opening into other spaces, it wasn't anywhere near as conventional as I'd expected. The walls were the color of fresh cream, and covering the shiny hardwood floors were priceless Navajo rugs in an endless variety of hues.

One living room wall held some kind of altar, a table covered by a crocheted shawl, on which she'd placed stones and candles and seashells, as well as a couple of daggers with decorative handles.

There were fresh flowers there, too. I didn't get close enough to see whether those flowers held any fairy bugs. Two or three bees and a couple of other bugs buzzed around the room, to which

Haggerty paid no attention. So the crazy chick made honey indoors. Whatever.

Other surfaces held candles, too, as well as the sconces built into most of the walls. And scattered on a number of surfaces were fruit bowls, filled with apples in dark red and brilliant yellow. And here and there a bowl held plain water. This was where Haggerty's true nature came out. Unless what she displayed at the office was also true.

The most arresting aspects of the décor were the paintings. Dominating each wall of the sprawling living, dining, and family room areas were large unframed canvases. I'd never seen anything as striking as those paintings, nor as hard to describe. They weren't abstracts, exactly, yet they weren't realistic, either. And they kept changing right before my eyes. At one moment they looked like eddies of bright colors, more like swirling mists, if fog came in brilliant hues. Then it would seem as if the mists would part a bit, to hint at a place beyond. I found myself staring at one painting after another, longing to see past the swirling colors, and almost feeling as if I did for an instant now and then. But I never felt able to hold on to what lay beyond those veils of pigment.

I couldn't say how long I stood gazing into those paintings. Only when, with a wistful sigh, did I accept that I would never see what might be hidden beyond the mists, did I blink rapidly to break their spell. When I did, I spied the name "Haggerty" painted in bold strokes in the lower corners.

I stabbed a finger toward one of the paintings. "You? You painted them?"

Haggerty tossed her purse and a ring with her house and car keys on a slim walnut table just past the foyer. A spare set of keys hung from a hook above it. As she shed her suit jacket and tossed it onto an ivory pillow on an oak futon, she shook her head. "My mother is the artist in the family."

I sank onto a floor pillow tossed on a Navajo rug in deep crimson and coral and teal. "You have a mother?" My jaw fell.

With a droll tilt of her lips, Haggerty said, "That's the usual vessel for arrival. Of course, I have a mother. I even have a grandmother."

"Have a father, too?" I asked.

"Somewhere, I suppose." She gave her head a stiff shake.

"He didn't stay around very long."

With a knowing sigh, I said, "There's a lot of that going around. Getting back to this mother and grandmother business. I don't get it. You were born, you can die…"

"I'm as much flesh-and-blood as you are, Samantha. It's just that I'm also…something more."

I nodded sagely. "You take human form."

She choked. "Take it? I'll have you know we had it before you folks started swinging in trees."

I hated superior deities. I gestured toward her mother's artwork. "What is that place in the paintings?"

"Tir na n'Og, our homeland."

"Oh, yeah. Heaven. You haven't been there, have you? Nor your mom?"

Haggerty shook her head. "Not till we're called home." She turned to face the largest of the paintings, and all the day's strain evaporated from her face. "But this is what we see in our dreams."

I slipped off the pillow onto the rug, and clutched the rough ivory fabric covering the cushion to my chest. "So where is your mom? Does she live locally?"

"No, she prefers the weather of the Southwest to our coastal climate."

I breathed an envious sigh. "Sedona, I'll bet. Or Santa Fe." Places for people like me, and the real thing.

Haggerty chuckled. "Try Las Vegas."

I snorted. "Don't tell me your mother likes to play the slots."

With a sardonic grin, Haggerty said, "It's more accurate to say she plays havoc *with* them. Mom doesn't like the casino's advantage—she considers it her mission to create more winners."

"She sounds like my kinda girl."

Haggerty frowned. I sensed my remark hit a truth she hadn't noticed before, and she didn't like it.

My hostess provided me with a pair of pastel sweats, socks and sneakers, a T-shirt to sleep in, as well as a fresh toothbrush and comb. While I changed, Haggerty made us hot chocolate.

When we gathered in the small family room off her kitchen, she wore jeans and a sweater, and her auburn hair waved loosely over her shoulders.

Cozy in my borrowed sweats, I cupped my hands around the hot mug of chocolate. "So, Haggerty, tell me about Angus."

She gave her wavy hair a shake. "Angus isn't for you, Samantha."

"Not good enough for your family, huh?"

She frowned at me. "Believe it or not, I was thinking of you. Angus is *Danaans,* one of the original gods."

"You can't go to *Tir na n'Og,* but Angus can come here?"

"The *Danaans* can go to any world they wish. Their powers are unlimited."

Other worlds? How many were there? No, don't tell me. I turned it around on her. "How long do you have to stay here? Before you're called home to...Avalon?"

She shrugged. "Until I discover whatever I'm here to learn. But I'm in no rush. The same is true for you, Samantha. You're here to work through something, too, before you move on to the next plane."

I wrinkled my nose at her. Too heavy for me.

"Don't you ever wonder why we're here?" Haggerty went on. "Don't you think about karma?"

"Karma? I thought that was a club in West Hollywood." I swiftly changed the subject. "Let's get back to Angus."

"Angus really isn't someone you want to get involved with. I can't imagine why my mother sent him to me. I know you seem like a good-time girl, but I'm betting you still want something more than that. Believe me, when the going gets tough, Angus, that good-time boy, will be long gone."

I shook my head. "Men. They're all the same. Angus sounds like my ex."

"You were married?"

"Don't remind me." I snorted. "I gave that bastard the best week of my life, but did he appreciate it? Not a bit."

Haggerty laughed.

"What's so funny?"

"I'm sorry," Haggerty said. "I thought you were joking." When she saw I wasn't, she asked. "How long were you married?"

"Eight days. But it felt longer."

"Like nine, I bet."

"You know it." I swatted at a bee that kept circling my head.

Haggerty quickly came out of her chair. "Please let the bees alone, Samantha." She extended her palm; the bee settled in it. She carried it away and gently deposited it on a leaf of a potted begonia.

"You *want* bees in your house?"

"Who else would transport the flower fairies?"

O-kay. Before I dismissed that ridiculous idea, a dragonfly buzzed the surface of one of the water-filled bowls, as if it had been placed there for that purpose. After a moment, I realized it probably had.

I studied her across the surface of my hot chocolate. "Detective Azar seems nice."

"Ummm," she muttered. Without warning, Haggerty squeezed her eyes closed and pressed her hand to her head.

I quickly put my mug on the oak coffee table before the sofa and rushed to her. "What is it?"

Haggerty held her head in her hands. "Molly again," she muttered. "That same image in the cellar."

"You know, I've read that Molly Claire considers herself sensitive. Is it possible she's trying to send you, or someone, a message?"

With a sigh, Haggerty sat up again. "If she is, I wish she could have provided better directions." She pinched her eyes closed. "What do you know about her?"

I shrugged. "Just what I read while waiting to pay for my groceries, so you gotta consider the source. Her co-stars always report that she's the nicest person in Hollywood, but the little people behind the scenes say it doesn't extend to their level. Especially not after her old man dumped her for a newer and better Molly." I studied her. "You've been in that basement with her—what do you know about her?"

Haggerty's facial contraction eased, and I gathered the vision had faded. "Just that she's so very intense. I'm going to call the office. See if the night crew has turned up anything." She struggled to rise from the sofa; it seemed to take a great effort.

"Wait. Tell me something. Your powers—why do they weaken you like this?"

Haggerty spoke absently as she hunted for her cordless phone. "They're diluted, by being too many generations removed from the *Danaans,* too much intermarrying with mortals. And because we're not worshiped by many people anymore. We draw strength from our believers."

I snorted. "Not many? You mean there are actually *some* people alive today who worship Celtic gods?"

When she dug the cordless phone handset out from behind a pillow on the sofa, she suppressed a smile. "One or two."

Something seemed to happen then. She proceeded with that call, but her mind appeared to be somewhere else, and she kept glancing at her watch. I sensed that I'd given her an idea she was eager to put into effect. She concluded the call as quickly as she could, with nothing to report. Then, all at once, she became hurried with me. She snatched away my mug and carried it along with her own to the kitchen.

"What a day we've had," Haggerty said on her return. Only she seemed more rejuvenated than she had only a few minutes before. "You must think I'm an awful hostess. Let me show you to the guestroom, Samantha."

I was tired, but the tequila had worn off, and I was still too wound up for sleep. Besides, I was comfortable there. Well, I'd have been more comfortable if I still had the dregs of my hot chocolate. I shrugged to show my indifference to seeing the guestroom. But once Haggerty made up her mind about something, I'd discovered there was no dissuading her. She took hold of my hand, tugging me to my feet. She dragged me to a room at the front of the house.

Her small guestroom had been furnished with a double bed, a single oak nightstand and a low dresser. Laid out on the dresser was a model of Stonehenge in England. I'd never been there in person, but it looked just like the pictures I'd seen. I reached out to touch it.

"Uh-uh, Samantha. That's fragile. Why don't I move it out of here, so you don't have to worry about it."

She leaned against the doorframe and clenched her eyes closed. All at once, the model disappeared. It totally vanished.

"What...?"

"Don't worry, I just moved it to a storage closet, where it wouldn't be in your way."

"Holy shit. When they transport on Star Trek, they get beams and those lines. And that's not real, but this here—" I kept stammering. "I've never seen anything like that."

This was a day of firsts, way too many for my comfort level.

I sank onto the striped bedspread and just looked up at Haggerty, who leaned against the doorframe. She wore a superior smile—she was showing off. Why was she willing to drain her precious powers just to dazzle me?

My sense before that something had occurred to her grew stronger. And Haggerty didn't want me to know anything about it.

Obviously, she had a lot to learn about me.

CHAPTER TEN

Even if I hadn't been too agitated by the day's events to sleep, there was no way I would close my eyes now that I knew Haggerty was pulling something. To lure her into putting the operation into effect, I gave every appearance of falling in with her plan. I yawned and told her I couldn't stay awake a minute longer. Despite her poker face when she bid me goodnight, I saw an easing of her facial muscles, confirming for me that I'd told her precisely what she wanted to hear.

Fooling people comes easily to me. I'd been doing it all my life. But a goddess? For all I knew she had x-ray vision, like Superman. If I sat there waiting for her to go into action, she might just hunker down in the living room and watch me through the wall. Though I generally believed that corners wouldn't exist if we weren't meant to cut them, I decided tonight I had to play my act straight. Well, pretty straight—after all, it was still an act.

I slipped off the pair of sneakers that Haggerty had loaned me, but I kept on her sweats and socks. She'd already laid out an oversized T-shirt for me to sleep in, but I placed that into an empty nightstand drawer. Then I peeled back the covers on the bed and climbed in. The last thing I did was to turn out the bedside light.

I must have waited in the dark for a good twenty minutes. I began to think I'd misread her. Then the hardwood floor outside the guestroom creaked, as someone tiptoed toward it. The footsteps stopped, and I imagined her standing by my door, listening. A minute or two later, I heard the sound of the doorknob turning, and then, through my cracked eyelids, I saw a beam of light when the door opened a few inches.

I'd learned what *not* to do the first time I tried faking sleep, back in my early teens when I wanted to sneak out to a concert. It seemed an easy enough ruse to pull off. The trouble is we never see ourselves when we're asleep. Like everything else, a successful fake-sleep lies in the details.

Since I couldn't crack my eyelids much now, I felt, more

than saw, when Haggerty peered into the room. I immediately went into a routine I'd been perfecting since that night in my teens when I failed to show up at a concert. Though my heart raced with excitement, I slowed my breathing, keeping it as shallow as possible. As expected, Haggerty was thorough—the door didn't close. After a while, my lungs demanded a big honking breath, but I'm nothing if not a professional con-girl. I refused to let my chest swell as it demanded. I even produced a soft, contented snore. When she still didn't leave, it was time to show her the light disturbed me. I began to toss, and even muttered a bit. Haggerty must have accurately read the signs of my restlessness because she quickly shut the door.

I grinned into the darkness with satisfaction. I swear, that routine works so well, I should patent it.

A short time later, I heard the front door closing. I slipped out of bed. Within the darkened room, I carefully parted the drapes and peered out.

The combination of Haggerty's porch lamp and a street light in front of the house next door lit the scene so well, it couldn't have been clearer if it had been played out on stage. I watched as my hostess, dressed now in a floor-length, loose-fitting gown in some white gauzy fabric, skipped down her front steps. She paused long enough to quietly open and close the gate on her picket fence, before slipping off to a dark minivan that waited for her in the street.

As soon as the minivan pulled away, I threw on my borrowed sneakers and sprinted from the guestroom. Out in the living room, I saw that Haggerty had taken the set of keys she'd dropped next to her purse when we came in. Her purse was still there.

I had to go after her. But how? I'd left Lady Stang at the Federal Building. My eyes drifted to another set of keys dangling from a small hook over the table. I'd borrow Haggerty's car!

I raced from the house so fast, I forgot to look at the flower bug-fairies. But when I backed the Honda out of the driveway, I couldn't help but notice the gnome was gone.

The minivan had a head start, but lucky for me, the driver drove slowly, even in the middle of the night when there was no reason not to speed. Besides, Haggerty's Honda had some muscle—was that true for all new cars? Unless I started making some serious bucks, I'd never find out. Sometimes I feared they'd bury Stangie and me together. Still, I've followed people loads of times—well, clients I feared might be sneaking off to see another spiritual advisor. And I'd learned it helps to guess about their destination. While I didn't know where they were headed, I had a good idea of the route they might take. I drove to the closest freeway entrance, and I spotted the minivan just before it turned onto the entrance ramp.

The minivan followed the 101 Freeway into the 134. The freeways are never really empty in Southern California, no matter what the hour, so other cars provided me with good cover. I just tucked into the next lane and hovered in the minivan's blind spot.

With its tinted windows, I couldn't make out much about the driver, other than that it appeared to be a woman with long hair. Given the car, and the cautious way she drove, I pegged Haggerty's friend as a suburban mother. Except that soccer moms don't ordinarily whisk FBI agents away in the middle of the night.

The van took the Griffith Park exit. I had to be careful there. That park must encompass several thousand sprawling acres, much of it uncultivated and largely unlit. So the driver didn't wonder why someone was tailing her through the wilderness at that hour, I turned off the Honda's headlights and struggled to keep the minivan's taillights in view.

Both cars climbed high into the park's hills, on unlit, unmarked roads. When ours were the only vehicles there, I had to let it gain more ground. Once it was out of sight, and I feared I'd lost it. I circled around those winding roads until I finally came upon the minivan parked along with other cars on the fringe of a wooded area at the side of the road. I tucked the Honda around the next bend, so Haggerty wouldn't see it if she finished her business before I had a chance to make my getaway.

What business could she possibly have out there at that hour?

CHAPTER ELEVEN

Not wanting to risk sending out the noise of dried brush crunched underfoot, I skirted the fringe of the wooded area until I found a narrow trail. The trail climbed more steeply than I expected, through a thick grove; at points, no wider than my hips. With the trees towering over me and pressing against my sides, the place felt dark and creepy.

Until I looked up. Like most urban areas, L.A. throws too much incandescence at the night sky for the stars to glow in all their glory. But this high up, in the midst of such darkness, the stars burned brighter against the pitch sky than I had ever seen them. Once I let my eyes adjust to it, the full moon lit the way for me.

When the trail leveled out and the trees became sparse around me, I heard voices carried on the breeze that blew my way. Melodic voices, mostly high-pitched, but with some lower timbres. The wind also carried the pungent scent of smoldering herbs. Lavender, I thought, and roses, with maybe a dash of lemon—I used essential oils during some of my readings, so I knew their scents well. The trees gave way to a clearing at the top of the mountain.

I slipped off the trail, creeping behind a row of bushes that ringed the open area, and peered through. A group of people, alternating gender, danced in a circle and chanted aloud. Some of them were naked, while others wore loose-fitting robes in a variety of colors. Within that ring, a cauldron smoked and gave off more intense smells than downwind.

And at the center of the circle, adored and revered by those worshippers, with her arms raised and her head thrown back—stood Haggerty.

One woman's voice rose above the soft chanting, calling out, "Bide ye the Wiccan laws ye must, in perfect love and perfect trust."

I watched, mesmerized as they danced around Haggerty's swaying form, faster and faster, working themselves into a frenzy. And I listened, without understanding, to the words that voice continued to proclaim.

"Heed ye flower, bush and tree, by the Lady, blessed be."

Transfixed by the scene, my head growing woozy from the scent of those smoldering herbs, I began to sway to their rhythm.

"True in love ye must ever be, lest thy love be false to thee," the voice cried.

Some forgotten scene from a movie floated into my head to provide identification. "It's a witches' coven," I whispered aloud, though to myself.

"Aye, that it 'tis," came a returning whisper from right behind me.

With a gasp, I turned, certain I'd been caught.

Surprised again—Angus knelt there.

How was it possible that I hadn't heard his approach? Sure, the scene in the clearing had riveted me, but survival had to be my strongest instinct. I would have heard it if anyone had approached through that dried bush. If they'd approached in any normal way, that is.

"Angus, how...?"

He heard it before I did, a rustle in the bushes, headed our way. He pressed his finger to his lips as a signal for silence. When he turned his head in the direction of the sound, I saw the top of his ears weren't rounded as ours are, but came to a pixyish point. Not a weird point like Mr. Spock or anything, just enough to give him an elfin quality when his ear tips peaked through his soft blonde waves. I wondered what it would feel like to nibble on them.

The sound of footsteps grew louder. Before anyone came into view, however, his face grew taut with concentration. In the next instant, he disappeared. One second he was there, and then, poof—he was invisible. I glanced down at myself—and I saw *I* was invisible, too!

Yet I felt no different. When a passing cloud drifted away, I saw in the moon's bright, light, that we weren't absolutely transparent; our bodies glistened as clearly as water, but with the slightest ripple. Unless someone was looking, though, they would never notice.

Before I could question what form I came to be in, several figures approached. They appeared to be young girls, nude below gray-white cloaks that seemed to be spun of ash and cobwebs. Lacy wings peeked out from under their cloaks. Their faces looked human, but unnaturally pale, with dark eyes so reddened, it looked as if they'd spent years crying. And though they seemed quite young, the hair that hung down their backs to the ground was a shiny gray, which shimmered in the moonlight like the rippling skin of a seal.

Once the creatures appeared assured that nobody inhabited this part of the woods, they glided past us, patrolling another stretch. After they moved well beyond us, with no warning, Angus and I became visible again.

Angus gave one last look after them to be sure they were gone.

"What—?" I began.

"Banshees," he whispered.

"Banshees?" I said in a hushed gasp.

"No worries, dear girl. They're not keening." Angus went on to explain that they cried when someone from the families they guard died. "Annabelle enlists them to protect these rituals of hers from view. Our girl leaves nothing to chance."

I hesitated. So many questions, yet I wasn't sure I wanted the answers. But my curiosity still ruled. "Where does she get them from?"

Angus frowned. "From? They're always here."

I shook my head. "No. I refuse to believe all this exists—gods and goddesses, banshees and fairies—and I didn't know about it."

Angus smiled at me with amused tolerance. "Banshees, fairies of all sorts, take many forms, dear girl. Have you never seen a crow or a weasel or a hare?"

"Of course, I have."

"Then, my darling Samantha, you've seen a banshee in one of her disguises."

I suddenly felt as if something sucked all the air from me. So it was true. There really was a magical realm right here. How could so much exist that I knew nothing about? I must have looked as stunned as I felt when I muttered as much to Angus.

With an expression that combined superior knowledge with an eagerness to share, Angus said, "This world holds more than you can imagine. Why don't you let me show you some of it?"

He took my hand and quietly led me away. Angus brought

me to a clearing in the thickest part of the forest, which was about the size of a Las Vegas high roller's bed and just as round. Though we'd only walked for a few minutes, our hideaway was far enough away from the coven's spot that I could no longer hear their voices, and the air's only scent was the crisp evergreen spice given off by the pine trees surrounding our honeymoon bed.

Though still dazed by what I'd seen, when I stood facing Angus, my breath began to quicken in anticipation. He placed his hands on my waist, sending a tingle throughout my whole body.

"How magnificent a woman you are," he said, his melodic voice growing husky with emotion.

And when he took me in his arms, I felt magnificent. For the first time in my life I didn't feel like pudgy Samantha, squeezed-into-last-season's-clothes Samantha, I felt like the most divine woman on Earth. The touch of his lips on mine made me drunk with desire, the movement of his hands as they explored my body made me dizzy. And my body positively ignited when Angus left a trail of kisses, as soft as the breeze, from my neck to my breasts.

Our garments seemed to be shed with no more than a touch. We stood apart for a moment, drinking in each other's bodies with our eyes. If I had a man made to order, he could not have been any more perfect than Angus. His chest was broad and strong, with just enough strawberry blonde hair to tickle my fingers when I ran them through it. His lean, muscular thighs were taut when he pressed them to mine. Yet filling his soft blue-and-silver eyes was an expression of caring and appreciation. Never had I felt more desirable, more cherished. Never had I felt more a woman.

Our bodies fell together to our bed of fallen leaves and pine needles. But the charm ended briefly then, when the pine needles jabbed at my writhing back.

Angus drew away from me. "The ground is too rough for skin as soft as yours."

"That's okay, I don't mind," I said breathlessly, drawing his hard chest back to mine.

Angus had another solution. He simply elevated our joined bodies until they floated in the air a few feet off the ground.

"But you won't have any leverage without—" I protested. "You can't —"

Smiling with the knowledge that he had no limits, Angus

said simply, "I can."

And he did.

"Omigod, omigod, omigod, omigod," I whispered again and again to an accelerating beat. Until I realized what I was saying. After that I just screamed the word in my head.

Then I saw lights, colors like the ones in those paintings in Haggerty's home. And for one single moment of pure ecstasy, those mists parted to reveal a place exquisite and ethereal beyond description. We might just have been hovering a few feet from the ground, but let me tell you, that god took me all the way to the stars.

CHAPTER TWELVE

The next thing I remembered, someone broke into my sleep by pounding on a door and shouting, "Wake up, Samantha."

My body stirred. I found I was sleeping on something more comfortable than the ground, but also more substantial than air. I opened my bleary eyes and saw nothing but a jaundiced blur, until I wiped my curly blonde hair from before my eyes. Then, though it was dark, I recognized the room as Haggerty's guestroom.

The events of the night before came back to me in a rush. After our romantic tryst, Angus and I parted at Haggerty's Honda, just as the Wiccan ritual seemed to be breaking up. I rushed back to Haggerty's place. I wasn't there more than ten minutes before the minivan dropped her off, and I heard my hostess sail through her front door.

I knew she had no more sleep than I had last night. Yet once again, she banged on the guestroom door, and cried in an annoyingly upbeat voice, "Time to rise, Sleepyhead."

I didn't see why I should rise, when the sun hadn't yet seen fit to. Glancing at the digital clock on the nightstand, I saw I hadn't been asleep for even two hours.

Then I remembered my time with Angus. With a smile, I shifted lazily and stretched. Nothing as mundane as sleep could trouble me today. I carried the sun inside of me now.

When I heard footsteps approach the guestroom door for the third time, I shouted, "I'm up."

After rising unsteadily to my feet and shaking out my wild hair, I drifted from the room. When I passed one of those paintings Haggerty's mom did, I suppressed a smug smile. Okay, maybe I couldn't remember what it looked like beyond that swirling colored mist, but I saw past it once. I knew that.

In her modern kitchen, with its white cabinets and appliances, Haggerty stood at the stove and told me to take a seat at the round pine table in the breakfast nook. She placed before me a plate of eggs and toast, with a few slices of fresh apples. Suddenly discovering I was ravenous, I shoveled it in.

"You're a good cook," I said.

"This? It's nothing," she said, over her shoulder, while plating her own breakfast. "You should try my 'Fit for a Goddess French Toast.'"

Was she offering another course? Fortunately, I can always fit it in.

Already dressed in a navy suit, Haggerty slipped into the chair across from mine. One look in my direction, and she scowled. "Samantha, why couldn't you have listened to my warning about Angus?"

Huh? How did she do that? "Angus? Your...uh...cousin, you mean? I haven't seen Angus." Man, I put that one across with such innocence, anyone would have bought it.

Haggerty's scowl just deepened.

"How did you know?" I asked sheepishly, while wiping some egg yolk from my chin with a napkin.

She snapped, "You asked me about auras. Yours, yesterday—pale yellow. Today—bright gold. What mortal man could do that?"

"I don't know, but if you find him, send him my way."

Hey, I wasn't the only one who had experienced a metamorphosis during the hours when we were supposed to be sleeping. I might not know an aura from a brick wall, but I could see the change in her, too. Her skin glowed brightly this morning, her body gleamed with vitality. Her worshipers had done the trick; they were like a drug for Haggerty. As Angus was for me.

"Will Angus age?"

"The *Danaans* age, but too slowly for your time to measure. They're eternal."

"So when I'm an old bag with crepe skin flapping under my arms, Angus will be..." I shrugged. "Maybe it won't matter. Maybe I'll still make him my own."

Haggerty just gave her head a sad shake and concentrated on eating her breakfast.

We stopped at my place on the way to the Federal Building. I rent a guesthouse behind the main house of a gated estate in Santa Monica, as I have since I first went out on my own. Haggerty said she needed to make some phone calls. With her cell phone in hand, she waited in the car, while I went inside to change and pack some things.

My first reaction when I unlocked my door was to cringe, and that surprised me because I'd always taken pride in what I'd done with my place. The guesthouse only contains a bedroom, living room, kitchen and bath, but all the rooms are unexpectedly large. I'd painted each a different, vibrant color. The living room was a dusky rose, with a deeper and glossier tone painted on the crown and floor moldings. I filled every possible space with crystals and candles and aromatherapy warmers, and covered the walls with paintings of unicorns and dreamy stuff like that. I mean, I see a lot of clients here—my place has to look the part.

I'd picked those intense colors because I thought they radiated life. And though my metaphysical doodads were hokey, I thought I'd created such a tasteful effect. Now, with Haggerty's home in mind, this looked so cheesy to me.

I'd gotten a deal on the place when I first took it. My landlady, who lived in the main house, was an aging widow struggling to hold onto the home her husband had left her, along with his debts. Badly in need of repairs, the whole place had begun to look seedy. Despite her financial bind, when she learned I was psychic, she let me have the guesthouse for less than she planned to ask, with the understanding that I would give her readings whenever she wanted.

Naturally, I jumped at the deal. Even after her demands for readings grew, I still felt I was ahead of the game. I mean, it wasn't like they cost me anything. I did find it odd that she didn't ask any of the things clients typically do. She didn't want to know about her husband in the Great Beyond, or what the future held for her. Instead, she asked questions of a cultural or sociological nature, about what direction we, as a people, were headed in.

I didn't find out for some time that my landlady had pegged me for a charlatan from the get-go, and not a good one at that. Whenever I made a cultural prediction, she took her meager savings and invested it in precisely the opposite way. She used me as a negative barometer, in effect. Worse yet, it worked.

I mean, who could have predicted there would be a Starbucks on every corner, that chefs would become stars, or that people would crave truffles? Have you ever *seen* those things? What can I say? Not really psychic, remember?

By inverting my predictions my landlady had made enough to keep the estate in pristine condition. Once I caught on to what she was doing, I renegotiated our rental agreement. I live there rent-free now, though naturally, my readings are still part of the bargain. The sad thing is we both continue to pretend I really do have the gift. If I had any shame, I'd gag on it.

Just as I finished changing, I heard a knock on the door. Today, I wore a knee-length prom gown from the '50s. Who was going to know how special I was if I didn't look it? My dress had a billowing skirt made of several layers of organdy, striped with bands of turquoise, peach and coral. And as the skirt shifted, the stripes seemed to jump around. Fun, huh? I liked that dress too much to care that some people insisted it gave them vertigo.

I threw the door open. Haggerty stood on the doorstep.

Her blue eyes widened briefly. She recovered fast, though. "Nice getup, Gidget. Are you ready?"

I told her I just had a few more things to toss in the suitcase, and I returned to the bedroom to finish. When I left Haggerty, she was standing in the middle of my living room, taking it in. And she'd seemed irritated. When I returned, she appeared more relaxed, as she fussed happily among my trinkets.

With a big smile of approval, she said, "This place really suits you."

How did she mean that?

She gestured to a bookcase filled with crystals. "This is why you live a charmed life. All these crystals—you're protected."

Yeah, right. It took all I had not to snort at her. Once again, our contrast struck me as ironic. Here she was, Ms. Uptight in her dorky suit, and she believed that crystals could keep a person safe. While I dressed the part of the cool, metaphysical chick, yet I didn't count on those rocks for anything.

There had to be a moral there. I just didn't know what it was.

When we left my place, Haggerty started down Wilshire, toward the Federal Building. Then, without warning, she went into a U-turn, as if the impulse had just struck her.

"Where...?" I started to ask.

"Just humor me, okay?"

Hey, it was not like I had a schedule. Besides, after what I spied on last night in the park, any diversion of hers promised to be interesting.

We headed up the coast and pulled alongside a vacant lot overlooking a sheltered Pacific cove. Since it was a weekday, when Haggerty cut the Honda's engine, there were only a couple of people sitting on the bluff, an elderly pair just packing up their blanket.

"No dolphins today," the man called cheerfully to us. "We've been watching for 'em since first light."

He and his wife paused when they came abreast of us, as if they expected their experience to short-circuit ours.

"We'll just give it a few minutes," Haggerty said.

"Suit yourself," the elderly man said with a sniff, though it clearly didn't suit him that we wouldn't rely on his judgment.

Haggerty stood near the edge of the cliff staring down at the ocean. I followed her glance to where gentle waves crashed against rocks in a small inlet. A little farther out, a diving platform, so new the ocean hadn't yet weathered its redwood planks, rolled gently on the swells.

Though Haggerty never turned back to watch the old couple leave, I could tell from her posture that she was listening for the sound of their car starting up. The old guy really took his time packing up the white Buick we'd seen parked near where Haggerty left her Honda.

Only when they were gone did she glance over her shoulder toward the Coast Highway. She waited till she saw a big gap in the traffic, and then turned back to the ocean. She raised her head into the air—and let fly the loudest screech I'd ever heard.

It startled me so much, I nearly fell over the bluff. "What the hell was that?" I cried.

With a smile, Haggerty directed my attention out to the horizon. All at once, dolphin heads started popping to the surface way in the distance. Pod upon pod of them rushed closer.

"Watch for intruders, will you, Samantha?"

"Huh?"

With a trace of a frown, she said, "People. Will you watch the road and warn me if anyone comes?"

"Oh…yeah, sure."

I kept watch as she asked. Still, I couldn't resist sneaking glances over my shoulder. Naturally, living at the beach, I'd seen dolphins and passing whales loads of times, though never the number now gathered out there in response to Haggerty's shriek. When she began making other chirrups and squeaks and whistles, I recognized those sounds for what they were. She was speaking their language! A couple among the vast pod of dolphins responded in kind, while others made different sounds in the background, like people murmuring during speeches.

The whole exchange only lasted a few minutes. One second they were all there, squeaking and crying back to her; the next, they were leaping into the air as they rushed back out to sea. Haggerty turned away from the shore. Since I seemed incapable of movement, she nudged me toward the car.

"I guess you want an explanation," Haggerty said.

Ya think?

"It occurred to me that being so close to the coast, it's possible Molly's abductors might move her by boat." With a toss of her head, Haggerty indicated the dolphins. "They'll watch for it and alert me."

"You broke the code," I stammered. "To their language. Scientists have been trying to communicate with them for decades."

"Right," Haggerty said with a snicker.

I came to a stop outside the passenger door to her car. "No, don't tell me—they're gods, too, or fairies of some sort."

When another car pulled up behind us, Haggerty indicated with a nod that I should get into the Honda. Even after we were on our way, she still hadn't answered.

"They say dolphins used to walk on land," I said. "Is that just a myth?"

Finally, she said, "They were shape-shifters, capable of surviving on land, in the sea, and in the air. They gave up their changeling powers to live for eternity in the water."

"They loved it that much? I mean, me—I love a long soak, too, but the puckering..." I made a face.

"Apparently, they gave themselves a pucker-proof skin," Haggerty said with a laugh, then added in a more serious tone, "and they didn't want to live among humans anymore."

"But they love humans," I protested. "Look at the smiles they always give us."

Haggerty shot me a glance that said I was naïve. Me? Hah! I was as jaded as they come.

"That's just the way their faces look," she said. "But you're right, they do like humans. They just don't trust them."

From the intense stare Haggerty directed through the windshield, something told me that neither did she.

Everyone was already gathered when we made it to the Bureau. Jake was there, still dressed in the same black jeans and scuffed leather jacket from yesterday, and his five o'clock shadow was on overtime. Ironically, Rusler was the one who had changed his clothes, but his weary demeanor made him, not Jake, look like he'd never left. Rusler had already shed his suit jacket, and underarm crescents were spreading down the sides of his limp blue shirt. But they all looked so haggard. Fortunately, those weary people seemed to cheer right up when they saw my dress.

In contrast to those tired souls, Haggerty's vitality looked obscene. Jake followed her into her office and perched his fine firm butt on the corner of her desk.

"Annabelle, you look like you just came off a vacation. How do you do it?"

"It's a new makeup," she said, flushing. "And I took a pill last night so I could close my eyes for a few hours."

With a shrug, he said, "Whatever works."

She sent a careful look my way, to check whether I knew otherwise. I didn't give her—or myself—away.

Jake twisted my way. "How 'bout you, Your Highness. Any more visions?"

I described Haggerty's impression of Molly's imprisonment in that smelly basement, making sure I never looked at her.

"I'd have called it in if there had been anything there to identify it," Haggerty said when I concluded.

Jake didn't pay attention to her. He just kept staring at me, as if with his forceful glare he could get me to tell him how I really obtained that picture. For Haggerty's sake, as well as my own, I'd never tell. Cynics, ya gotta love 'em.

The taskforce returned to work, sifting through the crime scene report from the cabin where Molly's Clowns were shot. The good citizens of the city had also started calling in sightings of

Molly. Overnight she'd achieved the status of Elvis and Bigfoot. When you put together all the places she was said to be seen, and the times, and the distances, it was clear she couldn't have been in any of those places, not to mention all. I was a flake, too, but at least I knew it.

Since there wasn't anything I could do to help, they put me in a small office with a TV and a stack of magazines so old the pages had yellowed. The TV rested on a VCR, but the tape in it was blank.

Before he left, Jake said with a suppressed smile, "You get any more of those impressions of Miss Molly, you give a shout, huh, Madame Samantha?" He ended with a smug chuckle.

You know, if I were the real thing, I'd find skeptics like him—and me—a pain in the butt.

I killed some time with the magazines, wondering how people happened to fall off *People* magazine's *100 Most Beautiful People* list when their TV shows went off the air. Do they lose their looks along with their jobs?

Finally, with nothing else to read and nowhere to go, I felt desperate enough for daytime TV. The local news was showing a special report on *The Power of the Pyramid* exhibit. A popular female anchor, whose blonde hair was coifed to within an inch of its life and whose aging face had been shot with so much Botox they probably wouldn't need to embalm her when she died, accompanied a curator for a sneak peak at the treasures that awaited those lucky enough to get tickets. Since the only museums I frequented were vintage clothing stores, I hadn't even tried.

The curator was a tall elegant man who looked like Prince Charles, only without those ears, who walked in front of the exhibit cases with kind of a leap to his step. Either he was really excited about the exhibit, or he was one of those oppressively optimistic souls just high on life. He did talk down to the anchor, explaining everything in simple language, as if to a small child. He must have sensed he was dealing there with the fundamentally stupid.

When the camera panned over one small display, so much gold gleamed into the lens I had to divert my eyes. He opened the case, so the camera could draw closer. When the anchor extended a manicured hand toward an ancient scroll, I thought Prince Charles would tackle her. As it was, he leaped a good foot into the air when he put himself between her hand and that scroll, all the while explaining that the natural oils on her hands would break down that delicate papyrus.

I couldn't blame her for the impulse. Those items were so captivating, so otherworldly, that I also longed to reach through the TV and touch them. There was one little gold cat that I desperately wanted to cradle in my arms and keep forever. Not because it was so valuable, as it must have been, but simply because it bewitched me. As Angus was to mortal men, that statue was to house cats—a more perfect version.

Though the golden cat remained my favorite, other pieces mesmerized me nearly as much. I became so captivated by those treasures, I tuned out the curator's droning lecture mentally, since it was starting to patronize me, a smart blonde, along with the dumb blonde anchor. If I'd seen a remote control anywhere in that room, I would have muted it, but I was too lazy to get up and turn down the sound.

Except that, as long as the sound kept playing, I couldn't entirely tune it out. I didn't pay much attention to it, but after the fact, when Charlie's words filtered through to me, I realized I might have missed something significant.

Fortunately, the dumb anchor repeated the gist for others of her ilk out here in TV-land, as well as me. "So what you're saying is that many believe the pharaohs weren't mortals, but gods? Is that it?" she asked, tilting her head attractively for the camera.

"That was the belief generally held in ancient Egypt. In the modern world, it's somewhat rarer." The curator ended with a superior chuckle.

Given all I'd seen in the last day, I'd say the modern world should do a reality check. But gods, huh? I began to feel a connection, and it made me uneasy. Like that feeling you get when you drink too many Margaritas while watching *Ghostbusters*. Surely, everyone has experienced that.

Haggerty picked that moment to drop in.

I looked past her to make sure we were alone before asking, "*Celtic* Gods?"

Her face paled and she performed the same check over her shoulder, before whispering tightly, "What about them?"

"Are *Celtic* gods really separate and unique?" Not that I was completely convinced they existed, you understand, despite everything I'd seen. For all I knew she was just better at my scam than I was. "Didn't every ethnic group back in the ancient world just rename another group's gods? The Romans renamed the Greek gods, and the Celts renamed the Romans'. And maybe the Greeks borrowed initially from the...Egyptians." Whoa! Where did that come from? I'd like to tell Mr. Kempler from tenth grade history that I did more in his class than apply my makeup—only he'd taken out that restraining order on me.

Haggerty gave her big blue eyes a dramatic roll. "You wouldn't say that if you could see what it's like when all the clans get together."

I didn't know why what she said made me feel worse. Or what I was afraid of.

Still, I persisted. "The Egyptian pharaohs—were they gods?"

"They were till sometime around the Twentieth Dynasty. Then they left Egypt in the hands of mortals." She hesitated. "Well, near-mortals. The original pharaoh-gods left their descendents, and those who would guard the pharaohs to come, with some powers." She paused in what was starting to sound like a lecture. I resisted the desire to tune it out—look what happened when I did that with Mr. Kempler. "Actually, their guards had more powers than the pharaohs themselves, so that they could protect their kings. Nothing like those the original pharaohs possessed, though. Then, after leaving Egypt in semi-mortal hands, they decamped to another region."

Distracted from my original intent, I said, "No kidding. To where?"

"The area that's now the southwestern part of the U.S. The Egyptian gods became the ancient tribes known today as the Anasazi and the Sinagua."

No, this was all too much. I rubbed my face quickly with my hands, hoping Haggerty would disappear by the time I removed them. Not only hadn't she, Jake had popped into the room, so I couldn't even question her any more.

"The seer want anything?" he asked Haggerty with a thrust of his thumb at me.

"I didn't ask her yet." Haggerty turned to me. "We're sending out for lunch. Can we get you anything?"

The thought of food made me queasy. That was a first. "Just get me whatever you're having." With a pair of nods, they walked away.

On the TV, the curator held another artifact for the camera, a painted bowl, almost as beautiful as the cat I thought of as my own. Now it failed to hold me. I felt I had to shut it all out: the thoughts that made me uncomfortable, but wouldn't quite jell; all the creatures whose existence I'd learned about since yesterday—I had to block it all out before my head burst. Finally, something overcame my laziness. I actually rose to turn the set off. I started for it, so desperate that my arm stretched out before me, with my finger pointed at the power switch.

Just then a live reporter broke into the special. A man whose tie was yanked down and top shirt button undone, to show he really was toiling away in the news trenches, stared intently into the camera. "We interrupt regular programming for this live report. Just moments ago a gang robbed a bank at Olympic and Bundy, leaving two tellers dead and the manager pistol-whipped."

While I listened to his report, sad as it was, I didn't get too worked up about it. L.A. was the bank robbery capital of the country. Robberies only made the news when they were especially violent, like this one. Actually, now that I thought about it, even with the level of violence reported, it was odd that the station bothered to interrupt their special for it.

The reporter might have been reading my mind—sometimes I believed everyone was psychic but me.

"Unique about this robbery was that four of the five robbers dressed as clowns. The fifth, who was undisguised, seems to have been a prominent Angeleno. This station has obtained an exclusive copy of the bank's security tape."

The station switched to the grainy black-and-white tape. Sure enough, four people—men, judging by their builds—were dressed as circus clowns. All of them held automatic weapons. The fifth robber, a slight, blonde woman with a quirky haircut—looked like Molly Claire.

The image so shocked me, I stumbled backwards, unable to stop until I bumped into a chair. Good thing my dress padded my tush, or that would have hurt.

"Haggerty," I screamed. "Get back here. Now!"

She rushed in, followed closely by Jake. "What's with all the noise?" he demanded.

I gestured toward the screen. Words poured from my mouth without pausing in my brain. Less than usual, even. I couldn't be sure what I said, but my rambling account must have made some sense, because it made Haggerty jump to the VCR and press the record button.

Rusler came to the doorway. "What's that...?"

Jake told him, nearly as incoherently as I had.

"Get that security tape," Rusler roared.

The TV station returned the camera to the reporter, who just recapped what he'd already said.

Haggerty switched to the tape she'd made. We all drew close to the small screen to scrutinize an image that now was one generation grainier.

"That *is* Molly Claire, isn't it?" Haggerty asked.

If not, it was her exact double. Same little heart-shaped face, same turned-up nose dotted with tiny freckles. She wore a dark sweater over a pair of gray knit pants. Her layered haircut didn't look much different whether she spent the night tied up in some smelly cellar, or if she just stepped from the chair of a pricey Beverly Hills salon. Her unmade-up face was slick with sweat and locked in a pained grimace. Like the other robbers, she held an automatic weapon, but not in a way that indicated she knew how to handle it. And she alone never fired hers.

At one point Molly stole a look at the security camera, and mouthed a couple of words.

"What's that she said?" Haggerty demanded. She rewound and replayed the tape.

"I can't tell," Jake snapped.

Since my job required me to know things people didn't tell me, I'd perfected the art of lip-reading ages ago. Unlike the others, I had no trouble making out what Molly mouthed on the tape.

"Help me," I muttered. When they all turned to me, I said, "The words she said were—*help me.*"

CHAPTER THIRTEEN
Haggerty

What a grueling, frustrating day. After hours of investigation, they'd determined that Molly Claire had actually participated in that bizarre bank robbery, as they'd gathered from watching the tape. Since Molly alone of the robbers had not worn latex gloves, she'd left her fingerprints at the scene. The bonding company that had insured her last motion picture sent over a set of her prints for comparison. And when the taskforce viewed the original tape, it was easier to read Molly's lips. She did indeed beg the camera for help. For now, the taskforce operated on the premise that she was a hostage forced to participate in the robbery. Despite a scouring of the bank branch by crime scene techs, no usable evidence had been turned up on the other robbers, the men dressed as clowns.

Worse still, that surreal crime had attracted a national media spotlight. All the networks reran the surveillance tape nonstop. The Bureau had contacted the headquarters of all the major California banks with a stern warning that any future tapes were to be turned over to them immediately, rather than the media. But the cat was out of the bag, and the public frenzy associated with Molly Claire's kidnapping kept escalating.

Now, finally, she and Samantha had returned to Haggerty's house for dinner. As always, the peace her home provided cut through the tension Haggerty carried within her.

She had thought having Samantha stay with her would add to the ordeal. But she found the girl surprisingly good company. Though Samantha insisted she never cooked, she cheerfully pitched in. Since Haggerty told her she planned a stir-fry dinner, while she went to change her clothes, Samantha found a box of rice in the pantry and started it simmering, and she pulled plastic bags full of vegetables from the crisper. She'd also discovered a bottle of wine in the refrigerator and was searching for a corkscrew when Haggerty entered the kitchen.

"One drawer to your left," Haggerty said. "Near the back."

Before inserting the corkscrew into the cork, Samantha took a moment to move a bowl of apples on the counter. "What's with all the apples?" she asked. "You've got bowls in every room, trees in the yard—you're not buying into that 'keep the doctor away' business, are you?"

Haggerty surprised herself by feeling an unexpected eagerness to share. She reached across the counter and took an apple from the bowl at Samantha's side. "Apples are sacred to us." Yanking a knife from the knife block next to the stove, she cut through it and held both halves out for Samantha. "You see, when it's cut crosswise, the seeds form a pentagram. That's a symbol of regeneration to us. Immortality."

Haggerty took a bite from one of the halves and held the other out to Samantha. Samantha slowly bit into the apple piece. Haggerty wondered whether her roomie was frightened of the fruit, or awed by it.

Despite her street-wise ways, Samantha seemed awfully naïve to Haggerty. Well, more of an odd combination of guile and innocence. There wasn't much harm in her, despite her dubious professional choice. And she had such a fun outlook. Haggerty couldn't say what had possessed her to reveal her true nature to Samantha. It hadn't been necessary—she could have used the con artist as a vehicle for her own visions without revealing to Samantha the actual source of those psychic impressions. Beyond the Wicca followers, she almost never told mortals. Strangely, she wasn't sorry—at least not yet. Let the girl go to the media with the story, and she'd sing another tune. For now, it was a relief to be herself with another person, yet not be revered as she was by the witches.

Haggerty sensed Samantha's gaze on her when she cleaned the counter after she finished chopping.

"You're not just neat, you're *really* neat," Samantha said.

"Because I'm disposing of vegetable scraps? What do you do, compost yours on the floor?"

Samantha laughed. "Not quite. But your place really is so clean, you must have a cleaning lady come in every day."

Haggerty set up her wok on the stove. "On my salary? I've never had a cleaning lady. Fortunately, I have a good brownie."

Samantha's eyes bulge with shock. "You exploit a child?" She snorted. "And people disapprove of me."

Struggling not to laugh, Haggerty explained, "Not a brownie as in a little girl scout. My kind of brownie is fairy."

Samantha turned a trifle green. "Bees and dragonflies in the house, brownies." She ended with a groan.

Then, as if on cue, Haggerty heard a scratching sound from beyond the kitchen wall. Prattling on to Samantha as if she sensed nothing, Haggerty reached into a cabinet for a glass and went to the refrigerator, where she filled the glass with milk. She placed the milk at the end of the kitchen counter, while ignoring Samantha's questioning glance.

Just when she turned away, Haggerty heard a scurrying behind her. She caught Samantha's eye and urgently mouthed the words, *Don't look at him.* She knew what Samantha must have seen before turning away. A tiny brown man dressed in a fur loincloth. Haggerty knew he would glance around furtively, before whisking the milk away.

"Your brownie?" Samantha asked in a meek voice, once the small creature had gone.

Haggerty nodded. "I must warn you never to appear to notice him. Brownies are terribly shy. They won't permit thanks, or even acknowledgment, from the people whose homes they clean. All they want in return is an occasional glass of milk, or maybe a cookie. I'm glad you saw him, though. If you spotted him when I wasn't around to warn you, you could freak and stomp on him, as you might a mouse or something."

"I wouldn't stomp on a mouse," Samantha said in a small voice.

"Good. They're fairies, too."

A swaying Samantha looked like she was trying not to faint. Taking pity on the girl, Haggerty suggested that Samantha check her answering machine, directing her to its location in her bedroom.

Only after Samantha left, did she question another curious impulse. She, with her intense need for privacy, had just offered to share her personal sanctum and her private calls with a con artist. Why did she trust Samantha so much?

Samantha returned a short time later to report there had been a call from Molly Claire's manager, saying he was having the items she requested sent to her house by messenger later that night.

"He's sending them here? I thought he'd send them to the

office." With a shrug, Haggerty dismissed it, but explained the message to Samantha. "It occurred to me that Molly's abductors have awfully good intelligence about her. So I asked her manager for copies of any tapes and photos taken behind the scenes on her movie shoots."

"Good idea," Samantha said. "Oh, Detective Azar also called to say he'd be stopping by."

"Here?" Haggerty asked, her voice rising. "Now?"

Clearly misunderstanding her concern, Samantha said, "Don't worry. You look great."

She didn't, she knew. Not in her jeans and ratty old sweater. But she wasn't worried about herself as much as her house. She always prepared it before mortals came. Whisked away the...oddities. Did she have time for that now?

The doorbell rang before she had a chance to think of a way to head Jake off. Samantha shooed her away to answer it. Haggerty hesitated only a moment more, before running to the door.

When she threw the door open, Jake stood on the doorstep. With the harsh porch light shining down on him, creating dark lines on his fatigue-hardened face, he looked more menacing than normal. Like someone she didn't know. The momentary impression changed when he walked past her into the house. If anything, with his shoulders bowed by fatigue, he looked more unsure than usual.

He threw an absent glance around the living room, and muttered a perfunctory, "Nice place," before taking the seat on the futon that Haggerty offered. Even then, he sat on the edge of the cushion with his hands nervously clasped before him.

"I just came from the hospital. Plotnik's hanging in there. I told them to get in touch with us the instant he regains consciousness. And I made sure the cop on duty knows that nobody gets past him who's not on the visitor list."

She just nodded. She'd left the same message with the hospital.

As a bee floated past him, Jake leaned away from it. He reached into his bomber jacket and pulled out a sheaf of rolled-up papers. But when a second bee flew by, he looked askance at her.

Haggerty held her hands out in a helpless way. "One of my neighbors keeps a hive."

"Want me to get someone in the Department to talk to them?

That can't be code in this neighborhood."

That was all she needed. When they didn't find any beehive, Jake would hear about it. To distract him, she hastily asked about the papers he held.

"I thought you'd want to see the final crime scene report. I knew you wouldn't want to wait till tomorrow, so I thought I'd bring them by."

Samantha rushed in, carrying Haggerty's wine glass along with one for Jake. She plopped the glasses before them, with a comment that she was needed back in the kitchen. Cheerful little matchmaker, Haggerty thought irritably, as Samantha scurried away. What would happen if a dragonfly buzzed Jake's glass?

While seeming to scan the report, Haggerty took a moment to quiet the flower fairies on a bouquet at his side. She'd told Samantha the truth. Mortals almost never noticed them. When they did, they usually believed they needed to get their eyeglass prescriptions checked. But Jake was a skilled investigator. She couldn't take that chance.

She wondered why she was never able to pick up any impressions from him. Apart from his aura, which was darkish and restrained, but that was typical for a cop. Some days, even when the sun gleamed brightly outside, it was as if her office was filled with thunderclouds from all the shadowy auras. And she picked up his melody, which was atonal and jazzy. But she couldn't see inside of him. Cops were notoriously closed off, to everyone. Wives, friends, and even goddesses. She couldn't grasp any hint to how he'd handle learning the truth about her.

Their eyes met. When Haggerty looked away, an awkward silence settled between them. She wasn't sorry when Samantha broke the mood with her sudden screams. Haggerty rushed to the kitchen with Jake on her heels.

"Help!" Samantha shouted before the sizzling wok. "This thing is spitting at me."

Haggerty nudged her aside and lowered the flame. "You're supposed to wok on a high flame, Samantha, but not hell-high." When the doorbell rang again, Haggerty added, "Why don't you get that and leave the cooking to me."

Samantha returned moments later with her arms wrapped around Angus, who nuzzled her neck and muttered about the perfection of his "Sammy-girl."

Great, Haggerty thought, now it was officially a double date.

Haggerty jumped in fast with an introduction. "Jake, this is...Samantha's boyfriend." She shot Angus a look to reinforce that it was his relationship with Samantha, rather than the one he shared with her, they would acknowledge.

Just as the dinner was ready to serve, another headache struck. Haggerty carefully moved the wok to a different burner, before sinking against the stove in pain, as a vision floated into her mind. Even as she wondered how she would attract Samantha's attention, she was surprised to find Samantha there at her side. And it was Samantha who touched her to ease the passage of the vision.

Samantha went into her psychic act. Haggerty had to admit it was better than the show she'd put on if she dared reveal her gifts to people.

"I see something. Molly," Samantha said, swaying.

"Do tell," Jake said. He sent Haggerty a jaded look over Samantha's head. "Still in that cellar you told me about, or is she counting the loot they took today?"

"She's in a different place now." Samantha stole a glance at Haggerty to confirm what she was seeing. "A white windowless room, with one knob-less door. She's screaming and scratching the walls, but she's trapped."

"You really see that?" Jake asked, in a hushed voice.

"Really," Samantha snapped.

Hostility and cynicism stole over his face. "Where is this room?" he demanded.

"I don't know," Samantha said with a stifled sob that sounded genuine.

Haggerty threw a quick questioning look to Angus, to see if he could tell anything she could not. He answered with the barest shake of his head. He could discern more if he chose to, she knew. His powers were strong. But Angus never bothered using them unless it was to create more fun for himself. Haggerty felt like shaking him.

"If she can send this, why, oh-why, can't she send anything else?" Samantha cried.

"Good question," Haggerty said.

CHAPTER FOURTEEN
Samantha

Jake left right after dinner. Too bad for Haggerty; I was hoping she'd get some. Workaholic that she was, she didn't seem too concerned, claiming she needed to make calls from her room.

I took Angus to the guestroom to see if lightning could strike twice between us. I'm happy to report it can strike twice, all right; it can strike as many times as you have stamina for, if you get my drift. And gods have endless stamina. I wasn't sure whether we would still feel that magic. Sometimes the second time with a guy wasn't so wonderful, as if you spent all the fireworks on the first go-around. Amazingly, it was just as glorious for Angus and me, and I started to think maybe it always would be.

During the throes of passion, I admitted something to Angus that I might not have, had my brain been doing my thinking, rather than my hormones. "You are the perfect man," I shouted, before my voice broke into a moan.

Angus made an admission of his own. "Samantha, my love, do you know how many eons I've been searching for a woman like you?"

Later, while basking in the afterglow, his words came back to me, and they filled me with as much pleasure as making love had. Eons! He'd been searching eons for someone like me. Not that I believed him. During those moments, men will say anything. It felt good to hear those words nonetheless.

We giggled together beneath the covers. I doodled pictures with my fingers on his broad chest, while challenging him to guess what I'd written. For all I knew, he could read the thoughts in my mind before I began writing, but he gallantly pretended to be stumped every time.

"What kind of a god are you?" I asked.

"Why one of youth and love and laughter, of course," he said as if it were self-evident. "All of which manifest themselves in my music. It's been said for millenniums that no one who has heard my sweet harp could fail to follow it."

Having heard it myself, I believed that.

"That's why you're so perfect for me, my girl," he went on. "There's as much lightness and depth in you as a great piece of music. Just as much joy and playfulness, juxtaposed with a great swell of drama."

Depth? Drama? Wow! No one ever said those things about me. And no one else ever would, I knew. With a silent sigh, I acknowledged that I was really falling for this guy. Uh...god. So hard. If Angus would inevitably leave me, as Haggerty had said, I knew I was headed for heartbreak. But there wasn't a thing I could do about it.

I couldn't say when I drifted off to sleep. I had no conscious awareness of the hours that passed until I awoke, without Haggerty's prompting, the next morning. Angus wasn't there when I opened my eyes, but he had left a shamrock on his pillow. Though I felt stupid doing it, I kissed it. And I knew I'd wear it in my bra all day, pressing it to my heart, even though the very idea made me feel hopelessly lame.

I realized it was the smell of smoke that had awakened me. Once I was more aware, I identified it as burning incense.

I popped my head out the guestroom door and saw Haggerty standing before her altar. Tracing a pattern in the air with a dagger she held, Haggerty softly chanted some words.

"This is a time that is not a time," she cried. "In a place that is not a place, on a day that is not a day."

Then what was it?

"I stand at the threshold between the worlds, before the veil of the Mysteries. May the Ancient Ones hold and protect me on my magical journey."

And me, too, I thought, chastened. Really—me, too.

Haggerty and I planned to go by the hospital on the way to the Field Office to check on Plotnik. We stopped for gas on the way. While she pumped it, I wandered into the station's food store for some Coke and Mentos. I needed to balance her hearty meals with my usual food source.

At the cash register there was a display of those cheap Celtic necklaces you see sometimes. That basket weave pattern in silver hanging from a black cord. On impulse I bought a necklace and put it on while waiting for my change. I had to say, it looked pretty good with the pink crepe bridesmaid's gown from the '40s that I had on.

Haggerty might have noticed it when I climbed back into the car—unless she laughed to herself all the time for no reason.

Haggerty had to show her ID to the cop at Plotnik's door before we could enter his room. We'd learned from the nurses on the ICU floor that his condition had been reclassified as stable. However, he hadn't regained consciousness, and apparently, that surprised his doctors.

We stood next to that hospital bed, staring down at the still form in it. Plotnik was more attractive in his clown makeup than lying there without it. He had one of those faces you just naturally want to laugh at. His head was an elongated egg, his bulbous nose a squishy sponge. And his thin, wide lips were perpetually curved, so it looked as if he was always grinning like an idiot. Even while unconscious.

I couldn't interpret all the machines that monitored his condition, but his skin looked pinker now than the ashen tone I'd seen beneath the clown makeup after he'd been shot. He really looked awfully healthy for a gunshot victim who wouldn't wake up. Though his eyelids were closed, they kept twitching. Occasionally, the lids rose enough for me to see movement below. He was dreaming. Do people dream in comas?

I looked to Haggerty on the other side of the bed. "Can't you do something to bring him out of this? Wake him up somehow, so we can question him."

"Me? No."

I bet she could. She could probably perform lots more magic than she admitted. She just feared someone would guess.

I propped my fists on my hips. "I see. So your powers have no useful application, they're just flash and sizzle." Like the way she moved that Stonehenge model.

Haggerty's delicate nose wrinkled with amusement. "Frankly, Samantha, I'd expect flash and sizzle to be more your style."

She had me there.

"Come on," Haggerty said. "Let's see if the doctor's skills have more substance."

We waited for Plotnik's physician to meet with us just outside of ICU. A small Asian woman in a white coat, who looked too young to have finished junior high, not to mention med school, joined us there. But when she opened her mouth, Dr. Chan had the kind of gravelly voice that old blues babes envy.

"Mr. Plotnik is making an excellent recovery," she said. "Faster than we expected. But it troubles me that he isn't conscious yet. His brain activity is strong. We don't know what's keeping him unconscious."

"Drugs?" Haggerty asked.

Dr. Chan shrugged. "No one but our staff and your crew has been in there. And we've tested for just about everything. Whatever is keeping him under—it's a new one to us."

The questions raised by Plotnik's condition kept us both quiet during the drive back to the Field Office. Once there, they put me in front of the TV again. Only now I wasn't killing time, I had the responsible job of monitoring it. Oddly enough, it felt exactly the same. I didn't even get to see that little gold cat, which I'd loved so much yesterday, since there were no specials on *The Power of the Pyramid* today.

Of course, it wasn't much of an exaggeration to say I watched Molly Claire rob that bank a thousand times. Regular news programming was pre-empted, in favor of endless numbers of talking heads telling us what we were seeing when we watched that tape. After a while, I would almost have rather seen her as Haggerty had in her vision, in that smelly basement. But that image was Haggerty's alone.

That basement must have been here in Southern California, after all. Even if I never saw anything like it. The cops were watching the airports, the train and bus stations, so how could they have moved her from somewhere else to rob that bank? I refused to consider the matter of the dolphins, since I no longer felt as sure I'd seen what I thought I saw. Talking to dolphins? Right.

It was so boring, I almost fell asleep on my watch. Well, that and the fact that I hadn't gotten much rest during what proved to be quite an athletic night. Angus was positively indefatigable, but I, sadly, was all too mortal when it came to energy.

My eyelids were just drooping, when a sudden thought

jerked them back open. Dodi Drake! I'd made an appointment with her for this morning. Was I late? I glanced at my wrist—which was naked, of course, devoid of a watch. Maybe Dodi's Secret Service agent, Gus, was right; maybe I should wear a watch. I knew now it was possible to be psychic, while appearing totally ordinary—look at Haggerty.

All thought of Dodi vanished from my head just as fast as it had appeared, when the TV station switched to another urgent update. Despite the Bureau's demand that it receive all security tapes first, once again, another bank had delivered its robbery video to a local news show. This time I hit the record button on the VCR as soon as it began to play, while shouting for the members of the taskforce to join me.

"Not again," Billy muttered behind me after a moment.

My own eyes remained glued to that screen. This tape wasn't much different from the last one. The bank branch was different, but the robbers still wore clown suits. Though one thing struck me as odd: judging by their builds, they might not have been the same men as the day before.

And, of course, Molly was there. She wore the same clothes as yesterday, but she looked a day more ragged. And dirty—her face was streaked with soot and her hair was starting to look greasy. And today, when she stole a look at the security camera, one of the clowns jammed an automatic rifle against her back. There would be no begging this time, unless you counted the haunted look in that poor woman's eyes.

Several members of the taskforce rushed to that bank, including Jake and Haggerty. And me. Naturally, it was at Haggerty's insistence that I was dragged along with them.

A couple of LAPD patrol cars were already on the scene when we arrived.

"Hey, Azar, we're doing your job for you," said a patrolman with a brown moustache and the inevitable mirrored aviator glasses that cops favor.

"Yeah? Then I can leave?" Jake asked sourly. "What do you got for us, O'Neill?"

Jake left with the patrolman and his more rotund partner. Haggerty went to speak to the branch manager, whose head gash was being patched by the paramedics at the ambulance parked outside.

I stood alone, leaning against the counter near the teller windows. Until Special Agent Lisa Lorne joined me, the female agent who'd asked me to tell her fortune the day before. She of the matching sweaters, and now I knew, the coordinated name.

"To think I gave up my first career choice for this," she said with a sorry shake of her chestnut hair.

She took hold of one of the pens chained to the counter and began doodling her name on a deposit slip. Not surprisingly, she had a real girly handwriting, with lots of swirls. My only surprise came when she dotted the *i* in her first name, rather than capping it with a smiley face or heart. She had that kind of penmanship.

I'd given her high marks for the individualistic twin set she'd worn the day before. Well, individualistic for this dark-suited bunch. Today I began to think she was taking her singular—and terribly dowdy—taste too far. She wore a loose-fitting shift of a dress, patterned with tiny blue flowers.

I wanted to ask why she was hanging there with me instead of doing her job, but I got a feeling about her. The Bureau is strictly Skepticism-Central. That was why Haggerty had to disguise her secret—she'd be laughed out. When Lisa kidded me about telling her fortune, she was just trying to fit into that macho world. I sensed now that she really did want a reading.

I broached the subject directly. She confirmed it by giving her bowed head a slight nod.

The only flamboyant thing about Lisa was her exquisite Australian opal ring. I love Aussie opals, those shimmering turquoise-colored stones with so much fire.

"Let me hold your ring," I said and held out my palm.

"Ooh, psychometry. I've heard some psychics do their readings by feeling the emanations that come off the subject's possession."

Right. I had no more ability at psychometry than I did at cashing a check at the grocery store, now that I'd bounced a few there. I just wanted to hold that ring.

Naturally, with absolutely no psychic impressions coming off it, I based what I told her on my guesses about her. "I see you in a classroom, filled with eager young minds." Who other than a grade school teacher would wear that dress?

"Do you really?" she trilled. "Because you know, I started out to be a kindergarten teacher, only my dad was with the Bureau and he thought…"

I tuned out what Dad had thought, since he'd obviously missed the mark in his daughter's case by light-years.

"I'm convinced of it," I said emphatically. Conviction came easily to me, since I didn't take it seriously.

"I still keep kids in my life. I volunteer with gang members and at-risk teens," Lisa said.

I was cynical enough to believe she did that to get in good with Rusler, by adopting his pet cause. It had to be tough competing with Haggerty, the way Rusler felt about her. When Lisa went back to yakking about her old man, I figured she had confused our exchange with a fifty-minute hour. I wasn't her therapist, I was a fake psychic giving away a valuable reading for free.

Someone screamed from the back room of the bank. With loads of cops and fibbies on my heels, I followed the sound to a small lunchroom behind the teller area, where I found some bank employees huddled around a TV.

"It happened again," a gray-haired woman shrieked. "At another bank."

The taskforce members pushed to the front of the pack, and I let them carry me in their wake. On the screen we saw what was becoming the rerun of the day: Molly, clowns, bank, and automatic weapons used with abandon. Only this tape was from a different bank, in another part of the city.

They divided the taskforce, with some members staying behind at this crime scene, and others going to the new one. Haggerty's forehead was corrugated, I noticed, like she was starting to get another vision. With Jake between us, I couldn't make contact with her.

He swore a lot in the car during the ride there. With impotent rage, I sensed. If it was going to go on like this, the good guys didn't stand a chance. There were thousands of banks in Southern California—no way could they guard them all.

When we arrived at the second bank, we found another murdered man there. Apparently, the security guard had had the poor sense to draw his weapon on four clowns armed with automatic weapons. But I wondered about something. The violence unleashed at the first robbery was so outrageous. But in the one we'd just come from, the manager had merely sustained a slight wound. And no one would have been hurt at this crime scene, if the guard hadn't behaved stupidly. Had the clowns just been trying to get the cops' attention with that first robbery? To convey how serious they were? Or was I giving them too much credit for orchestration?

Haggerty put her hand down on a counter by the teller windows. She didn't place it there casually, but in a very deliberate manner. Her forehead wrinkled tightly. I placed my hand on her arm. A cascade of images floated into my mind. Since Jake approached us, I went straight into my act.

"I see something..." I said, going into my swoon.

"Can it, willya, Madame Phony," he snapped.

"Hear her out, Jake," Haggerty ordered, though her tone sounded too soft to carry much punch. The vision made her weak.

I sped up my report. "Men changing into those clown suits."

For once, he seemed to take me seriously. His swarthy skin grew pale, and I could hear his emotion in his voice when he asked, "Faces? Can you see faces?"

I shook my head to indicate I couldn't. "Just hands and arms. And tattoos. Gang tattoos." I'd lived in L.A., Gang-City, for too long not to recognize many of those tattoos. I'd also seen some of them captured in the photos in Rusler's office.

"Which gangs?" Jake asked. "Tell me about those tattoos."

When I described all the various designs I saw, Jake shook his head. "Not possible. You're describing the markings of the Sixteen Streeters, the Crazy Boyz, and the Asia Hoods. The Crazy Boyz and the Asia Hoods are mortal enemies—they'd kill each other on sight. And you've got all different ethnic gangs there. That just doesn't happen."

I remembered that he had worked the LAPD gang detail until recently, so he had to know what he was talking about. Yet I couldn't shake the clarity of the image Haggerty sent to me, nor my sense that those men were working as a team. The coordination I saw looked too practiced. The tattoos were also quite clear. No mistake.

"They're united," I said, having no idea where that certainty had come from.

Jake almost choked. "United?" He ran a hand through his hair, smoothing down his wiry cowlicks. "May the gods have mercy on us," he whispered.

I looked to Haggerty and saw undisguised fear written across her pale, drawn face. "Something tells me it's gonna take a lot more than that," I muttered.

CHAPTER FIFTEEN

My bombshell that the rival Southern California gangs had united to perpetrate this insane crime spree, of which Molly Claire was the centerpiece—was met with waves of reactions. While stunned at first, the taskforce folks quickly moved on to outrage. Half of them directed their anger at me, certain I had made it up. The others seemed to believe it, but they were the type to blame the messenger. Jake absolutely refused to accept it. Haggerty alone, the one who sent those images to me, remained quiet during the shout-fest her revelation had unleashed.

The first thing they had to do, Rusler insisted, while shooting eye-darts at me, was to verify my theory. Everyone with contacts in the gang world made calls. Rusler made his on his cell phone, while pacing the corridors of the Field Office, supposedly in search of a solid signal. Occasionally, I caught sight of him with his hand cupped around his mouth as he whispered into the phone. Despite all the hours he'd put into his anti-gang efforts, he didn't come up with anything useful. Nothing he felt like sharing anyway.

At one point, while on my return from the ladies room, where I'd gone to straighten the seams of the nylons I wore beneath my calf-length gown, I passed Rusler's office. Absently tossing his cell phone in his hand, he caught sight of me through the open office door. With a crick of his hand, he indicated for me to come in.

He didn't invite me to sit. He simply unhinged his lower lip to produce what I took to be a threatening smile, but which looked more like the display I imagined they used in dental school.

"You better not be dragging us off-course, little lady," he warned.

This was so great. Angus considered me the perfect woman, and Rusler thought I was *little*. Imagine that. If everyone kept turning my head like this, it wouldn't be long before I'd start singing "I Feel Pretty."

"I just tell 'em like I see 'em," I said, with a straight face. That was the truth. Thanks to Haggerty, I really was seeing this stuff.

"We'll know soon enough. Special Agent Haggerty should come up with something that will either prove or disprove your prediction."

Haggerty, huh? That was choice. Let's see her try to disprove her own vision.

Rusler's stiff jaw relaxed into something resembling a curve, producing the first semi-genuine smile I'd seen on him. "She can communicate with all those boys, you know. It was her faculty for languages that brought her into the Bureau. And she has such rapport with gang members, she'll learn the truth."

I wouldn't have predicted that about her. So far, I hadn't seen her display much rapport with anyone, apart from the witches. Then again, after watching her with the dolphins, I couldn't question her language skills.

"I have good harmony with them myself." He pointed to a photo of him and another man on the wall behind his desk, both looking like sharks saying *cheese*. "I found a job for this man in the Holm's supermarket chain." He pointed to another picture. "And I placed this young fella as a records clerk with a big Beverly Hills dentist."

Funny, Jake said the same thing. Were Beverly Hills dentists actively recruiting these losers? Maybe the same kid got mileage outta two advisors. Fortunately, the jingling of Rusler's phone relieved me of having to respond. He pushed past me, walking into the hall, whispering into the phone as he went. I wandered back to Haggerty's office.

When I got there, she was just hanging up the phone, which she glared at it in anger.

"No luck, huh?"

Still distracted, she absently shook her head.

"Rusler says you're a whiz at languages. Is that true? Say something in…" Which language should I choose? "Vietnamese."

Still lost in thought, Haggerty slowly turned her troubled blue eyes my way. "What? Oh, sure, I pick up languages, you know, when I focus on the thoughts of someone who doesn't think in English. But I forget them just as fast."

Sounded like the way my brain worked, only with everything. "But you do have a great rapport with gang-bangers, right? Rusler said so."

She glanced behind me, before saying softly, "Mr. Rusler doesn't understand *how* I discover the information I do. He assumes it's by building relationships with suspects." She tapped another number into the phone.

So she did use her powers on occasion. Good to know. She built cases against suspects by taking a reading of them. Was that Constitutional? Were Celtic goddesses bound by it? Funny, I always considered myself a big-picture person—only to discover the real picture was way bigger than I could ever have thought.

Haggerty ended the unanswered call with a frustrated sigh. She returned to the bullpen where several taskforce members were at work. I trailed along. Rusler wasn't there now, and neither were Billy and Lisa. Jake was, though, and apparently had as little luck as everyone else. After each call, he slammed the receiver down. He had a pocket-sized address book open next to the phone, which he turned to after each angry slam. The address book didn't surprise me. He had seemed like a retro-kinda guy. No Blackberry for him.

Finally, his luck turned, when he reached the director of a clubhouse that offered gang members an alternative to the street.

"Hey, Rod," he said. "Anything strange happening with your charges?" When others around the table looked his way, Jake put the call on speaker.

"Uh...yeah, Jake. I was gonna call you, but I heard you got kicked up to Homicide. It's odd, but nobody's coming around anymore. The bad boys—they've just vanished. They're not here at the clubhouse, not on the street. And the kids on the fringe, they're making themselves scarce, too. Like they're afraid to be seen. Something's coming down, Jake. Something bad."

Jake schmoozed the guy a bit longer, but wasn't able to extract anything more specific. "Thanks, Rod," he said at last. "Let me know if you hear anything else, okay? The minute you hear it."

Rod cleared his throat. "The thing is, I might be taking a little trip soon."

A slouching Jake suddenly sat up. "Rod, be straight with me here. What—"

"Gotta go now, Jake," Rod said hastily. "Keep your head down, bud. I mean it, ya hear?" With that, he hung up.

Jake scowled at the phone for a long minute. When the dial tone came through the speaker, he clicked it off.

From the other end of the table, Rusler said, "Maybe you'd have more success with an in-person approach, Detective."

Strange, Rusler hadn't told anyone else to hit the streets. It almost sounded like he wanted to get rid of Jake.

With a shrug, Jake accepted the suggestion. "Come on, Annabelle, Ms. Brennan, let's go rattle some cages." He headed for the elevator.

Haggerty didn't hesitate to follow him. After a moment, I tagged along. Just as he appeared to accept me, I began to feel weird about the three of us always being together. I wanted *them* to be together, alone. Still, that was my deal with Haggerty.

Jake didn't say much during our drive. Other than to mutter occasionally, "Vanished, huh? My snitches can't have *all* vanished."

We went to a house in the South Central section of Los Angeles.

A slight African-American woman answered the door, her dark eyes brightening at the sight of Jake. "Detective Azar, how nice to see you. Won't you and your friends come in?"

He told her we were in a hurry, but he said it in a less-rushed, more gracious manner than I expected. He must have liked this woman.

"I need to see Mickey, Mrs. Terry."

"My Mickey, he packed a bag about a week or so back. Wouldn't tell me where he was going, neither. Just that it was gonna pay off for him." She gave her short gray hair a shake. "I don't know where I went wrong with that boy, Detective."

He gave Mrs. Terry one of his business cards and asked her to call if her son returned. When she glanced at his card, for just a second, twinkling surfaced in her dark eyes. Haggerty had told me he'd doodled on his cards. Whatever little sketch she saw there momentarily lifted that woman's burden. But a grim set to her jaw immediately replaced it.

Jake squeezed his lips together, a cross between a frustrated smile and one of sympathy. "I'm hoping things work out okay for you and Mickey, ma'am."

Jake's kindness blew me away. Given his flinty edge, I wouldn't have thought he had it in him.

Back in the car, he directed Haggerty to drive to another house in a different neighborhood. "Might as well try another gang,"

Jake said with a shrug.

Nobody answered the door at the next house we visited. We split up and checked out some windows around the sides and back of the house. Haggerty reported seeing clothes scattered in the bedrooms and signs of hurried packing. I wondered whether she actually *saw* that, or discerned it by some other means. And if she knew the occupants of this house had left, why couldn't she figure out where they'd gone? Psychic abilities weren't worth as much as I'd always thought.

"Where to?" Haggerty asked when we returned to the car.

Jake placed another call to Rod, the director of that clubhouse. Now there was no answer.

He asked Haggerty to jump on the freeway and head for the Valley. He didn't say anything more until he directed her to exit in an industrial neighborhood in Van Nuys. He barked out orders that caused her to make a bunch of turns on streets I didn't know, before telling her to pull into the empty parking lot of an industrial complex of three or four connected buildings. The driveway took us around the largest of the structures.

"Hey," I said. "This is a foundry." I pointed to a faded sign on two posts stuck in a seedy planted area next to a receiving entrance door.

"The foundry's closed, long time now," Jake explained. "The owner is retired, and doesn't need the money. He's converted most of the place into a clubhouse for the kids. The smelter is still functional, but it hasn't been fired up in years." With a gesture, he directed Haggerty to continue driving around to the rear of the complex.

We parked next to a boxy building that looked like it must have been a warehouse at one time. A plaque over the door identified it as "The Hanover Street Clubhouse." Smaller lettering below that read, "An Activity Center Sponsored by the Lorne Foundation."

The door, which Jake said was almost always open, was locked now. A note scratched on a sheet of paper taped to the door read, "Back in five."

In silence, we waited five; minutes, that is. Then another five, and a few more after that.

Finally, Jake said, "You two wait here. I'll see if I can find another way in."

He wasn't gone long before he reappeared and whistled for

us to join him around the other side. While we all walked back to the door next to the receiving entrance, he explained that he remembered where they kept an emergency key.

He unlocked the door to the old foundry and held it open for Haggerty and me. I'd never seen a smelter before, but it looked like I would have imagined. A huge metal vat over giant-sized burners. Of course, everything was cool now, not fiery as it must have been while operational. And it was quiet there. The only sounds I heard were the ones our shoes made tapping against the concrete floor.

Jake led us through a passage that joined the foundry with what must have been the offices at one time. Bunk beds now filled some of those rooms; places for kids to crash. Other rooms held TVs, computers and video games. While the foundry portion was remarkably clean and looked abandoned, all these messy rooms showed signs of recent use. Containers from fast food places littered many surfaces, and some garments had been dropped here and there; sweatshirts, gang bandanas, baseball caps. There was even a woman's designer purse. The kind whose surface is stamped again and again with some snooty logo. I couldn't have said which one— my income didn't lend itself to a familiarity with high-priced designers. A kid probably clipped it somewhere with the idea of giving it to his mom or his girlfriend.

It occurred to me that I might as well give the poor thing a home. I inched back down the hall, till I reached the doorway where I'd seen the purse.

Without turning my way, Haggerty asked over her shoulder, "Lose your way, Samantha?"

Sheesh! This was worse than when I was a kid and thought my mom had eyes in the back of her head. Why was it okay to rescue dogs and cats, but not purses?

"Hurry it up now," Haggerty insisted.

"Wasn't doing anything," I muttered, but I quickened my step.

I caught up to Haggerty and Jake in what must have been the inside of the warehouse portion we'd parked near. That voluminous room had been converted into a basketball gym, with a wooden floor and an electronic scoreboard. But the scoreboard was dark now, and the floor was dusty, as if it hadn't seen any traffic in a while.

"Rod," Jake muttered softly, "did you let someone chase you

off?"

It scared me that this guy, who worked regularly with bad guys, felt frightened enough now to run away.

When no one answered, we slowly let ourselves out the gym door and piled back into the car.

After a few more futile stops, Jake said, "This is hopeless."

"Don't quit now, Jake. With all the gang members you know, there has to be someone else we can try."

Jake's head twitched as if he'd just gotten an idea. "Just a sec," he muttered. He punched a number into his cell phone.

When someone answered with a cautious, "Yeah?" that I could hear from the backseat, he thrust the phone at me, while mouthing the words, *wrong number.* I took the phone and went into a routine of asking for someone and apologizing for my mistake. The guy on the other end of the line had already hung up before I could finish.

Jake's lips twisted into a smug set when he took the phone back from me. "At least we know where someone will be on our next visit."

He directed Haggerty to an apartment building more rundown than most of its neighbors in Echo Park. Instead of parking, Jake told Haggerty to drive by. He craned his neck to stare up at the front windows of a second floor apartment. The windows were open and a yellowing rag of a curtain hung out.

He had us park around the corner, in front of a storefront pizza parlor. The three of us started for the building where his snitch lived. But before we'd reached the corner, Jake asked us to wait, and he sprinted back to the pizza place. He emerged a few moments later tossing a pizza box into the air.

"Samantha," he said, "Feel like making a little delivery?" He held the box out to me.

Samantha, huh? My family had never been particularly cozy with the cops. Some of them actually consider what we do as fraud. Can you believe it? I'd noticed when they want something from you, they get all chummy. Now I was "Samantha," rather than Ms. Fake Psychic or any of the other names he called me. But after seeing him with that poor mother, I didn't mind. Cop or not, I decided he was one of the good guys. I held out my palm for the box.

"Too cool and too light to be holding any pizza," I said.

"Nothing gets past you, Madame Psychic." He offered me a grin to take away any sting. "No sense wasting good food on a dirtbag."

Jake explained his plan to draw the reticent informant from his apartment. While he and Haggerty hid behind a pair of the city's oversized garbage cans, I marched up to the door and tapped a little tune on the buzzer of the apartment marked "Jorge Ramirez."

When no one responded, I shouted to the open windows on the second floor. "Yoo-hoo, up there." I punctuated my remarks with a few more taps on the buzzer.

A wiry Hispanic man, sporting a pencil-thin moustache and hair shaved to about an eighth of an inch all over his head, peered out the window. "Yeah?" The same voice I'd heard on the phone when Jake had called. "What'a'ya want?"

While holding up the pizza box, I thrust my chest out to give him a glance at the major league cleavage peeking out the top of my gown.

While he didn't refuse a look, he said sourly, "I didn't order no pizza."

I gave him a coquettish shrug. "Maybe someone else ordered it for you. All I know is it's paid for. It's plenty big to share, too."

"Yeah?" He hesitated. "I'll be right down."

Once Jorge Ramirez's head popped back through those yellowing curtains, Jake leaped from his hiding spot and raced to the door. He and Haggerty nudged me aside.

The instant the building's door opened, Jake pushed Jorge back inside and pinned him against the wall of the small, dark lobby. Haggerty came up behind him, and I stood behind her. Though I was the closest one to the fresh air coming through the open door, the combined stench of fried onions, beer, and urine in that lobby made me want to add fresh vomit to the mix.

"Ain't been coming around anymore, huh, Jorge?" Jake asked. "Not like you not to need bread."

Jorge struggled against his hold, but though he was a larger man than Jake, he didn't manage to loosen himself. When he couldn't break free, he spit at the detective, landing a big glob right on his face.

Jake didn't let go of Jorge to wipe it away. He just let that goo drip from his face, while he said, "Shouldn't have done that,

Georgy-boy." The soft fierceness in his voice scared me more than shouting would have.

"Hey, man, I don't need you no more. There's a war already started that you don't have a chance of winning," Jorge shouted.

To my surprise, Haggerty reached across Jake's shoulder and placed her palm on Jorge's forehead. "You seem agitated by it. Tell us about it."

Jake's head spun around to her. His full lower lip hung open. It startled me just as much. She sounded like some TV shrink inviting him to share his feelings. He had spit at a cop—his feelings weren't in doubt.

Jorge tried to shake off her hand. "Get that paw off me, bitch."

Freeing one hand, Jake stuffed his card in Jorge's shirt pocket. "When you need help, Jorge—and you're gonna need it—you call me."

Did thugs have card files? I know TV police officers hand out business cards like snowflakes in a blizzard, but it surprised me to see that real ones did, too. What did I know? Not cool with cops, remember?

Jake released his hold on Jorge, and that gang-goon tried so hard to get away, he tripped over his own big feet. Eventually, he made it up the stairs.

Jake gave Haggerty an incredulous look, before blowing out the front door with a frustrated sigh. After a "duh!" moment, I finally understood why Haggerty had touched Jorge.

I slipped my hand around the crook of her elbow and held her in that smelly lobby for a moment longer. "Did you see anything in his mind?" I hissed. "Did you get anything?"

"He was lying to us," she whispered back.

"About what? A gang war? No lie there. That ship has already sailed, Haggerty."

"No, not that." She threw an anxious glance through the open door to where Jake must have been waiting out of view.

"That's all he said," I reminded her.

"I know. I can't explain it, Samantha. I just sensed that somehow, he was trying to deceive us."

No shit. For that, she got to be a goddess?

Back at the Field Office, Jake filled the taskforce in on our limited progress.

Everyone spoke at once, firing out suggestions, until Rusler silenced them by patting the air before him with his outstretched palms, like he was flattening an imaginary down pillow. "I think aggressive action is called for. It's time to use the weapon we've kept in reserve." He lowered his jaw in my direction, producing a smile totally devoid of sincerity. "How about it, Ms. Brennan? Ready to take a turn at bat?"

Whenever possible I avoid men who use sports metaphors, since I never know what they mean.

Fortunately, Rusler rephrased his question before I proved how dense one of us could be. "Would you be willing to hold a press conference challenging the bad guys with what you know? Unofficial, you understand, no connection to the Bureau."

Haggerty shouted, "No!" Just as I said, "You bet!" Our voices blended.

She sent me a silencing scowl before turning to Rusler. "With all due respect, sir—"

The way I figured it, that meant none.

"We can't allow Samantha to be made into a target," Haggerty went on. "She's a civilian. It wouldn't be right to use her as bait."

When she put it that way... No, this was my chance. "I said I'd do it."

"We'll protect her, Annabelle," Rusler went on. "Naturally, she'll have to be moved out of your home, though."

Oh, naturally. We couldn't endanger the agent who was paid to put herself in the line of fire, just the dispensable civilian nutwad. That reasoning still didn't dissuade me.

Over the growing swell of voices, I shouted, "Listen, it's my choice."

Haggerty leaned into my face. "May I see you alone in my office?" She gave my arm a yank.

Once we reached her office, Haggerty's brusque manner softened. She gestured for me to take the guest chair, and she leaned against the edge of the desk.

"Samantha, you've seen what these men are doing to Molly Claire, and they apparently think she serves some purpose for them.

You would be nothing but a threat. Do you want to end up like Plotnik? Or worse?"

I let my head fall forward until my long hair hung into my lap. "I hear what you're saying, okay? But look at me. I'm twenty-eight and three-quarters, and I'm not exactly setting the world on fire. Hah! I'm not even setting a *match* on fire."

Haggerty pressed her hand to my shoulder. "I'm only a year younger than you, and I'm not doing that much better."

"A year *younger?*" I shrieked. "I thought for sure, you'd have passed the big 3-0. And you are too doing great. You might not have been so high up before this all started, but you're on the fast track now, babe." I nodded my head in the direction of taskforce's command post. "If you'd do the nasty with Rusler, you'd be his second in command in no time."

Now she squeezed my shoulder till it hurt. "Would you do that?"

"Me? No. But when you consider Angus—"

"Samantha!" After a short hesitation, she said. "I have a really bad feeling about this."

"I stared at her. How do you mean that? Your kinda feeling, or mine?"

"What does it matter?"

"With yours, there's a higher probability it'll happen." After a moment, I gave my wild hair a swift shake. "Either way, I gotta do this. Don't try to talk me out of it. Opportunity doesn't *keep* knocking, you know. You have to catch it while it's there." I faltered. "Unless you see something really bad in my future." Before she could respond, I stuffed my fingers into my ears. "No, don't tell me."

Even with my fingers in my ears, I could still hear her say, "Samantha, it doesn't take a psychic to know this. Nothing good will come of what you're planning to do."

I snatched one of the apples from the silver bowl on her desk and took a swift bite. Hey, they worked for her, right? That bite sank like a stone, as the acid churning in my stomach rose up to meet it.

CHAPTER SIXTEEN

Once Haggerty accepted that she wasn't going to change my mind, she threw herself into planning my press conference with the same vigor as Jake, who'd warmed to the idea much earlier. The three of us had gathered in Haggerty's small office, though Rusler popped in regularly to check the progress. Oh, yeah—they shoehorned Lisa Lorne in there, too, though she just hummed softly to herself.

After we worked out what I would say, we addressed where we would hold it. I nixed Haggerty's suggestion of a hotel function room.

"Why not?" she asked. "It's done all the time. Reporters expect it."

I shook my head.

"Where then?" Jake asked.

"The steps to the Museum of the Antiquities," I said.

"Why there?" Lisa asked, wrinkling her cute little nose.

Since she hadn't contributed anything valuable up to that point—or ever, that I could see—I ignored her.

Jake drummed his fingertips against Haggerty's desk. "Where *The Power of the Pyramid* is set to open? How come?"

I looked to Haggerty for help, but she refused to meet my eyes. How could I explain it? The timing of it all weirded me out. What were the odds of some deities crossing my path just when the relics of other, earlier gods were headed our way? But what could I say without ratting out what I knew about Haggerty?

I finally just tweaked the truth. "When the world is about to descend on Los Angeles for the most priceless show ever—a crime spree breaks out all over the city. Coincidence? I think not."

Haggerty seemed to be biting her tongue. Probably suppressing a remark that I truly *did not think.*

Jake gave his wiry dark hair an indignant toss. "Madame Samantha, the guys holding Molly Claire are robbing *banks*, not museums. They're after money, not ancient artifacts. They can't even spell *artifacts.*"

I yanked my full skirt away from where he kept kicking it with his dusty boot. "Come on. You're a cop—aren't you trained to distrust coincidence?" Now his boot only connected with my dress about half the time.

"I'm not buying it, kid. Still, the museum might not be such a bad locale for the press conference." Haggerty started to argue against it, but Jake held up his hand to cut her off. "I know what you're gonna say, Annabelle, that the security arrangements will be a bear. But look at it this way: It's a showy enough stunt to attract all the reporters in town. And it gives us a big open space where we can watch her without attracting any attention ourselves."

Haggerty chewed her lip; I sensed she wasn't convinced. Nobody else shared her reservations, however. When Jake, and a suddenly vocal Lisa, presented the idea to Rusler, he was so taken with the location, he claimed credit for it.

But there were great security obstacles to overcome. Fortunately, the onsite security for the exhibit was the province of the LAPD, and Jake was tight with the guy in charge. He even wangled a short tour for us.

When the time came, we headed out together again. Like the three pigs. Lisa stayed back at the office to finish coordinating the details. During the drive, the tension in the front seat was so thick, you could cut it with those edgy, clipped responses Haggerty and Jake kept hurling at each other. Now me, stretched out alone in the backseat—I had succeeded in purging myself of all of Haggerty's negativity. I was getting my wish, I was finally on the cusp of becoming a celebrity psychic. I just wished I could have been wearing my tattered Renaissance gown instead of my pink one, which would have made a stronger statement on the news. Nothing more substantial concerned me.

My heart felt so light in my chest, my mind too lost in my dreams, that I scarcely noticed the drive there, until Jake caused us to make a couple of stops. The first was at some donut joint, where he bought six oversized boxes—and failed to share any with us. His second stop was a coffee shop. There, before entering, he did ask Haggerty and me if we wanted anything. Haggerty asked for a coffee, black. I just shook my head. Coffee, right—when the car was filled with the heady sweet scent of warm fat.

The coffee shop was out of our way, and I couldn't see why

we had to waste time going there. We'd passed up a few more convenient independents, as well as the usual three Starbucks that you find on every block in L.A.

Jake spent about a week in there, or so it felt to me. In that proximity to the donuts, the smell drove me nuts. When he emerged it was with four huge trays of coffees in different sized containers. But above the trays, Jake wore a scowl. Once he climbed back into the car, he explained that he'd gotten a job there for one of his ex-bangers, and he'd wanted to see if that guy had picked up any rumors. Too bad his protégé had already ditched that job.

Since his stops were cutting into my time in the spotlight, I sourly asked why he had to raid the town's snack reserve, especially since he obviously wasn't sharing. In between gulps of java, Jake finally explained his purchases. "The guys on that detail aren't allowed to leave the museum for meals. They gotta eat what's provided there or starve. Even if they bring something from home, it's searched so thoroughly, it's not worth eating anymore." Jake paused for another chug of coffee. "Theoretically, outsiders are not supposed to bring anything in, either. But Matt, the Loot in charge, and I went to the Academy together. And he knows the constraints are wearing at the guys. He'll turn a blind eye."

I hoped not, if it meant those donuts weren't going to be mine.

The news vans were already assembled when we drove past the museum entrance, and reporters ambled about the area set aside for them outside the museum. Haggerty drove around to the rear of the building, as Jake's friend had directed.

After parking the car, Jake stepped up to the speaker box at the museum's rear entry and announced our arrival. An automatic door opened for us. Once we walked through that door, it sealed shut behind us. Two LAPD officers, one male and one female, waited for us in a secure entry chamber. Though Jake flashed his badge, and Haggerty also provided identification, the unsmiling pair made no acknowledgment of their brethren in law enforcement. The man ran a metal detector wand over all three of us. Then he searched Jake, while the woman officer frisked first me, then Haggerty. And more thoroughly than Angus had explored my body cavities the night before, let me tell you.

The donuts and coffee got the least scrutiny; all they did was drool over them. Although those two never cracked a smile, Jake told them they could help themselves to the goodies, once their superior gave his approval.

After we were released from that security chamber, Jake's friend, Lieutenant Matt Nobel, met us in the museum. He was a tall muscular man with the thick shock of wheat blonde hair over steady gray eyes, which he'd partially obscured by tinted frameless glasses. With his charcoal herringbone jacket and blue oxford shirt, Nobel looked more professorial than the street-wise cop Jake said he was. By contrast, the curator types rushing around in their overalls and painter pants, looked like farmers, or bums. Was it any wonder I dressed as I did?

Jake submitted his gifts for Nobel's scrutiny. The donut boxes were taped shut and had clearly not been opened. And the coffee containers, while not sealed, looked like standard-issue stuff. The cardboard cups were marked with their contents the way they always were, and in the few Lieutenant Noble checked, the foam looked undisturbed.

After Nobel approved it, Jake and I put the goodie-fest out on a plywood board spread between two sawhorses in corner.

Before I snatched one perfect glazed donut for myself, I whispered to Jake. "What does he think? That you're gonna poison everyone?"

He gave an unconcerned shrug. "Could happen. He's trusting me more than anyone else."

I looked over my shoulder at Nobel. "Your friend, he seems a bit stiff."

"He's carrying quite a load o' responsibility here. Something a lily of the field like yourself might not understand, Madame Samantha."

Had I actually said I liked him? I toiled, too. Let him try figuring out what some of my clients want to hear.

Nobel drew Jake away. "You've got to see some of these artifacts, my friend. The gold, the papyrus...glorious pieces. Most of my guys don't appreciate them, but I know you will. Of course, you've already seen most of them."

"Only in photos. And at museums over there, during visits with my grandparents in the old country. We'd sail from port to port along what the Ancients called the River Aur..."

A female worker, arms laden with boxes that obscured her view, nearly toppled the goodies table when she crashed into it. "Save the donuts!" I shrieked. I rescued a couple from annihilation.

Jake returned just as I was licking the last of the powdered sugar off my fingers.

"Did you share my theory with your friend?" I asked. I just heard him showing off.

"We shared," he assured me. His mouth twitched with amusement. I didn't get the joke, beyond sensing that it was at my expense.

Not until my promised tour, that is. Which didn't live up to my expectations, by the way. It amounted to a test to see whether a problem they were having with one display case had been fixed. Then again, it did involve the case I'd seen on the TV, the one where the gold cat had caught my eye.

As Nobel led us toward it, my heart rose to my throat with excitement. Then I saw that covering the case was a layer of glass. And what a layer.

"An inch thick," Noble announced. "Now watch this." He looked my way. "You might want to step back, miss,"

"Madame," Jake said with a straight face.

Nobel blinked a couple of times, but he just nodded. He took what looked like a car remote from his pocket. I stepped back. With a flick of the remote, a row of thick metal bars came down before the display with a loud "whomp."

"Titanium," Nobel said, obviously being a man of few words.

Another push of his thumb and a metal sheet rolled down between the bars and the glass.

A frosty smile flickered across Nobel's pale lips. "What do you say, Jake? Think your homies have a chance here?"

"Wouldn't wanna make book on it," Jake agreed.

They both looked at me with pity. Fortunately, I was used to that.

Then, it was time for my press conference. Only the first of many, I felt sure, now that I was finally getting the attention I'd been itching for. Before I made my entrance, the two cops who had vetted us through the entrance chambers, escorted Jake and Haggerty outside, along with some others from the security detail.

The museum's outdoor plaza was a grand affair, modern but with the kind of dignity you'd expect from the Parthenon or some such place. What did I know? I never paid attention during history classes. Stairs rose from the street way below in clusters of eight steps between long, deep platforms, before moving up in another step cluster. The press folks were corralled within velvet ropes on the last platform below the museum entrance level. Large square columns, at least three feet on a side, supported the upper floors, before the recessed entry. Jake and Haggerty stood behind those columns on either side of me.

The museum spokesman, the Prince Charles clone I'd seen on TV, was to introduce me to the media. For all the droll kidding I'd taken from Jake and Nobel, I didn't expect much from this guy, either. I mean, he didn't seem the type to even know anyone who had a spiritual advisor, not to mention having one of his own. But I had to admit, he handled it straight, with respect yet. Even if he was a little stingy with his praise. I fixed that by leaning around his bony shoulders and embellishing what he said into the microphone before him.

"…want to introduce Madame Samantha Brennan, a person with paranormal—"

"Psychic to the stars," I shouted at full voice into a microphone already set to project quite loudly.

"Uh, yes. She—"

"And Celtic goddess," I added, though I lowered my voice a decibel or two. When it came through the mike, it still just about broke the sound barrier.

Ol' Charley gave me a long look at that point, and he swayed as far back as he could without moving his feet. Hey, I didn't ask to stand next to him, either. He finished up my intro so fast, he'd have left an Indie car in his dust.

Stepping up to the microphone, I gave a flirty little toss of my shoulders, and I tapped the heels of my open-toed pumps together. Before starting, I gave the crowd a quick sweep, in search of Angus. When he'd insisted he wanted to help, Haggerty had seized on my theory of the connection between our present troubles and the museum opening, and she'd told him to get a job playing his harp at a nearby bar, so he could pick up any scuttlebutt the locals might drop.

Since she didn't buy the theory herself, I knew she just made busywork for him. And I guessed he was busy at it now, since I didn't see him out there. I stifled a stab of disappointment and pumped myself back up for the opportunity of my life.

"Good morning," I shouted, once again forgetting how loudly that microphone projected. I might have been a bit close to it, too. A squeal went out that probably decimated the bird population for a five mile radius. "I know you're concerned about the fate of actress Molly Claire. I'm in touch with her and I want you to know she's okay."

Off to my left, I saw Haggerty frown. I wasn't supposed to open with Molly. And when I did mention her, I was expected to pop out some carefully worded bilge. But Molly Claire was the one those folks out there wanted to hear about. And talk of her was what was going to get my face on a city full of TV screens tonight.

"Molly is a hostage, of course, but she's being treated well, and she prays for this reign of terror to end."

"Who's holding her?" someone in the audience shouted.

I love a press corps that knows when to cue. Remembering the last time I was on the verge of gaining exposure, and how Haggerty had put a halt to that interview, I glanced her way. With her head pressed to the gray marble column that she stood behind, and her knees bent into it, pain clearly hobbled her. So much for my protector. Fortunately, Jake kept a lookout from the other side. But danger could strike from so many areas; too many for one person to watch. I might have felt a shiver of fear if I weren't so thoroughly jazzed.

Since I figured Haggerty was in no shape to stop me, I abandoned the script entirely, rushing on with my own remarks. "From the visions that have come to me, I have learned—"

To my surprise, despite her weakened state, Haggerty came tearing out from behind the column, shouting, "Down! Guns in the street."

I stared at the street below. A black Mercedes sedan, with deeply darkened windows, rolled past at a snail's pace. The windows had been lowered several inches. Suddenly, the barrels of what I later learned to be automatic rifles were thrust out those windows.

Still, I stood there, stupidly staring. When the car moved into position directly before me, I continued to gawk at it, as reporters scrambled, and few savvy cameramen pointed their lenses at the car. Haggerty threw me to the ground, sheltering my body with her own.

She was in pain—I'd seen that. But she overcame it, and she risked her life to save mine. Nobody had ever done as much. Still, I filed away for later the fact that, even in a weakened condition, she was not to be counted out.

A hail of gunfire filled the museum entryway, with a storm of bullets that ricocheted off the marble surfaces just above where I lay.

Only when the sound of gunfire faded away, did I think: If this was how all press conferences ended, they could keep 'em.

CHAPTER SEVENTEEN

Amazingly, nobody was killed, thanks to Haggerty's quick reactions. Though a few reporters were hurt in the scramble to escape the rain of bullets. The paramedics had arrived and were working their way through the crowd's injuries. Next time someone came gunning for me, remind me to have a goddess at my side.

Surviving the experience had totally turned my brain to mush. I didn't ask myself any of the questions that must have occurred to the other survivors of that onslaught. What did it matter? If I had asked, I could never have heard the answers. All that gunfire in a confined space had caused me to temporarily lose my hearing.

Apparently, I wasn't the only one. At that moment Jake appeared to be shouting into his cell phone. His mouth opened wide enough for shouting, anyway. High color brightened his dark features, fury at his inability to hear, I'd bet.

Fortunately, nothing was expected of me, so I just plopped my fleshy heinie down on the marble step where I almost left my life and flattened my crinolines so I could check out the aftermath of the attack across the top of my full skirt.

The one upshot was that I had finally made the news. Once my hearing returned, I planned to start giving interviews. Trouble was, one of the cops wrote me a note to let me know that Haggerty had vetoed any more appearances by me. Even worse, I began to notice reporters taping interviews with *each other.* By the time those stories went on the air, I feared I wouldn't even be a footnote. Damn, when would it be my turn?

Damn Haggerty, too. Where was she anyway? When I finally spotted her on the sidewalk down by the street, she was talking to some little boy. Sure, make nice with the kid, but nix the phony psychic's chance at the brass ring.

A pair of paramedics swooped down on me where I sat. They poked and prodded and apparently found me to be okay.

"When will I get my hearing back?" I shouted, though all I heard was the ringing that seemed to be coming from within my own head.

One of them raised a hand with five fingers held up. Then he did that wavy side-to-side move which generally meant, *more or less.* Five what? Five hours, days? Five *years?* I couldn't peddle my trade like this, and something told me that Haggerty wouldn't want to keep me around as a permanent vehicle for her visions. It's hard enough making your way on your wits, without finding yourself totally witless.

By the time the paramedics moved on to someone else, I saw Haggerty nearby with Jake. As if life had become a silent movie, I watched when she handed him the keys to her Bureau-issued car. And the short wave he gave us both, before heading back to the museum entrance. With a jerk of her head, Haggerty indicated that I should follow her.

I staggered to my feet with all the grace of a rhino. And I tried to keep up with her swift steps. Somehow my knees kept shaking, making my feet wobbly. Funny, but I walked okay that morning—before my twenty-eight and three-quarter years had passed before my eyes. I asked her to wait up, and with more of an understanding nod than I expected, Haggerty slowed down.

We left the museum grounds and walked into a mid-Wilshire neighborhood. Where were we going anyway? I put the question to her, but I just saw her lips move.

"What?" I shouted.

With an irritated grimace, Haggerty stopped and faced me. She brushed my hair aside and placed her hands over my ears. Then she closed her eyes, as a look of concentration came over her face. In an instant, the ringing stopped and I could hear again.

"To think I had to use my powers for that," she said, swiftly moving on again.

Like I asked to be deafened.

Our walk came to a halt beside a park across the street from an elementary school. While I collapsed on a park bench, Haggerty remained on the sidewalk, pacing anxiously.

In the distance a man and a woman headed towards us. The couple walked right past Haggerty without any sign of recognition, however. Only when they moved on did I notice that their larger bodies had blocked the approach of a pair of small boys, maybe seven or eight years old. To my surprise, it was those little kids who stopped and met with Haggerty.

When I joined them, Haggerty stopped speaking briefly, but she didn't introduce me to the boys. I just stood and gawked. Never before had I seen such beautiful children. One boy's golden blonde hair looked like spun gold. While the tresses falling over the other kid's forehead were as rich and dark as sable. Framing their sparkling blue eyes were rows of those thick lashes that, by a wicked twist of genetics, only males seem to end up with. And they both had the cutest little turned-up noses, which copper-colored freckles danced across. Those little angels were perfect enough to star in sitcoms. I swear, they looked that good.

"Thanks for coming, guys," Haggerty said. "What do you hear?"

Before they could answer, I dragged her a few feet away. Aghast, I said, "You *do* exploit kids! How can you?"

With a sigh, Haggerty whispered, "Those aren't children, Samantha, they're leprechauns. They've gone undercover in schools all over the city for me, to keep track of the younger gang members."

Huh? I looked at the pair again. They did reflect the kind of confidence that having a pot of gold hidden behind a rainbow somewhere might create. But what was I thinking? I mean, they were three feet tall.

"They're too big to be leprechauns," I said. "There's a reason my grandmother always called them 'the Little People'"

Haggerty rolled her eyes. "They're projecting themselves larger. It's an illusion." She returned to her friends.

By the time I caught up to her, the blonde one said, "They've been cut off entirely from the higher-ups. No contact, no communication."

Who did? What were they talking about? He spoke in a small boy's voice, but the lift of one shoulder looked oddly mature, even jaded.

"They're not needed anymore," the other boy added with a sage nod.

The boys, or whatever they were, looked so real at that size, so solid. How could they project that? Were they like holograms? Or had their tiny bodies expanded somehow? I wondered what they would feel like to the touch. My hand drifted out toward one of them. Without appearing to look at me, Haggerty pushed it away.

"But the young kids are their future," Haggerty said. "Given their attrition rate on the street, they need to keep recruiting."

The dark-haired boy gave another cosmopolitan flick of his shoulder. "The future has ceased to matter, apparently. They've restructured. The hierarchy has changed."

I tried touching one of them again. The boys inched away, before casting annoyed glances my way.

"The hierarchy has changed," Haggerty repeated softly to herself. Then she gasped and said, "They have a leader."

The blonde kid snapped his fingers. "Of course. It stands to reason. If they're united now, you have to ask yourself: Behind whom?"

My hand started drifting out again. This time Haggerty paused long enough to say, "Samantha, if you don't lower your arm, I'll freeze it like that."

I lowered it.

They ended their conversation with a promise to get in touch with Haggerty, if they learned anything more.

Haggerty turned and started walking back toward Wilshire. Only after a few steps did she remember me. She turned and flipped a finger to indicate I should tag along. As she continued walking, she dialed a cab company on her cell phone and asked to be picked up outside the museum.

"How do they project their tiny bodies bigger?" I asked.

Okay, I happened to ask it just as the taxi dispatcher confirmed our pickup, so she had to ask him to repeat what he said. Was that any reason to shoot me that exasperated look?

Once she ended that call, she asked, "Samantha, how would you like me to turn your hearing off again, along with your speech?"

Me without a mouth? Couldn't happen. "Okay, but what the hell were you talking about with them?"

"Gangs need to keep bringing in new soldiers. They start appealing to the young ones when they're easily awed by the big boys, and lock them in before the little ones know what they're getting into. Now, apparently, the older gang members have ceased all recruitment efforts. Probably because their focus has changed. Because they've been united by a leader who has channeled gang activity in a new direction."

My shoe knocked a stone down the sidewalk. "There must be

hundreds of gangs in this city."

"More than twelve thousand, actually." When my stone landed in her path, Haggerty gave it a vicious kick. "And more than a hundred and fifty thousand members."

I lengthened my stride so I could reach the stone first. I gave it a gentle tap designed to keep it on my side of the sidewalk. "That many, huh? So they can't all be tied into this scam, whatever it is."

Haggerty shook her head. "All our man needs is to rope in the leaders. The troops will follow them anywhere."

"This is bad, huh?" I asked.

"Always the master of understatement, Samantha."

My natural impulse was to top her droll sarcasm with my own snappy comeback. Only, before I could, I saw Haggerty wrap her arms around herself. She shivered, though it wasn't cold. I realized this was too serious to joke about.

She must have been doing battle with her own demons. And won. She suddenly squared her shoulders and lengthened her stride, as if she were marching into battle. "At least we know what we're dealing with now," she announced in a strong voice.

Did we, though?

Apparently, Haggerty's excuse for sending Jake back to the Federal Building alone was that I wanted to go back to my place to change. To cover the lie, we actually did it. Insisting that I lower my profile, she made me change into a pair of jeans and a baggy jersey top. She also made me pack another bag, filled with dowdy duds, to bring along.

When we arrived back at the Bureau, Haggerty went to her office to return some calls. I wandered in the direction of the bullpen, drawn by the shouting I heard coming from there, and the fact that I kept hearing my name.

I stood between a pair of cubicles, facing the table. Dressed down as I was, as I'd always predicted, everybody ignored me. Of course, tempers were also flaring. Especially Jake's. He'd planted himself near one end of the table, while Rusler stood at the other. Apart from it being a modern conference table, and all the suited individuals in between them, it smacked of the O-K Corral.

"I'm telling you," Jake shouted, indicating his hearing wasn't returning quite as fast as mine had, "that the people in this room were the only ones who knew what Samantha told us about the gangs uniting. We were also the only ones who knew what she was about to reveal at that press conference. There was no reason for them to take her out—unless someone leaked why she was a danger to them."

So that was why the people in that car had shot at me. My brain had become so gooey, it never occurred to me to question why it had happened.

My gray cells were sharpening now. I wondered, for instance, why Jake's focus had narrowed in on Rusler. And why Agent Billy's beady little eyes were drawn to someone across the table from him—she of the coordinated sweaters and names—Lisa Lorne, who sunk down in her seat, maybe so nobody would notice her.

And I wondered why the unspoken possibilities now surfacing in my mind hadn't occurred to me before.

CHAPTER EIGHTEEN

Hours later, still in my cruddy jeans, I huddled with Haggerty before the television in her family room. On the floor next to the TV cart sat the cardboard box of tapes and photos that Molly's manager had sent over. We hadn't yet had a chance to review that stuff. Since a couple of dragonflies rested on that carton now, I knew, even if I were in any shape to view that material tonight, there was no way I would try. The bees, of course, just buzzed between the flowers.

The ramifications of the target I'd made of myself kept hitting me. Why hadn't I listened to Haggerty when she advised against my going public? Why did I think she kept her powers secret, if not for her own protection?

What felt even lousier was the idea that someone I knew had ratted me out. My thoughts drifted to Rusler, then Lisa, and even Billy. Billy was always off somewhere, maybe following Rusler's orders, but I'd never seen those orders given.

Haggerty didn't buy Jake's theory. "The taskforce personnel weren't the only ones who knew what you planned to say. You blabbed to the staff at the Bureau, and I overheard you hinting to the museum employees around the donut table." She paused to consider more possibilities. "Lisa went to the hospital today to check on Plotnik—she could have mentioned something there. Loads of people could have dropped the dime on you."

I wasn't sure whether it felt better or worse to learn the pool of my potential enemies had widened. Nor was I convinced. "The people at the museum can't leave during their shifts."

"They have phones, don't they?" Haggerty hesitated. "One among them might even have another form of communication."

An all-too-brief sighting of myself on the news momentarily drew my attention away. It was only after my fifteen milliseconds of fame flickered and died that I realized she'd said something intriguing.

When I turned to her, Haggerty raised her eyebrows and

121

shoulders at the same time, a double-barreled shrug that drove home the point that she thought her remark should have been obvious. "Come on, Samantha. If I'd been stuck in the museum, I could have sent a message out, even without a phone."

"Sure, *you* could have. You're a goddess—you have all kinds of powers." Which she was mostly too stingy to use. "But you're unique."

"Not as much as you think," she said in a pensive tone.

"Wouldn't you know if someone there was...special?"

She shrugged. "Most of us can hide what we are from each other quite well, just as you mortals deceive each other."

Haggerty rose and walked to a small plaster shelf jutting out from the wall, which held an amber-colored candle. Striking a match from the matchbook beside the candle, she lit the wick and stood drawing in the candle's orange blossom scent.

But her hand had shaken too much for my comfort when she lit it. I mean, she was my rock. Your rock's not supposed to be scared. I drew my bare feet under me, tightening myself until I felt like a pretzel, and not a secure one at that.

In a small voice, I asked, "What are you saying? You think whoever's behind this is...like you?"

Haggerty whirled around. "Look at the evidence. These gangs have killed each other for generations. No one has ever succeeded in maintaining a truce for long. Now they're all working together. Only an evil genius could have accomplished that. You can't really believe he's mortal?"

I choked. "Are you suggesting mortal humans can't be evil? Look at Stalin, at Hitler. What would you call them?"

"Not human—that's for sure." She snorted. "Really, Samantha. How naïve can you be?"

I hated it when she challenged everything I knew about the world. What if she was pulling my leg? What if she wasn't?

She obviously wasn't feeling all that secure, either. When her candle-power hadn't been enough to chase her willies away, Haggerty picked up an apple from a bowl at the side of the couch and absently clutched it in her hands.

"It's a demon, I know it is," she said with feverish intensity. "It's Bile, the god of hell, or Elathan, the god of darkness. Or maybe Baal, the god of pain. Or one of their descendents. Maybe we've lost track of some of them."

I stood facing her. "Do you really believe—"

Haggerty's gaze jerked to the TV. She gasped and dropped the apple to the floor. I followed her startled glance to the screen— where a man pressed a knife to Molly Claire's throat.

This man wasn't dressed like a clown, unless that would be how you'd describe Rambo. His face was disguised with combat paint, and he wore a headband tied around his shoulder-length inky black hair. His athletic arms bulged, when he kept Molly pressed against his well-built bare chest, digging that knife deeper into her neck.

"Listen up, people. If the cops keep out of our way, the movie bitch lives. If the pigs keep doggin' us, then not only does she die, but so do a whole lotta youse."

He jerked the knife. When its blade broke her skin, a trickle of blood ran into the soiled, oversized T-shirt she wore. Despite the graphic image of blood soaking into the white shirt, what got to me was Molly's expression. The fear in her eyes, and the look of suffering trapped in her taut muscles, was enough to make my own chin quiver with imminent tears.

Rambo spat out his demands. Fifty million smackers from the city of Los Angeles to keep its people safe. One hundred million from the combined studios and movie distributors Molly had made money for over the course of her career. And from the police, the county sheriff's department, the DA's office, and the FBI—absolute amnesty from arrest or prosecution for any and all gang members.

"Glad he's not greedy," I muttered.

The TV switched back to the anchor, who solemnly announced that the preceding tape had just been received by their station and they rushed it onto the air. So much for the FBI's edict. Good to know law enforcement carried such weight. They ran the tape again, and then the one of Molly in the bank robbery, when she had begged for help. The all-Molly network.

I tried to erase the image of that frightened woman from my mind, but it refused to leave. Molly Claire had always seemed like one of those people who had it all, yet she was never satisfied. She enjoyed huge success in the movies. But she was always going on talk shows, complaining because they never took her seriously as an actress, offering her only the lightweight parts, not the meaty stuff.

Frankly, I never understood why anyone would want to play those gutsy parts, which invariably demanded emotional bloodletting from the actor. Nor why the audience enjoyed them. I never liked feeling anything that deeply. And I figured that, despite her moaning, Molly wasn't so different from me. I mean, why else would she have been good at fluff, if she wasn't basically shallow? The irony was that now, when there was an excellent chance she wouldn't survive, she'd probably become more of an expert on pain than she ever planned. And, I feared, so had I.

"They really have us between a rock and a hard place, huh, Haggerty?" I asked. Us? Like I was one of them.

Haggerty absently shook her head. "They've already achieved much of what they claim to want. By default, the city is a police-free zone for them." She gestured at the TV. "The rest of the demands—that's all smoke. I wish I knew why they sent it out."

"Duh!" I said. "It's about the money. A hundred and fifty really big ones."

"Why then are they robbing banks for really small hauls?" Haggerty asked.

I shrugged. "To show everyone how tough they are?"

"To terrorize us, you mean? Maybe," she answered thoughtfully.

The doorbell rang. "That has to be Angus," I said, leaping to my feet, eager to put as much distance as possible between me and the dark stuff I'd seen on TV. But a thought stopped me. "Haggerty, did you get a vision of Molly before that tape ran?"

"Nothing," Haggerty said. "Maybe she's too exhausted to send anything out."

That wouldn't have been my take on her. Anxiety and adrenaline still seemed to be pushing Molly toward the breaking point. If only she could have known that there was someone out here ready to receive whatever she could send. But how could she know that?

I opened the door. When Angus stepped through it, I threw myself into his arms.

"What's this? Sammy-girl, you're shaking." His brawny arms curled around me.

I almost let the story burst out, but I remembered Haggerty's caution about how little staying power Angus would exhibit during tough times. Instead, I pressed my head against his chest and gave it a shake.

I couldn't entirely hold things back, though. "What do you do when life gets too real?"

He laughed effortlessly, that musical sound I loved. "Why, I just go off to another realm where it's not so damned genuine."

I fervently wished I could. More than ever, I envied him— and Haggerty—their freedom.

CHAPTER NINETEEN
Haggerty

Haggerty did everything required of her after seeing the ransom demand on the news. She remembered to tape the Rambo-warning the next time it appeared, she telephoned the station manager and chewed him out for not bringing it straight to the Bureau, and she called the taskforce command post to tell them to send someone to get that tape from the TV station. Through it all, her mind wasn't on those actions. She didn't think about Molly Claire, or how impotent the Bureau had become. All she really thought about was how happy Samantha seemed when she skipped to the door to let Angus in. And how much she envied Samantha her freedom.

Samantha, who wasn't saddled with a family that often behaved less than mortal, instead of more than as they should have; Samantha, who hadn't committed herself to making this realm more fair than it was. Samantha, who could just disappear if things got too ugly.

With a sigh, Haggerty tried to dispel the negative thoughts. She knew that what she really envied most about Samantha was that she had someone like Angus in her life. Someone—period. She tried not to notice the sounds coming from the guestroom.

As if on some cosmic cue, the doorbell rang. Haggerty dragged herself to the front of the house to answer it. Even before she opened the door, she sensed Jake's agitated presence on the other side. She threw the door open and watched as he proved her impression right. He'd turned away from the door, frantically tapping his foot. He finally noticed the open door and blew in past her.

"I just came from Plotnik's bedside," he said. "Guy looks healthier than I do. No change, though. Still can't wake up."

He paced in such frustration on her shiny floor that Haggerty thought he would wear through the finish. She'd noticed before that he scuffed his shoes, especially when he felt strained, but never as heavily as tonight.

"Lisa was already there, chatting up the cop guarding him,

giving him treats. The moron hadn't even checked her ID, just took her word for who she was," Jake went on, oblivious to his scuffing boots. "I reamed him a new one for that, lemme tell you. I told that patrolman he can't trust no one. We gotta keep Plotnik alive till he can tell us who plugged him."

Haggerty didn't remind him that she understood that as well as he did. She sensed talking was his way of dealing with his agitation.

"You heard the latest? Their demands?" he asked, barely pausing his tense stride. "So they think they can hold this entire city hostage, instead of just one woman. Do they really believe this will make us back off?"

How strange, she thought. Jake took the threat as literally as Samantha had.

"And the money." He snorted as ferociously as an angry bull. "As if the city would pay extortion to keep its citizens safe. That's why they pay us cops. The movie folks—that'd be chump change to them. But they're still not going to part with it."

Was she the only one who believed the demand to be no more than a device? A device that hid something more sinister, even if she couldn't tell what it was? She would have presented her theory, only she sensed Jake was in no shape to absorb anything new now. Instead, she just offered him a beer.

She returned from the kitchen with a couple of beers and a plate of meatloaf, leftover from the dinner she'd made for herself and Samantha. "I thought you could use some comfort food. Meatloaf always does it for me."

She found Jake slouched on the futon. "Comfort food, huh?" He grabbed the fork and cut two meatloaf slices in half, and stuffed two pieces into his mouth. After a quick swallow, he said, "In that case, got any koushry? When I want comfort, it's my mom's koushry."

Koushry? Someone she should remember had served her that. What was it? On overload herself, Haggerty shook her head. "Sorry, just meatloaf."

Jake shoveled the last of the meatloaf into his mouth. Then, rapidly switching gears, he eyed the guestroom door. With a nod of his head in that direction, he asked, "Our girl pick up anything new?"

That was interesting. Jake might have said that in a

derogatory way, but it sounded like cover. He wasn't so much the skeptic now when it came to Samantha's purported psychic impressions.

Jake squinted at her. "Do you think she really—you know, sees things?"

An impulse flashed in Haggerty, a desire to share the truth with him. Then reason returned. If he wasn't ready to hear her theory about the case, he really couldn't take her personal story.

Looking down at the wooden floor, she said, "It's hard to explain what she knows any other way."

"She picked up nothing tonight, huh?"

The sound of laughter coming from the guestroom softened the electric charge building up between them. "She's been a little occupied," Haggerty said, sitting beside him.

Jake glanced down at the beer bottle he held between his tightly clenched fingers. "Lucky her," he muttered. He cast a speculative glance at Haggerty through his dark lashes. "Do you ever wish the world would just go away?"

"You mean, no tomorrow, no yesterday, only now? Oh, yes," she said with feeling.

He shook his head. "The world won't stop. Sometimes you just gotta seize your timeout."

He placed her beer bottle alongside his own on the coffee table. Then he stood, awkwardly shifting from foot to foot. Finally, he took Haggerty's hand and drew her into his arms.

Though her mind cried out for her to stop this while she still could, her body drifted along with him. So effortlessly, she might have considered it all a dream, if the sense of anticipation hadn't taken her breath away. His soft, demanding lips found hers and claimed them. She felt her own parting in response, and her tongue flicking out, inviting him in. His arms wrapped around her so tightly, she couldn't breathe. Her body arched into his. It was hard to for Haggerty to surrender completely to any man, given all her powers. Yet she felt herself submitting totally to him.

When his hands began to explore her body, she felt her breath catch, then quicken. Her loins ignited in liquid fire. For the first time in longer than she could remember, she felt herself living in the moment. And it was a moment she fervently hoped would never end.

The doorbell rang. Then again, and again. It wasn't until the fourth demanding burst of sound that the reality sank in for Haggerty; their moment had been shattered. They came apart, awkwardly and abruptly. Neither knowing where to look, or what to do with their hands. Haggerty concentrated on trying to still her racing lungs. Jake tried to shift his clothing to cover the appearance of his arousal, but his faded jeans were tight.

She slipped through the tiny entry to the door. Too suffused with emotion now, she didn't even try to read who might be on the other side of the door, peering instead through the peephole.

She raced back to Jake. "It's the SAC, Agent Rusler."

Jake swore. "How did I know that bastard would have perfect timing?" He shoved his hands into his pockets.

When the bell rang again, Haggerty absently patted down her rumpled sweater and went to open the door. At the sight of her, Rusler's jaw dropped to form such a huge smile, it displayed nearly all of his thick white teeth.

"Annabelle, my dear, I wanted to see how Samantha is taking this latest volley," he said in a jovial tone that belied the serious nature of his excuse. He eased past her without waiting to be invited, still smiling—until he caught sight of Jake. The hinged jaw snapped shut.

"Detective Azar," he said in clipped tones.

Jake gave him a tight nod.

In the silence that followed, Rusler's gaze moved from Jake, to Haggerty, and back again. He lifted his head as if to smell the animal charge still present in the air.

Haggerty would have felt mortified, if she weren't awfully angry. "Detective Azar was also worried about Samantha," she explained, determined to brazen it out. "She felt so overwhelmed, she went to bed."

No lie there. Haggerty hoped Samantha kept the laughter down. Despite her determination to make strong eye contact with Rusler alone, her gaze found Jake's. A tired look of acceptance had come into his dark eyes. They both knew what they experienced was gone for now. Even if Rusler left, they couldn't recapture it.

"Detective Azar was just leaving, sir. Perhaps—" Haggerty stopped. What could she say? *Perhaps you should leave, too.* The man was her boss. But this was her home. She showed Jake out, stealing a moment at the door to whisper conventional remarks, in which she hoped he found greater meaning.

Haggerty would have thought nothing could make that awkward situation worse—only to return to the living room to see Angus casually strolling from the kitchen, wearing nothing but the guestroom blanket wrapped around his narrow waist. He clutched the blanket with one hand, while in the other he held a pair of wine glasses; he carried a bottle of wine between his inner arm and his body.

Though she had never felt more embarrassed, Haggerty resolved to keep it impersonal, as she introduced Angus as Samantha's dear friend. Before Angus could respond, Rusler held his hands up in a stop position insisting that they not shake hands. While Rusler chuckled softly at his own joke, Angus seemed not to understand. Giving his shoulder-length hair an indifferent toss, Angus passed around Rusler and disappeared into the guestroom.

Still not ready to deal with Rusler, Haggerty excused herself and carried the beer bottles to the kitchen. She was so lost in thought, she failed to notice he had followed her. She placed the bottles in the sink. Before she could move away from the counter, Rusler's arms came around her, pinning her between the counter and his body.

"Annabelle," he muttered, pressing his face between her shoulder blades.

Why *now?* Haggerty agonized. From a desert to a flood zone in mere moments.

"Surely, you've guessed my feelings for you," Rusler murmured against her neck. "With tensions running so high, I need you now as I never—"

"No!" Haggerty roared. Using the extraordinary physical strength she possessed, though rarely used, she broke free of his hold.

"Annabelle...?" Rusler's jaw hung slackly for once, as if in shock.

"That's Special Agent Haggerty, sir. I've never given you any reason to think of me in any other way."

Anger narrowed Rusler's eyes into menacing slits. "I've done a lot for you. Where's your gratitude?"

There were so many things she could say: That she'd earned every opportunity that came her way; that he had no right sexually harassing someone under his command; that she could turn him to stone as easily as looking at him.

She could have said so many things. But all she said was, "Agent Rusler, I am not your Twinkie."

"Not anymore, you're not." He ran his hand through his thick hair. "I'll show myself out." Moments later, the front door slammed hard enough to shake the house.

Haggerty might have turned to stone herself. She stood that still, until long after the sound of that slam faded away. Then, finally, she dragged herself to her breakfast table and slumped into a chair, holding her heavy head in her hands. It all felt like too much for her. Being strong all the time. Why was she the one that always had to support everyone else? Wouldn't anyone ever be there for her?

An image drifted into her mind. She knew what she needed tonight. At least, what she needed if she couldn't have Jake. Her sense of anticipated comfort began to offset much of her exhaustion, even as she rushed to her bedroom, eager to get to sleep.

Stretched out on her bed, sleep came to her fast. Slowly, after she lost consciousness, she felt her spirit rise above her corporal body. With no more than a glance back at the form lying still beneath the bulky white down comforter, Haggerty's spirit drifted away from that room, from that house.

With full awareness of the out-of-body process, she rose high in the sky. Then she willed herself to begin floating in an east-by-northeasterly direction. She moved swiftly, deliberately, taking no note of her surroundings. Until she neared her destination—a casino on the Las Vegas Strip.

Only then did her movement slow to a drift. Haggerty, in spirit-form, floated into the vast casino and paused to orient herself. Though it was late night, the casino was far from empty. Haggerty finally spotted the person she was searching for.

Seated at a blackjack table with a few other gamblers was a woman who looked a young fifty. Her sandy red hair curled gently to her slender shoulders, and while she sat beneath the harsh artificial light of the casino, it looked like a glint of sunlight had been trapped in her sparkling blue-green eyes. Though her once tiny waist had thickened, the woman still looked lean and fit, despite the hours she spent warming the stool before that blackjack table. Her creamy skin clung firmly to her photogenic facial bones, though now it crinkled attractively in a fan of laugh lines around her eyes. Even in repose, a touch of humor was present in the serenity of her lovely face, and maybe a bit of mischief.

Though no words were uttered aloud, Haggerty felt her spirit saying, "Hi, Mom."

"Annie, darling," her mother's spirit said. "I've been expecting you."

Since both of Haggerty's grandparents were gods, a purer strain than Haggerty's own, her mother had inherited stronger powers than she possessed. And once Fionna reached the mother portion of a goddess's life, she maintained a constant connection to her child. Though she rarely interfered, she always knew what her daughter experienced.

"Give me just a second, will you, dear? This place has been quiet for too long," Fionna mentally told her daughter.

In some ways they were so much alike, Haggerty thought, both trying to make things better for someone else.

After only a short delay, elsewhere in the casino the lively sound of bells and whistles went off, and Haggerty heard shouts of "I won! I won!" Below her, she saw full lips that looked so much like her own, curve in satisfaction.

Haggerty watched as her mother's body said to the dealer, "Deal me out, will you, Tom. I'll just watch the others play for a few hands."

With nothing more demanded of her corporal form, Fionna's spirit drifted up into the voluminous space above the table and joined with her daughter's. Haggerty floated into her mother's arms. And though they were only together in spirit, it felt every bit as real as it would if their actual bodies were embracing.

After only a short time Haggerty sighed quietly to herself, with both relief and sadness. This is how you know you're an adult, she thought. When collapsing in your mother's arms still makes you feel good, but doesn't make everything all better anymore.

Planting a kiss on her daughter's forehead, which, even in the spirit realm felt like the caress of a breeze, Fionna said, "Things are so hard for you now, but someone has come into your life who will make it easier."

Even in her out-of-body form, Haggerty felt herself flushing, as she thought of Jake.

Her mother went on to clarify what she meant. "This girl sounds like quite the character."

"Samantha? Mom, you can't mean that. Samantha is unreliable, she's shady—and the sooner she's out of my life, the better it will be for both of us."

Fionna just shook her head. "Annabelle, the people who come into our lives aren't necessarily the ones we *want,* they're the people we *need.*" In both spirit and corporal form, her lips tightened into a stern line. "There's a reason why this young woman's path has crossed yours. Don't fight this connection, my darling."

Haggerty had never challenged her mother's psychic sense, but for the first time, she doubted it. She and Samantha were using each other, plain and simple.

"Mom, what do you see in the future? Can you tell me anything at all?"

Fionna closed her eyes, but an instant later, they popped open. Haggerty could see the horror reflected in Fionna's eyes now, as, even in spirit form, her mother's face grew pale.

"Mom, what is it?"

"I don't know. It's all too dark to see. But it's going to be very bad, Annabelle."

How much worse could it get?

"And—" her mother started to say. "I can't quite explain it, you know. It's just that I have a sense…"

"Yes?" Haggerty implored.

"That nothing is as it appears."

Before Haggerty could question her mother, a stabbing pain gripped her head. Almost instantly, she heard a bloodcurdling scream that seemed to go on without end. There was nothing to identify the source, but somehow she knew it came from Molly Claire.

Haggerty's spirit rushed home. As it did, her thoughts returned to what her mother had said only moments before. That what was about to happen would be very bad. Still hearing those screams, she didn't doubt that now.

But how could it be different from the way it appeared?

133

CHAPTER TWENTY
Samantha

I was back in high school again. I knew that because the version of me I saw in my mind's eye was thinner than the me I see in the mirror everyday. And because the clothes on the high school Samantha weren't as great then as the stuff I wore now. But Angus was there, too, and that made no sense.

I could see myself standing in front of my locker. Angus, with his hand nonchalantly pressed to the wall above it, circled me with his body. I could feel myself giving my head a coquettish tilt as I beamed up at him. And though the cool high school me, with my hot boyfriend, would never acknowledge them, I knew the unpopular girls were gathered across the hall in a little cluster, sending envious glances my way.

Once I acknowledged that, I had to admit this was not real high school, but a dream. If it were real, I would have been one of those girls across the hall, *yearning* to live like the cool girl with her hunky boyfriend, not actually living that life. With a mental shrug I dismissed that objection and just enjoyed the experience of basking in the spotlight of teenage envy.

Then the fire alarm went off. A relentless, tiring sound. All at once, Angus was gone, though I hadn't seen him leave. Other kids rushed down the hall, bumping into me in their hurry to escape. From what? I didn't smell any smoke. Must have been a false alarm.

Once again, I recognized that this had to be a dream. In real life high school, *I* was always the one setting off false alarms. Generally, before a test I hadn't studied for. In this dream world, I was practically caught in the stampede that someone else's subterfuge had generated.

With a sigh, the cool me in high school surrendered to necessity and started toward the exit. At the same moment, the even cooler, infinitely better dressed version of me—asleep in the guestroom of Haggerty's house—shook off the last of sleep, when I finally realized that the high school Samantha's fire alarm was

134

actually Haggerty's persistently ringing phone.

Though fully awake now, and really hating that annoying sound, I didn't rush to answer it. Haggerty would get it.

I rolled onto my side in bed. Angus was gone now, but once again he'd left something for me on his pillow. Not a shamrock this time, but a bouquet of wildflowers. Vibrant California poppies in every imaginable color were coupled together with delicate English cornflowers. The wild and the restrained, exactly what Angus had said about me after we made love last night. Okay, so maybe he was the only person who had ever seen any restraint in me, but I'd never object to praise, even if it wasn't true.

The flowers were gathered together with a piece of twisted straw. And though they were cut and not in water, they felt as fresh as they would on their stalks. I hugged that bundle to my naked breasts. Fairy flower bugs be damned.

That infuriating phone wouldn't quit. What was wrong with Haggerty? Didn't she want to spare her guest this annoyance?

Tossing the bouquet back onto the pillow, I hurled myself out of bed and threw on a robe, stomping from the room. The noise was even more irritating the closer I drew to it.

Before I reached the telephone, Haggerty suddenly came flying out of her room, tying the sash on her dressing gown as she ran. There was a furtive quality in the way she looked away from me when she grabbed for the phone, and maybe a trace of displeasure at having been dragged there. I remembered that night when she met with the witches, and I wondered if she'd left the house again. Yet her eyes looked puffy with sleep.

"Were you out?" I asked, remembering not to add *again*. She still didn't know I'd seen her that night in the park.

"Something like that," she muttered as she snatched up the phone and identified herself.

Something like that? How many ways were there? Realizing that my question might generate an answer I wouldn't want to hear, I started back toward the guestroom to rejoin my bouquet. I began to get the idea that what Angus called my "restraint," anyone else would describe as "denial."

Then from behind me, I heard her gasp. That simple sound contained such horror, it made me stop and turn back toward her. She didn't say much to her caller, she just listened. I watched as her dark blue eyes grew wide and her generous mouth tightened into an angry knot.

After a moment, she hung up. Without pausing, she started back toward her room, shouting over her shoulder, "Get dressed, Samantha. We have to leave. Right away."

"What is it?"

"A body. They think—" She stopped, but just bit her lip. "Better not to say anything, until we're sure."

A body? Whose? I thought about pestering her to tell me. But with each new blow, I realized I didn't want to know. I had to cling to my life and what worked for me.

With that in mind, when I returned to the guestroom, rather than slip on the drab clothes I'd discarded the night before, I reached into the closet for one of my special things. As if my hand had a mind of its own, it settled on a purple halter dress, in a gloriously rich satin. I'd bought that dress when one of the studios sold off their old costumes. Tinsel Town garage sale, with stuff from when stars ate more for dinner than some of them weighed now. I coupled the dress with my bright purple satin heels. I paused long enough to put on the Celtic necklace I'd bought at the gas station the other day, and I was out the door an instant after Haggerty, who, in her black knit outfit, didn't look a fraction as good.

The clock on the Honda's dashboard read 2:36. In the morning, I gathered, since it was pitch black out. We made good time getting to the freeway. To my surprise, instead of heading in the direction of the Federal Building, where I assumed we were going, Haggerty drove toward downtown.

I'd brought my bouquet with me, and now I clutched my flowers tightly in my arms, still amazed at how fresh they remained. Haggerty's palpable tension made me uneasy. "Did you see something about Molly tonight? Some other vision?"

Haggerty hesitated, before acknowledging with a slight nod that she had a vision.

"Bad?" I asked.

Though she was driving, and at breakneck speed, Haggerty pressed her eyes closed for an instant.

Confused and unsure of how much more I could take, I fluffed my full skirt, while exploring a lesser question. "How many ways are there to go out?" I asked.

She flashed a confused look my way. "Is that a riddle?"

"You'd know that better than me. You said, 'Something like that' when I asked you if you went out."

In the amber glow of the dashboard light, I could see her fingers tightening around the wheel. Finally, Haggerty said, "You really don't want to know, Samantha."

"Let me decide that, huh?"

She shrugged. "Okay. I went to Las Vegas."

I felt a big gaping silence form in my head. In a small voice, I asked, "By plane?"

"No," she answered shortly.

I hated it when she was right. I really didn't want to know.

Haggerty's Honda bypassed downtown and went a few exits into East L.A. She took the exit ramp fast, turning onto a street I didn't know. Less than a block from the freeway, she made a sharp right into a narrow driveway. There were some old brick buildings to one side of us, I noticed; quite a number of them, actually, in what seemed to be some kind of complex. I realized too late that there had been a lighted sign that we passed too fast to read. Haggerty careened into a parking space outside a modern building at the rear of the complex and leaped from the car, hurrying ahead.

Without paying much attention to where we'd ended up, I grasped my bouquet of flowers and toddled along behind her. My spiked heels were still clicking against the wide sidewalk, when Haggerty reached the glass double-door entrance and leaned on the buzzer alongside it. Only when I joined her there did I see, from the printing across those doors, that we'd gone to the L.A. County Morgue.

I peered through the glass doors. A tiny waiting room lay beyond them, filled with several navy chairs. Just past the waiting area was an opening to a receptionist's desk. Covering it was one of those sliding windows they always close in doctor's offices when you complain too loudly about the duration of your wait. Just like a doctor's office, only here, no one had any hope of getting better.

Before I could run back to the car, a gnarled old man carrying a wet mop, which had left a trail of drops along the drab vinyl floor, unlocked the door for us. That his dark eyes bulged unnaturally wide indicated to me that he knew more about this latest crisis than I did. And his obvious agitation scared me. You'd think it would be hard to rattle someone who worked at the morgue.

When Haggerty flashed her ID, the old man started to give her directions. She shut that down by telling him she knew the way. Man, this was a place I never wanted to know my way around.

Haggerty raced down a corridor that came off the waiting room. I dawdled behind her, afraid to look through the doors on both sides of us, until I realized they were only offices. The dominant smell in that area was copier toner, not...you know. I caught up to Haggerty at the elevator, as the elevator doors opened.

We only went as far as the second story. That floor smelled strongly of disinfectant and the kind of odors I vaguely remembered from high school biology, which were the reason I often cut it. We followed another hall around a couple of bends, until we arrived at a visitors' area. Most of the taskforce folks, except for Rusler and one or two others, waited there.

Haggerty jerked to a halt before the spot where Jake paced, scuffing his shoes against the floor. "Do we know anything yet?"

With his cowlicks stuck out worse than ever, Jake gave his head a shake. "Lisa has dental records. She should be along with them shortly."

Billy looked up from the molded plastic chair he'd squeezed his oversized bottom into, lifting his bushy eyebrows in disbelief. "Lisa? Did she stumble on them by accident?"

Jake gave him equally amazed shrug. "Had the sense to get 'em and kept them at the office. Go figure."

Obviously, they shared my low opinion of Lisa Lorne. I wasn't sure what they were talking about precisely, but I was starting to get the idea that Lisa might have a brighter future in law enforcement than I had predicted. What can I say? I'm not actually psychic.

Lisa came running around the corner, still wearing the sack-like dress and flat-heeled shoes she'd worn hours earlier. She clutched a manila envelope in her hand.

She stopped before Billy and thrust the envelope forward. "You take them in there." She gave her face a squeamish twist.

How did this chick ever secure her job? Nepotism must rule the Bureau.

Agent Billy popped up from the too-small chair with seemingly effortless ease. That big boy was full of surprises. He carried the envelope through a pair of swinging doors, accompanied by Jake, while the rest of us waited in a tight silence.

When they emerged, no more than twenty minutes later, Billy said, with a shake of his large, round head, "No surprises, kids. It's a match. That's Molly Claire in there."

"Molly—" I sputtered. "You mean she's...dead?"

Haggerty just stared off into space, while Jake turned my way and said, "That's right, Madame Samantha. Miss Molly has left the building."

"Not possible," I insisted, and I gave my bouquet of flowers a shake for emphasis.

Agent Billy stepped right into my face. "Kid, the bastards hacked her to death with knives and dumped her body on the steps of City Hall. You see anything there that leaves room for doubt?"

CHAPTER TWENTY-ONE

I refused to accept it. "No," I said, anxiously tapping my purple shoe against the floor. "She can't be dead. You don't kill your hostage. Not if you want your demands met."

Haggerty had left the house with her hair loose, a way she never wore it while working. Though her auburn hair looked good against her tight black knit top, she found a rubber band someplace and was now tying it back at the nape of her neck.

"Those demands were never going to be met," Haggerty said. "They know it, and we know."

"I still can't believe they'd kill Molly Claire. There has to be some—" I started to say.

A strange voice from behind me interrupted with, "There's no mistake about the identity of the victim."

I turned to see a slim East Indian man in hospital scrubs. He kept drying his hands on a sheet of paper towel that he rapidly reduced to shreds.

Jake briefly introduced the man as Dr. Rasmi, the medical examiner who had confirmed the identification.

"We will have my finding verified by a forensic dentist, who'll compare the two sets of x-rays. But there is no question in my mind that the body found on the steps of City Hall is that of Molly Claire. Miss Claire was a celebrity—she took excellent care of her teeth. And her dentist kept accurate records. The body's teeth—they matched the x-rays precisely."

With that level of verification, I guessed they didn't bother with DNA. So much for the accuracy of TV dramas. I nodded absently, while watching the man further disintegrate the paper towel. "Wait. Dental records? That means there was no other way to…" My mind caught up to what Molly must have looked like now, how even her hands must have been hacked, making a fingerprint check impossible. My stomach acid rose up in revolt.

"Let's just say they did a number on Miss Molly, before they finished her off," Jake said.

Haggerty clenched her eyes closed. In sympathy, or was she feeling the effect of a vision? Maybe she just regretted what she hadn't managed to learn on time.

The taskforce folks decided to move to an all-night coffee shop. Calls were placed to Rusler and the missing members, who would meet us there.

During the drive, Haggerty related to me the last psychic impression she had of Molly, those unrelenting screams.

"I'd never felt such terror." She shook her ponytail. "My mom said something bad was about to happen. I should never have doubted her."

"Your mom? You called her?" I remembered her saying she went to Las Vegas, and that was where her mother lived. I groaned.

"I told you that you didn't want to know," Haggerty said, but her remark lacked its usual zing. Neither of us felt particularly jovial.

"Do you feel her somewhere out there? Molly, I mean. You know, on...the other side." Weird. When I didn't put any stock in those woo-woo words, I tossed them around like a billionaire giving tips. Now that I knew them to be real, it gave me the creeps to use them.

"I don't feel her at all. And that's strange. Once they pass over, I usually find it easier to connect with them. But my connection to Molly hasn't been typical from the start."

Haggerty drove into the parking lot, and we entered the coffee shop through the rear entrance. After following the corridor from the back door, past the restrooms and public telephone, we found everyone assembled inside. Rusler was there already. He sent Haggerty a look that would have flash-frozen a side of beef.

Ooh! There was a story there. I had hoped, for Haggerty's sake, that Rusler's interest in her would never move beyond the unexpressed longing stage. But it looked now like there was no putting that toothpaste back in the tube. Since the coffee shop was empty, the group pushed several tables together in the center. With only a few chairs open, I noticed Haggerty picked seats for us that were equal distance from both Rusler and Jake.

Lisa, on the other hand, the girl of the hour, shoved her chair so close to Rusler's, she might as well have climbed into his lap. Given the smug lift to her pointy little chin when she looked

Haggerty's way, I guessed that having been classified second best in the new-girl class of two had really chafed.

I'd reached my saturation point with all of them. Them and everything I'd encountered since I broke into Molly Claire's condo. Apart from Angus. *Still* clutching my unwiltable flowers, I went to the ladies room to be alone.

I sat in one of the stalls for a few minutes, but someone else entered while I was in there. Despite the appearance of solitude those stall sides created, the sounds that traveled over them shattered the illusion. When I emerged, I found Lisa standing at one of the two sinks in the vanity, touching up her makeup in the mirror.

I placed my bouquet on the counter, between the two sinks.

She glanced at it. "You look pretty silly, you know, clutching that bunch of flowers like it's your dead baby or something."

Considering where we had just been, I regarded allusions to anything dead to be pretty tacky.

"Oh, I almost forgot." Lisa fished around in her designer purse, a match for the one Haggerty forced me to abandon at the clubhouse. "I found a note for you stuck to the door at the Bureau."

I took the crumpled ivory envelope she extended. "Who would write to me there?" Once I saw it was addressed to *Sammy-girl*, I knew. "It's from my—guy." I almost said *god*.

I tore the envelope open. The note, which was from Angus as expected, read: "My girl, I've learned something. Meet me at 4502 Hanover Street in Van Nuys, and we'll explore it together. Wouldn't it be swell if we could present the solution to our Annabelle?"

I didn't recognize the address, so I read it off to Lisa.

She frowned at her reflection in the mirror. "That's the Hanover Street Clubhouse. Why would you go there?"

"Is it? Detective Azar took Annabelle and me there."

Lisa squeezed her reddened lips together, before smiling in approval. "I'm on the board of the Foundation that runs it. My uncle owns that property."

But who was keeping score? When I thought about it, I remembered the clubhouse as having been sponsored by something called "the Lorne Foundation."

I read my lover's note again, this time with less affection. Why couldn't he have been clearer? *When* did he want me to meet him? And wouldn't you think a guy who could leave cut flowers that wouldn't wilt would find a less pedestrian way of communicating? The handwriting looked awfully fussy, with its curlicues and swirls; quite old-fashioned. How old was Angus? Ancient, obviously. Clearly, he had learned to write during a more flowery time.

"Did you see him? Angus, I mean," I said.

She shook her head. "Agent Rusler said he did, though."

She giggled softly to herself and gave her head a tilt, as if she wanted me to fill her in on precisely how those two paths had crossed. I didn't know that story myself, but I wouldn't have told her if I had.

Instead, I said, "He's really cute."

She shrugged. "Maybe, if you like that type."

Right. Like she could do better. Rusler better quit gossiping about my boyfriend.

Lisa returned her overstuffed makeup case to her purse. "Gotta go. Agent Rusler wants one of the primary taskforce members to man the command center along with the night team now. I'm taking the first shift."

Whatever. That's the problem with being a spiritual advisor. The mugs believe that because you predict their future that you also give a rat's ass about it. Where did this chick get the idea her career mattered to me? All I could think about was Angus. Who cared if he was a little vague about meeting times? I'd just wait for him there. Anyplace away from those people was good enough for me.

"Who else is on duty with you?" I asked to be nasty, certain I could guess the answer.

Lisa fastidiously wrinkled her nose. "Special Agent Finkner."

Billy. So it wasn't exactly the A-team. That was what I figured. It occurred to me that, despite my aversion to cops, I hadn't minded getting personal with either Lisa or Billy. Proof, I guess, that I didn't take either of them seriously. I could do their jobs better than they did.

"Not that I have anything against overweight people, you understand," she hastened to add.

Why tell me?

Her eyes swept over my body. "I can't understand why Agent Rusler put him on the taskforce. What can that has-been contribute? It must have been a charitable gesture."

Yeah, Rusler struck me as a real charitable guy. Even so, I couldn't understand the entire composition of the taskforce. A few of them were obvious yes-men, Billy inspired no confidence, apart from his ability to jump in with the well-placed smartass remark and a stack of sandwiches, and nearly everyone else was too young to bring any seasoning to the work. Has-beens or never-weres. Apart from Jake, the one capable police detective, who had been thrust upon him—Rusler seemed to have assembled a team doomed to fail. So far, they were performing as expected.

"Billy's work is okay, I guess," Lisa went on. "But those breaks he takes a few times a day—forty-five minutes in the bathroom. What's that all about? Of course, he doesn't eat lunch. Who'd have figured that?"

Shut-up, already. She just wouldn't get the idea that I didn't care. Changing directions, I asked, "Hey, can you give me a lift? I left my car in the parking lot at the Federal Building."

"I don't know. Has Annabelle—"

The lie just rolled out. "It was her idea. She told me to take a cab, but you could save me a few bucks." Good to know I hadn't lost my touch.

Lisa tossed off an indifferent shrug. As I followed her out the coffee shop's back door, she said, "You know, Samantha, about that reading you did for me—I'm starting to think you were way off. Teaching's not right for me, after all. Something tells me I have a real bright future in the Bureau."

Now that Haggerty had cleared the way to Rusler, that was a prediction even I could make.

Lady Stang was mad when I climbed into her front seat at the Federal Building parking lot. And cold, of course, with busted springs that felt far worse under my behind than I remembered. So mad, she wouldn't start. I heard nothing but a feeble grind when I cranked the key. And it died away fast.

I looked over my shoulder to make sure no one lurked nearby. It was almost four in the morning, but you can never be sure. Then, confident I wouldn't be overheard, I patted Stangie's cracked dashboard. "Please, baby. I know some mean people have kept us apart, but it's you and me from now on, I promise." *Until I saved enough for a down payment on a Honda with leather seats*, I thought.

Fortunately, Lady Stang was no more telepathic than I was. This time, when I cranked it, her engine roared to life. With a bang loud enough to crack crystal for a two-block radius maybe, but no one was perfect. I threw her into drive and raced to Angus.

I wasn't certain I could find the foundry again, but I arrived without difficulty. I felt a little apprehensive driving around the darkened building to the clubhouse parking area. Why was I worried? Angus was a god; he could protect me from anything. Besides, I'd just wait in the car with the doors locked until he arrived.

When I cut the engine, I saw someone open the clubhouse door. With the lights out in the parking lot and the clubhouse behind him, I couldn't make out much. But the sky had started to brighten. In that low illumination, I saw a big man with long blonde hair coming toward me.

Angus! I leaped from Stangie and rushed toward him, nearly tripping in my spiked heels. It was only after I'd gone a few yards that I realized the silhouette's walk was wrong. Too stiff, without that joyous bounce Angus had.

It hit me all at once—what a fool I'd been. Like every moronic heroine who marches into the killer's trap, in every bad movie that ever made me laugh my ass off. What can I say? I was a girl in love. And that may have just signed my death warrant.

Before I could get away, the silhouette became a man who loomed over me. Rather than celebrating youth and love and laughter, as Angus did, this coarse-featured stranger commemorated beer breath and rotten teeth, I discovered when he leered at me. It was as if a Hollywood casting agent called for an Angus-type, and this was what he came up with. Someone with a superficial similarity, yet different in every way that mattered.

I started to turn away, only he took hold of my arm and held it in fingers that gripped like a vise. The man raised something in his hand—in the dark I couldn't make out what it was—which he brought down in the direction of my noggin. I think I let out a little squeak of protest. That was the last thing I remembered.

CHAPTER TWENTY-TWO

When, oh-when, would I learn to think before I acted? Not in this lifetime, obviously.

The last thing I remembered was rushing to the Hanover Street Clubhouse to meet Angus. Only instead of finding him there, a man who bore a superficial resemblance to my love knocked me unconscious.

When I came to my head felt like the night sky on the Fourth of July, with countless explosions going off. The difference was that mine were all trapped within the confines of my sore little skull.

The pain in my head was the least of it. When awareness first crept in, I felt as if my arms were being torn from their sockets by a pair of gorillas. Then I suffered a sensation of extreme heat, coming from somewhere close below me. And a peculiar smell—the odor was one I'd experienced before, though it took a while for me to say where. I finally identified it as an intense form of the smell in a friend's jewelry making workshop. I also felt my body swaying, as if it were floating in air. It was when I put all those elements together into a terrifying picture that my eyes flew open—and I found the reality of my situation to be even worse.

The smelter at the foundry was operational again. I knew that because, though I wasn't in a position to see it exactly, I could feel the giant vat of molten metal burning below me. My captor had strung me up above it, with my arms tied over my head and attached to an oversized rubber band, which, with the weight of my body, was gradually lowering me to the level of that hot liquid metal.

When, oh-when, was I going to *weigh less?* Not in this lifetime, considering how fast it was drawing to a close.

The heat of the molten metal billowed my skirt out. It had made my feet swell so much, my purple satin shoes pinched like the devil.

The devil? Haggerty had said a supernatural-type bad guy had to be behind all the inexplicable terror that kept coming our way.

True? All I could say for certain was that he was a sadist. There was such cruelty in all of these crimes. The way Molly's Clowns had been setup and discarded, and how Molly herself had been held in frightening conditions, only to be hacked to death. Now I was being forced to wait out what threatened to be a most agonizing death. I guessed the visions I'd passed on from Haggerty had really angered someone. But wasn't this overkill? What kind of person—what kind of *being*—considered this my just fate?

I didn't know how long I'd been hanging there. Even if I wore a watch, I wasn't in a position to read it. Time became measured in the distance I lost, as the elastic band that held my body lowered me closer to the vat below. I pressed my chin to my chest. That increased the agonizing tension on my arms, but I had to know how long I had.

No! What I saw spiked my fear even higher. My purple shoes now hung just above the lip of the vat, no more than four feet above the surface of the swirling metal. The soaring heat scorched the skin of my legs. I watched as my body sank lower. The elastic was losing its snap.

It wouldn't be long now. Despite my determination to go out on my own terms, in the spirit with which I'd lived my life, fear and dread overcame me. Tears began to fall. Big fat drops that splashed against my chest above my gown's halter neckline. My nose began to run, and I couldn't even wipe away the trail of snot that oozed down my face.

Despair overcame me completely, and the feeling of being terribly alone. Even now, I didn't put much stock in that metaphysical crap. Yet I found myself calling out to someone, silently, in my mind. It surprised me to discover who I cried for in this time of desperation. Not my mom. I'd miss her like the dickens, but she was never good in a crisis. Nor Angus. What we'd had was great, but I couldn't afford to cling to illusions. I know that when something burns as hot as what we'd shared, it cools off quickly.

It was Haggerty I cried out to. Tentatively, at first, like someone trying a telephone for the first time. *Haggerty*, I thought, *if you're there, if you can hear me, come and help me. Now, before all you can do is fish a sculpture of my padded form out of that vat below.*

As I broke into sobs, my thoughts burst into speech.

"Haggerty!" I swallowed hard, and my voice was reduced to a whisper. "Annabelle. Annabelle, *please.*"

CHAPTER TWENTY-THREE
Haggerty

Throughout that middle-of-the-night breakfast meeting in the coffee shop, Haggerty tried to focus on what mattered most. Molly Claire had been brutally slain—it was essential that they bring her killers to justice and put an end to this reign of terror. She tried not to let the personal issues interfere with those critical concerns. But Rusler kept glowering at her, as if her rejection of him were the *real* crime.

She had worked hard for her career in the Bureau, overcoming more obstacles than mortal agents faced. Fighting everyone in her family who believed the job to be too commonplace for one of their kind. Trying to make sure her cases got the benefit of her special skills, while hiding those gifts from the very people they benefited. Now it might all have been for nothing. Rusler was in a position to short-circuit her rise within the FBI. And judging by the fury he directed her way, it had become his most important goal.

And then there was Jake, seated just a few chairs away in the opposite direction. She tried not to look at him, knowing that would just anger Rusler more. But she couldn't help it. Never before had a man so thoroughly taken hold of her feelings. Unfortunately, coupling the giddy rush of intense attraction was the knowledge that it was hopelessly doomed. She felt forced to ride a roller coaster of emotions. The extremes exhausted her.

With so much on her mind, it wasn't surprising that she failed to notice the seat beside her had been empty for a long time.

When the meeting broke up, she threw the money she and Samantha owed onto the stack of bills at the center of the table, and rushed to the ladies room. Samantha was gone. Before panicking, Haggerty searched for clues. She found a single scarlet poppy petal between the sinks, as crisp as in the morning dew. Haggerty hadn't questioned that bouquet Samantha had been dragging around. It looked ridiculous, of course, but it fit her absurd wardrobe. Yet now that she touched the petal, Haggerty realized a flower so fresh had to have come from Angus. She considered asking the flower fairies for

Samantha's whereabouts, but decided to take a more mundane approach. She pulled her cell phone from her purse and called Lisa at the Field Office. Lisa confirmed that Samantha had gone to see her boyfriend.

At least she didn't have to worry about Samantha's safety. Angus wasn't the most responsible of her relatives, but he did seem genuinely taken with her. He wouldn't let anything happen to her. Why then was anxiety for Samantha gnawing its way through her stomach? Just the result of a shattering night, she assured herself. Samantha was fine.

With only a few hours left until she returned to duty, Haggerty went straight to her office, instead of detouring home. She found some of her co-workers gathered before the TV. Though it was barely eight a.m. on the East Coast, the President of the United States was holding a televised press conference at the White House. At his side stood the current Director of the FBI, Sheldon Norville.

Given the legacy of J. Edgar Hoover, Haggerty tried to break her own tension by imagining the stocky Norville in one of Samantha's ridiculous gowns. To her surprise, instead of the giggle she expected the idea to produce, the thought of Samantha gave her an uneasy feeling. As if she didn't have enough to worry about without scraping up needless concerns. Samantha was fine; she was with Angus.

The President expressed his outrage at the shocking murder of Molly Claire. With his sternest photo-op expression, he pledged all the resources of the FBI to fight the scourge that had overtaken Southern California, before it spread to the rest of the country.

A lot of good those resources had done so far, Haggerty grumbled to herself. Unable to stomach any more empty rhetoric, she slipped through the crowd of agents and went to her office.

She sank into her desk chair and covered her face with her hands. As a dull ache began to throb behind her forehead, she prepared herself to experience a vision of some kind, half-expecting to sense the spirit of Molly Claire.

Only that wasn't what came to her. The voice that drifted into her mind belonged to Angus. "Annabelle, luv, I've packed in the gig you asked me to take. That nightclub really isn't a happening kind of place, and you know what a groovy guy I am. That's the current lingo in this space, isn't it?"

Sure, if you were living in 1968. Angus had always had a fondness for slang, even if he could never get it right. An image drifted into her mind, that of Angus leaving the bar where she'd asked him to play, pushing his harp ahead of him. What did it matter? She'd only asked him to take the job because she wanted him out of her hair.

The chatterbox god's voice went on. "And I miss my Sammy-girl. You can't really need her more than I do, Annie. Send her to me, so we can play."

The truth hit Haggerty as a stunning blow—Samantha *wasn't* with Angus. Then where was she?

She considered questioning Lisa again, but Haggerty's own unique skills, as inexact as they were, were so much surer than mortal communication. She drew on all her powers. A weak voice drifted into her mind. "Annabelle, *please,*" she heard Samantha cry.

The desperation in Samantha's voice made Haggerty's eyes sting. She forced the reaction aside. Focusing again, she smelled an odd odor and felt a burning sensation in her nose. With a flicker of irritation at an impression that couldn't mean anything, she concentrated harder. The perception just grew stronger.

Sudden understanding caused Haggerty to choke in shock. She leaped to her feet and ran all the way to the elevators. When the elevator doors opened, Jake stepped out.

"Whoa," he said, breathlessly, seizing her arms. "What's the hurry?"

"Samantha's in trouble, Jake. She needs me."

He hesitated. "You know where she is?"

She gave him an absent nod. She started toward the elevator car, but he still held her.

"How?" he demanded. "I thought she went off with Angus."

Haggerty hesitated. "Rusler got a tip," she lied.

Jake stared back, as if he were debating whether to join her. Haggerty wondered if he would let his distrust of Rusler sway him. It didn't matter. She'd actually prefer to go alone. She'd have more freedom of action that way.

She broke free of his hold, jumping into the elevator car. To her surprise, Jake entered right after her, just before the doors closed. Okay, they'd just have to save Samantha mortal-style.

If they made it in time to save her at all.

CHAPTER TWENTY-FOUR
Samantha

The end was near. A bum in the park told me that, and I didn't listen. Sure, it was about five years ago, and he hadn't specified a time, so maybe I had an excuse. Now, on the verge of proving him right, I still couldn't accept it. I kept calling out to Haggerty, both aloud and in my mind, in between bouts of sniffling. My lower legs hung just below the lip of the giant lava bowl beneath me, as sweat ran down my sides and between my breasts, faster than rain in a winter storm.

Suddenly, I heard the screech of tires outside. Then voices, indistinguishable at first, but growing louder.

Finally, I heard Jake shout, "I'm telling you, Annabelle, the emergency key isn't where I left it."

The voices died out. *No, don't give up*! I wanted to cry. I couldn't get this close and still lose it all.

I started shouting, "I'm here. Don't leave me." As well as a few sloppy utterances too embarrassing to admit.

The sudden burst of gunfire drowned out my begging. The entry door splintered. Someone gave it a good kick and the door flew open.

"I'm here," I shouted.

They rushed in, Haggerty and Jake. Both halted several yards into the place. My gaze went to Haggerty. She came! She heard me somehow, and she came to my rescue. But it got too hard to stay focused on her stunned expression. She was a seasoned professional, but her obvious shock told me that my situation was worse than I imagined. When I finally glanced at Jake, it was clear, from his ricocheting eyes, that he wanted to be anywhere but here.

"We can't risk cutting her down," Haggerty snapped in response to some suggestion Jake made too softly for me to hear. "We'll have to move the vat,"

They wasted several precious minutes while determining there was no longer a forklift to be found that in facility. Then Jake squandered still more of my waning time trying to locate the foundry owner on his cell phone.

"Call Lisa. He's her uncle," I said through my sniffles.

They both looked at me. "Lisa Lorne?" Haggerty asked.

"Small world, huh?" Jake muttered.

Banalities yet, while I was about to become a statue!

Haggerty took a few steps closer to the vat. A steady look settled over her, a confidence that surprised me. "Jake, we passed a fire station a few blocks back. Why don't you go and see if they have a motorized platform?"

She was sending him away? When I needed all the help I could get? When she turned away from him, Haggerty winked at me. In a flash, I understood. She wanted to get rid of Jake so she could rescue me in her own way, with magic.

Unfortunately, Jake didn't seem to pay attention to her. "I have an idea," he said. "Annabelle, go down that hall to the bunk rooms and drag some mattresses back here. Spread them on the floor on the other side of the smelter."

Haggerty hesitated, clearly debating whether to out herself before him, or if she should just follow his lead. After a moment, she ran from the room and returned an instant later, dragging a twin-sized mattress.

Jake started to remove his leather jacket, but stopped and pulled the zipper up to chest height. In case I fell, he'd rather the liquid metal splashed on his jacket, not his thin shirt, I guessed. Despite the heat, I shivered.

While Haggerty continued bringing mattresses from the other room, Jake assessed various coils of thick, heavy rope that were wound up on the floor. He grabbed the end of one and started climbing up a ladder that was built into the far wall. I strained my neck to the side to watch his rise. The ladder connected to a catwalk at the top of that high space. It was there that my elastic band was anchored.

Jake ran across the catwalk until he stood about ten feet from where I dangled. He tied one end of his long rope to the railing, before twisting it twice around his own waist and tying it tightly. He reached into his pocket and pulled out a knife. Giving the handle a flick, a serious looking switchblade flew open.

Jake climbed over the catwalk railing. "Samantha, this is going to take some tricky timing. When I swing your way, I'll grab hold of you. Then I'm going to cut that line above you, and we're gonna fly out over the side of the bowl and drop onto the mattresses." He glanced at my feet, which had to be below the lip now. "You're going to have to raise your legs. Backwards, don't bring your knees up in front. Got it?"

In a shaky voice, I said, "Sure thing, Jake," with as much assurance as I could muster.

I secretly thought I was going to go down into that molten drink. Just me, not Jake; the rope around his waist should hold him.

Haggerty stood before the vat now. Her face still looked controlled. I'd have felt better about having her as Jake's backup, only I never really grasped how strong a goddess she was. If I took the plunge, I was guessing she couldn't reverse it.

Jake stuffed the switchblade between his front teeth. Then he jumped off the catwalk, letting his body hang from the rope. He pushed off against it to get the rope swinging, but he didn't go very far or very fast. Grumbling, he raised his leg and gave the catwalk a wicked kick, so strong I could feel the shake ripple down my sagging rubber band. That gave his rope the swing it needed.

Each moment took years to pass. As if in slow motion, I saw Jake's body hurl toward mine. I bent my stiffened legs back at the knees, wishing now I'd started that yoga regime like I always intended. He crashed into me and wrapped one arm around my waist. At the same time, he yanked the knife from between his teeth, and reached up and cut the band holding me.

I began to slip, as the arm wrapped around my waist slid away. "Jake, I'm falling," I cried. Though he'd cut the band, my hands were tied over my head, useless for grabbing him, even if they hadn't already lost all feeling.

He hurled the knife away. I heard a distant clang when it hit the concrete floor. He clutched fistfuls of my gown, but his fingers seemed to slide off the slippery fabric. I was going down!

To my shock, my body stopped sliding, even though Jake hadn't yet managed to take hold of me. Something suddenly attached me to him, yanking my neck so hard, I thought it would decapitate me.

After only an instant more, we swung over the side of the vat, and out of danger. We fell safely to the mattresses spread on the floor.

Whatever hooked me to Jake still held us firmly together. My Celtic necklace, I discovered, when Haggerty freed the cord from where it had caught in Jake's jacket zipper.

What luck! I thought. Until I saw a smug smile flickered across Haggerty's full lips. She did it! Jake would have lost me. She saved me, while keeping her own secret hidden.

Abandoning her dignity for once, Haggerty hurled herself at the two of us and shamelessly hugged us both. Jake was the first to pull out of our group love-fest. He went and retrieved the knife. When he returned to our landing pad, he cut the binding on my hands. Haggerty gently eased my useless arms down to my sides.

I looked at Jake. "Thanks, Tarzan." Even though I knew who my real savior was.

He touched the Celtic necklace. "Not me, kid. This sucker saved your life."

In more ways than he knew. I'd be grateful to Celtic power for the rest of my life.

Suddenly, I burst into wracking sobs. Jake's phone picked that moment to jingle. He went to a quieter spot to answer.

"How…?" I whispered to Haggerty.

"I heard you crying for help."

Not possible. Yet she was there. "You saved my life," I blubbered. "I know it was you who hooked my necklace into Jake's zipper."

She shrugged. "In some cultures that would mean I'm responsible for you now." With a droll twist to her lips, she added, "Fortunately, this isn't one of them."

Off in the corner, Jake answered his call. "Yeah? No way," he insisted after listening. "Okay, we'll be there as soon as we can." He slapped the phone closed and turned to us. "Think you can handle one more crazy thing?"

No! Of course, I can't, I wanted to shout. But I was alive, thanks to them. It seemed churlish not to share their burden.

He didn't wait for my answer anyway. "Here's the latest from the hospital—Plotnik isn't there now."

"They moved him?" Haggerty asked.

Jake shook his head. "Apparently, he walked out on his own steam."

CHAPTER TWENTY-FIVE

Wouldn't *somebody* slow this nightmare down? Just long enough for me to catch my breath. I mean, five minutes ago I stood on the brink of death—as surely as a virgin poised at the mouth of an angry volcano. Except for the virginal part, of course, and strictly speaking, the actual volcano. Apart from that, our situations were precisely the same.

And more than anything else right now, I yearned to put my swollen feet up somewhere, without the purple satin shoes that I would probably have to cut off, while knocking back a few cold ones. What I did *not* want to be doing was rushing off to the hospital to check on Plotnik's escape.

Yet that was precisely what we were doing. Or what we would be doing, once I made it to the car. I limped from the foundry at a snail's pace. Given that my feet had lost all feeling, how could my toes possibly pinch so badly? The trim of the rigid shoes cut so deeply into the swollen pinkish flesh of my insteps that I wouldn't be surprised if I began bleeding soon. Haggerty took my arm and tried to ease me along a bit faster. Speed was just not possible for me now.

Despite the sense of urgency she had to feel, Haggerty showed me some sympathy, but now that the danger had passed, I picked up anger coming from her, too. Jake simply refused to believe I couldn't hurry it up. He rushed to the car and stood shouting at me. "Come on, Samantha. Get the lead out."

Maybe I could get the lead out if I hadn't spent a few hours simmering over it. What did he expect me to do? But I understood. They were mad at me for sneaking off. Yet I sensed they were even angrier at themselves, about Plotnik. Someone had pulled a fast one on them, either Plotnik or his master. Sure, the taskforce had taken some precautions. They'd posted a cop at his hospital door, and various members of the group checked on him regularly. The truth was, while they desperately wanted to unlock what Plotnik knew, they didn't expect the unconscious man to give it up anytime soon. And that had made them careless.

Hell, Plotnik skunked his whole medical team. And they had science on their side. As someone who flunked more science classes than I could count—since I couldn't do math, either, unless it came with dollar signs—I found that impressive. How in the world did a man whose coma stymied his doctors suddenly come out of it, and with enough awareness to sneak away undetected? Had he been faking? If so, the medical types should have detected that. If someone had a way of bringing him out of it, why couldn't the doctors do it?

They decided we would leave in Haggerty's car. But she called the Bureau and ordered a couple of clerks to pick up my car and deliver it to her house. At least I'd have Miss Stang when I needed her, although I guessed I wasn't going to be sneaking off again anytime soon.

The sun was just rising now. I hadn't hung there as long as I thought. It's tough to judge time when each moment feels like a hellish eternity.

During the drive, Haggerty argued that, with their resources already stretched so thin, they couldn't afford to open another investigation into what happened to me, since it was clearly part of the same complex picture. What did that mean? That we were just going to keep an attempt on my life among ourselves? I was about to pipe up in outrage, when she threw a warning glance over her shoulder. Right—I got it now. She couldn't explain how she knew where to find me. Jake just grunted. As distracted as he seemed, I wasn't sure he even heard her. As for me, I'd keep my trap shut for now. What choice did I have? But I vowed that someday, someone and I were gonna rumble.

By the time we arrived at the hospital, Jake became even more impatient. "Annabelle, can't you get her to move any faster?"

So much for our newfound friendship. Like I was the elephant from the circus or something. We left Haggerty's car in a fire zone at the entrance to the ER. Closer even than the handicapped spots. The trip across the wide sidewalk just about hobbled me.

"Look at her, Jake," Haggerty said. "Her feet are swollen to the size of pontoons."

How flattering. But true, sadly. I was like some cartoon figure, with big puffy feet stuffed into little teeny shoes. I was just glad Angus wasn't there to see me. He might like his women full, but not necessarily full of hot air.

157

"Why don't I just carry her?" he suggested.

I'd like to see him try. He's a smallish man, while my body—well, as Angus had expressed it, it was not the favored form in this age of anorexic models.

"Just go on ahead," Haggerty said, the strain sharpening her voice. "We'll get there as soon as we can."

Though Haggerty remained with me while we inched our way through the hospital corridors, she was not kept out of the loop. She placed a call on her cell phone to someone on the hospital security staff. I thought about telling her cell phones shouldn't be used in hospitals, but I figured if I did one more thing to annoy her, she'd belt me for sure. By the time we reached the elevators, she had determined that the cop guarding Plotnik had been drugged and hidden in Plotnik's bed. The doctors were trying to rouse him now, so he could be questioned.

Haggerty commandeered an empty wheelchair she spotted. I let out an audible sigh of relief when I finally got off my poor puffy puppies.

"I *really* hope no one catches us and wants this wheelchair back," I said with feeling.

"Worrying about consequences, Samantha? What a novelty," she said with an angry bite. She hurled the chair into the deep elevator with enough force to send it to back wall.

Okay, I had that coming. Now that she had saved my life, and I endured her nastiness, I figured we were even.

I was still in possession of the chair when we made it to the ICU floor, where we found some of the taskforce people huddled around what had been Plotnik's bed. Rusler stood several feet away, with his arms crossed tightly over his chest. Several of the others paced around the room, while Jake had planted himself on the opposite side of the bed from Dr. Chan, the petite female doctor we had met earlier. Lisa huddled alone at the window, staring out. She wore another of her granny dresses. This one sported a yellow background with little teddy bears all over it. That pattern was so cavity-forming cute, I wondered whether she'd pulled a Scarlet O'Hara. You know, made the dress herself from her childhood bedroom curtains.

The drugged police officer was stretched out in Plotnik's bed, without his uniform. Someone had carelessly wrapped him in a hospital gown, which slipped off one of his bony shoulders. Had Plotnik made his escape in this guy's clothes? Judging by the length of the legs below the blanket, the cop, like Plotnik, was a tall, slender man. The uniform would have fit.

The cop was conscious now, sorta. His hazel eyes were glazed and a trickle of drool ran from the corner of his slack mouth. But he wasn't totally out of it. When Jake and the doctor argued, the poor guy's head slowly turned between them.

"I didn't say it *was* Rohypnol that someone gave him," Dr. Chan said. "I said it was *like* it in its effect. Like Ruffies, whatever had been administered to the officer has caused amnesia. Officer Ayers can't remember who gave it to him or how, or anything thereafter."

"It must have been someone on the hospital staff," Jake insisted. "He wouldn't have taken anything from a stranger. And who has better access to drugs?"

A nurse in bright blue scrubs came in, carrying an empty IV bag in her hand. She paused next to us and glanced down at me. For a second I thought she was going to demand my purloined wheelchair, and I was prepared to fight for it. Only it was my swollen extremities that she was staring at.

"Honey, have you had your feet looked at?" she asked. "That has to hurt."

No kidding. Before I could insist on a full exam, including an alphabet of letters—MRI, CT-scan, and any others they could come up with—Haggerty stepped between us. She clamped her hand on my shoulder. After a moment, she assured the nurse I would be fine.

Did she *know* that? Did she intend to do something to make it happen? I mean, in that special way of hers. Or was that hand on my shoulder just a warning to keep my trap shut, so I didn't slow them down any more than I already had? She released an annoyed sigh, as she had when she restored my hearing after the shootout at the museum. Relief slowly seeped through my scorched, swollen extremities.

Jake and the doctor kept going at it.

"Detective, our drug inventories are carefully monitored, and nothing is missing," the doctor said. "Whereas your people are in and out of here all day and night. If you're looking for a traitor, you might try your own camp."

Jake scowled. He leaned over the dazed cop. "You still don't remember anything, buddy?"

"Not a thing, John," Ayers said.

"Jake. My name is Jake. You've known me since you started at the Academy."

"Sorry...sir," Ayers said, obviously having forgotten Jake's name again.

Rusler approached the bed. "Forget about how Officer Ayers was drugged for now. What about Plotnik, Doctor? Any idea how he managed to come out of his coma?"

"I have a better idea about that." She extended her hand toward the nurse for the empty IV bag. "There's a syringe hole in Mr. Plotnik's IV bag. And we didn't have him on anything. We think whoever gave him something to keep him under, knew how to bring him out of it, too. The lab's having a little trouble identifying the residue."

Jake snorted. "Secret drugs that a lab can't identify? Come on, Doc."

"If you have a better explanation, Detective, I'd love to hear it," Dr. Chan snapped in her gravelly voice.

The nurse beside my wheelchair pointed at Lisa. "You there. You were here before the patient went missing."

Lisa spun around. "Me? No, you're mistaken."

The nurse gave her chin a firm snap. "Yeah, you were. I remember seeing that great dress when the elevator doors closed on you."

Great dress? Was she kidding? There I was in the best purple gown ever, and it was Lisa's crappy curtain dress she remembered. What happened to good taste?

"And there was a man with you in the elevator," the nurse said. "I wish I could have seen his face, but—"

"He wasn't *with* me," Lisa spat. "He was already—" She stopped abruptly, perhaps when she realized what she had just admitted.

"Agent Lorne? So you were here?" Rusler asked.

Lisa bristled. "What of it? We all checked on Plotnik. What's the difference?"

"Sure we did," Jake said. "I myself came at least once a day. More if I could. But the rest of us didn't lie about it. What's the big

160

secret, Lisa?"

"There's no secret. I just didn't want to complicate things," she insisted, before turning back to the window. "What secret could I have?"

All the eyes in that room zeroed in on Lisa. While they scrutinized her, the answer to her rhetorical question popped into my head: She had been trying to top them again, as she did with Molly Claire's dental records. The thought came with such a punch of certainty that it made my head spin. Whoa! Where was that coming from? I looked to see if Haggerty might be passing on some impression. But she just stared off into space, with her forehead knotted in a frown.

I looked to Jake in time to see his dark eyes gaze past Lisa and widen in shock. He stabbed a finger at the window. "For the love of... Look!"

Rusler took a swift glance out the window, before returning his attention to Lisa. "Yes, Detective, it's a beautiful sunrise. Don't we have more important concerns?"

The horizon looked more like a beautiful *sunset* than dawn. Swirling tones of orange, yellow and gray lit up the sky. Something was wrong there. I just couldn't say what.

Jake put his finger on it. "The sun rises in the *Eastern* sky, *sir,*" he said with exaggerated civility. "Given the colors in the *Western* sky now, something tells me we have another problem."

CHAPTER TWENTY-SIX

I sat curled up on Haggerty's family room couch, with my knees tightly clasped to my chest. I was alone in her house and scared silly. Not that anything threatened me. But after what happened with the lava tank, the specter of fear that had already taken hold of Haggerty, now clutched me in its grip as well.

It didn't help that I saw nothing particularly assuring on the news. The glow we'd witnessed along the Western horizon earlier today in Plotnik's hospital room wasn't some misguided sunset brought about by pinpricks in the ozone layer, but the result of a series of fires that had been set at points across the city. The fires continued to break out at various places throughout the rest of the day, and it was further taxing the city's resources and putting everyone's nerves on edge. It wasn't that the blazes themselves were so consuming, it was their random nature. The fire department never knew where another would spring up, and as soon as the overworked crews put one fire out, one or two more broke out somewhere else.

Fires weren't the only things igniting tonight, either. If we Angelenos know anything, it's how to riot and loot. Were we party animals or what? The crazy part was tonight's bursts of mob rule hadn't been triggered by some social grievance. Nor were they limited to any particular geographical area. They were breaking out randomly throughout Southern California, well beyond the city limits now.

No one could even say precisely where or how the mass hysteria had started. I had no doubts that our newest union shop, The United Gangs of Southern California, was behind it. With enough foot soldiers, which they certainly had, it wouldn't be hard to do. Set enough sparks ablaze, both the literal and figurative kind, and the good citizens of our city could be counted on to carry the ball from there.

The current footage on television showed flames sprouting from the roof of a mall department store, while a conga line of looters streamed out the door, their arms loaded down with all the booty they could carry.

I didn't understand the logic behind unleashing this unrest. What did the bad guys hope to gain by sparking mass lunacy? Not money, that was certain. Haggerty had been right about their demands; they were never more than a smokescreen. They didn't even keep Molly around long enough to try to collect. And tonight, it was the looters who were gaining, not the bad guys themselves. What was all that smoke hiding?

The scene on the screen switched to the charred remains of a strip mall not far from my place in Santa Monica. For the first time, I was glad to be stuck in Haggerty's house, in this sensible middle-class neighborhood. Then, as if someone out there could hear my thoughts and decided to mess with my head, I heard a few shots ring out from somewhere nearby.

So I was right to be afraid. My teeth chattered.

The only blessing I could count tonight was that, thanks to Haggerty, my tootsies had returned to normal size. They moved only a bit stiffly when I rose and, as I had several times already, padded to the front and back doors to check the locks. Both doors were safely dead-bolted, of course. Too bad whatever force was trying to take hold of this city wasn't going to be deterred by a door.

I half-wished I had a gun. And that was something I'd never thought before. Frankly, I'd always believed the problem with the Second Amendment was that it extended to people like me. Of course, if I had one, I'd probably shoot the only person likely to come through those doors—Haggerty. And I kinda wanted to keep her around.

She wasn't there now because Rusler had ordered the entire taskforce on eighteen-hour shifts, starting tonight. Naturally, Haggerty had argued that I should be included. I knew she was wringing herself dry trying to pick up on any psychic impression that might be floating around in the cosmos. And she still needed some way to share whatever she might pick up.

Rusler's reaction was, "I think we've all had enough of Samantha for now."

Like that feeling wasn't mutual. It didn't matter, since Haggerty's cosmic receiver didn't seem to be tuned to the right frequency.

Angus wasn't even around to keep me company. Haggerty said he'd been called home so he could perform some task for his mother. Called home? I found that term confusing. Was my lover *dead*—gods forbid—or not dead? Apparently, his mother, Boann, was some serious goddess, capable of hurling lightning bolts at people, or making their feet big again. Naturally, I didn't want to incur her wrath by whining. But I sure could have used her son tonight, to make me laugh and forget all our mortal troubles.

When my attention returned to the tube, the Talking Heads were discussing whether the National Guard should be called in to quell the revolt before it really got out of hand. Was that what this was? A revolt? Not in the political sense. No one was taking over. What did Mr. Big hope to gain from all this chaos?

Or was it *Ms.* Big? Back at the hospital, it sure looked like Lisa had something to hide. What was the deal with that chick? Every time I thought I had a handle on her, she morphed into something else. While I couldn't quite figure her out, I did feel certain she wasn't a leader. I could see her as someone's patsy, but not the one calling the shots. Yet what did I know? She kept fooling me. Maybe she fooled everyone.

How did I get mixed up with those people? Yeah, I know, I dealt myself into the game. How could I have foreseen where it would lead? What were the odds that my path would cross with someone like Haggerty's? We were oil and water. Laurel and Hardy—only one of us wasn't the least bit funny.

It was almost enough to make you believe in that woo-woo stuff. I looked across the room to where Haggerty had arranged some cut flowers in a crystal vase. I didn't even have to look hard now to see the colored fairies dancing on the petals. What had happened to me? It felt as if a door had opened that I couldn't slam shut.

"Can't you do something to stop all this nuttiness, you stupid fairy bugs," I shouted. I also remembered the brownie hidden somewhere in the house, and the garden gnome that had disappeared that first night. Maybe everyone had powers, everyone but me. It wasn't even a comfort to realize I wasn't alone in that house after all.

I wandered out to where Haggerty kept her altar, and stood before it, waiting to feel something. Zilch. I gently stroked the handle of a jewel-encrusted dagger. It was pretty, but I still felt nothing. This kinda crap might be the fake me, but not the real me underneath.

Was she right, was Mr. Big really a god of such evil proportions even Angus would be no match for him? The way he'd left me to die was pretty awful. How could I hope to fight someone like that? I felt an impulse to slip the dagger in my pocket, just in case. Only, despite all the beings inhabiting that house, I figured Haggerty would guess who took it.

When I returned to the family room, the TV station had split the screen into four quadrants. So we could keep up on four fires at once. Seeing those four flares like that made the fires seem more of a threat than they were.

I glanced at the cardboard box on the floor, the one Molly's manager had sent over. I wondered whether there might be a clue in that carton. Those tapes promised better diversion than the news. I yanked one off the top and popped it into the VCR.

In the days since her abduction, I came to feel as if I knew Molly Claire. When her cute little face came into view now on the screen, sitting in the guest chair on a talk show set, I felt a sense of loss. Maybe even guilt. If I'd set off the alarm sooner, would they have found her before the bad guys did away with her?

I focused on the screen, watching as Molly tilted her cute little towhead this way and that and wrinkling her small perky nose. Was she ever not playing a part, onscreen or off? What did that matter now?

The congenial talk show host fed Molly the expected lines, asking if she'd succeeded in putting the ugliness of her divorce behind her.

She blushed prettily. "Ancient history, Rick. I have a new man now, and he's making me very happy."

Rick, the talk show-guy, pressed for a name, which Molly coyly resisted. "I'll say this—he's in the biz, but he works behind the scenes, and not in a traditional way," she said. "He's such fun, and he says the most adorable things. Last night when I was a little blue about my career, he said, 'Good golly, Miss Molly. You gotta be jolly.' Isn't that cute?"

It was cute, all right. Barf-cute. Surely he wasn't the first guy to call her "Miss Molly." Even Jake referred to her that way.

Rick moved onto her campaign to play meatier parts.

Molly gave her quirky haircut an incredulous toss. "Rick, I can't tell you how much I long to play strong independent women.

People forget I started my career portraying characters like that, before I got stuck in the romantic comedy rut."

Not exactly true. While she had done more dramatic roles before Hollywood discovered she was the quintessential Sweet Young Thing, they were long suffering victim-types, not the butt-kickers she claimed to be going for today.

Dragging in her professed psychic abilities, Molly had tossed her slender hands airily above her. "They have to take me seriously soon, Rick. It's written in the stars. I know these things."

"Your future got erased, babe," I shouted at the TV. Enough with the woo-woo crap.

I immediately felt bad about what I said. After all, *she* got erased, too. I wondered again whether there was anything to fate. I mean, I never gave my choices much thought. I'd always been more of a *carpe diem*-kinda gal. But what if they hadn't been *my* choices? What if it had all been written in the stars?

For one thing, it would mean my destiny was a pretty piss-poor one, judging by my first twenty-eight and three-quarters years. I remembered again about the doornail-dead carpenter I'd stumbled across in Molly's condo. How I wondered at the time if he had handed off his fate to me.

Now I couldn't help but question whether our shared karma would get worse before it played out.

CHAPTER TWENTY-SEVEN

Angus returned to me sometime during the night, and we had quite a lusty reunion. But my euphoria wasn't so great that I failed to notice the thud of Haggerty's heavy steps when she returned home, shortly before daybreak.

My love god was still there when I awoke in the early morning. We faced each other, and amused ourselves by drawing designs on each other's chests. Naturally, that led to the inevitable diversion. Afterwards, while engaging in post-coital chatter, I told Angus about my near death experience the day before, editing out my big fat feet.

He showed me an uncharacteristically grave face. "That settles it, Sammy-girl. This place is too dangerous for you now. What do you say we go away to someplace where you can be safe, and we can have all the fun possible?"

I swallowed hard. "You mean…another world?"

Angus flexed one shoulder in a shrug. "If that's what you want. I was thinking more along the lines of Venice. Got a mate there who's owned the most glorious *palazzo* for centuries."

"Venice, *Italy?*" I asked, sending the words out on a wistful sigh. "How romantic." And a *palazzo* yet. I didn't exactly know what that was, but it sounded great. It occurred to me that if you got the chance to live for centuries, you could really make inroads on that upward mobility thing.

"So it's settled," Angus said. "All the seriousness around here is just bringing me down. You and me, Samantha, my girl—we're just not made to deal with all this trouble."

Maybe not, though one of us was made to cause it. "Say nothing about it to Annabelle, Angus, or she'll put the kibosh on it. Promise?"

He crossed his heart with his finger. "Absolutely. May neither of us ever be a fraction as earnest as our Annabelle."

Fat chance of that happening.

When we went to the kitchen, though it wasn't that long after

I heard Haggerty drag herself home, she was already dressed for work and seated at the table, listlessly eating a bowl of cereal.

Jake stood at the stove, where he'd finished making himself a bacon-and-egg sandwich. For a moment, I wondered whether he had spent the night, and I felt a rush of joy for Haggerty. But I only heard one set of footsteps the night before. And the jeans and the washed-out denim shirt he wore open over his T-shirt, weren't what he'd worn the day before.

Haggerty had moved a portable TV from her bedroom to the kitchen counter, and hooked it up to a satellite connector there. Though the volume was low, her gaze remained glued to the images projected on the screen. Things had gotten worse during the time when Angus and I frolicked. Jeeps filled with National Guard officers rolled through the streets now, though they hadn't quelled the sporadic rioting.

The TV switched to a sidewalk interview before an apartment building, between a male reporter in a flak jacket and a tearful blonde woman in her forties. Haggerty waved her cereal spoon in the direction of the TV. "Turn it up, will you, Samantha?"

When I did as she asked, the frantic voice of the petite woman filled the room. "That's right, my sister's missing, and the police just won't take it seriously."

The reporter, who kept looking over his shoulder as if he expected imminent ambush, reminded her that the police were too stressed by the gang revolt to devote resources to every missing person. "Besides, she might not actually be missing. Lots of people took cover wherever they could when the looting started. Your sister could be holed up with a friend."

The woman gave her curly fair hair an emphatic shake. "My sister's not just another missing person. She often worked with Molly Claire, as a... Oh, I forget what they call her job," she said in an exasperated Midwestern accent. "But she looked so much like Miss Claire that I'm afraid they've taken her hostage now."

Right. They took Molly hostage because of how she *looked*.

"I've driven all night to get here, and now the police have shut down the city, limiting movement to emergency personnel, so I can't even hunt for her," the woman said tearfully.

As cynical as I was, it struck me that it was more likely she'd driven just to have the chance to kick her sister's career into high gear. Normally I'd applaud that moxie, but since my own opportunistic efforts had yielded precisely zip, I didn't feel that generous now. I tuned her out.

Haggerty did as well when, with a sigh, she squeezed her eyes closed. Her eyelids were red-rimmed by fatigue; her auburn hair looked dull, and for the first time, strands escaped from her tight knot. Yet after only a moment's rest, her gaze returned to the screen. She was always focused on the case, one thousand percent. If I ever displayed that kind of staying power, I hoped someone would do the right thing and shoot me.

When the doorbell rang, Haggerty told me it was probably Billy Finkner and asked me to answer it. Apparently, before she left the command post, she'd arranged for Agent Billy to stop by with an update, before he took his few hours off.

Whenever I looked into Haggerty's yard, I always checked for the gnome I saw that first night. This time was no exception. Granted, when I opened the door, Billy's round form blocked most of my view. I stood to the side so I could take a gander around him. No gnome, though.

"How's it going, Billy?" I asked.

"Kid, if it got any worse, I'd welcome the gas chamber."

Billy's droll delivery sounded sincere, but I didn't buy it. I couldn't see someone so detached taking his cases that seriously. Proving my point was the wink he offered me. I sent a smile back into his twinkling little eyes, until I noticed something strange. Billy's eyes were green now. How was that possible? I knew damn well his eyes had been brown when I met him. Not the kind of hazel that looks brownish at some times and greenish at others, either, but sun-dried raisin brown versus Emerald Isle green.

He must have been wearing color contacts. How funny. I wouldn't have believed a man that sloppy could harbor such vanity. He never wore anything other than his lone suit, a baggy sack the color of poop. Though the contacts did fit with his silly comb-over.

I led him to the kitchen. Haggerty greeted Billy with a tight nod, while Jake asked him if anything new had happened.

"*The Power of the Pyramid* exhibit has been closed. All the dignitaries that planned to come have cancelled anyway. They can't move the stuff anywhere, though. The cops have the museum locked down until it's safe to ship everything on to the next venue." With a sigh, he added, "Like L.A. needs another black eye." He went on to say that they were keeping that information off the news.

Since that touched on my own pet theory, I asked, "Have the gangs shown any interest in the museum?"

"Not a bit," Billy said with a shake of his big head. "Those little pricks would rather steal five bucks from the till before torching a liquor store, than plan for a big haul."

Haggerty rose and deposited her empty bowl in the dishwasher. "Billy, can I get you anything to eat?"

I'd have thought Billy would be on that offer like a flea on a dog. He surprised me. With a pained expression, he rubbed his big round belly and said he didn't feel too good. He punctuated the remark with a burp that sounded like a bubble escaping from the bottom of a pool.

"Where's your john, Annabelle?" he asked.

Haggerty told him where to find it, allowing her attention to glom onto the news again almost instantly. When Jake asked whether she needed a coffee refill, she just nodded and absently drank the whole mug without appearing to notice she'd had a drop. Like I said, way too much staying power.

And speaking of staying power, Billy's powder room retreat went on awfully long as well. I remembered Lisa's crack about his lengthy bathroom breaks. Maybe he just suffered from bad digestion. When he didn't emerge in several times the usual stay, I began to wonder how bad it could be.

"Haggerty, do you think Billy could be sick?" I asked.

She glanced in the direction of the powder room and said, distractedly, "No, that's not it, it's—"

I alone was in a position to see a stricken expression come over her pale face. I sensed she had nearly slipped and made a remark that would have revealed something about herself, by virtue of her ability to perceive whatever was happening with Billy in another room. But what could her unique skills have to do with his toilet time?

Her abrupt halt drew vague interest from Jake. "It's what?"

Haggerty laughed nervously. "Don't mind me. I don't know what I'm saying anymore. Of course, he could be sick. I'm a mess, and Billy is a lot older and in worse shape."

Having lost interest, Jake just glanced at his watch. "Time to hit the road, Annabelle."

Haggerty told Jake that she'd follow his car to the Field Office. While she gathered her purse and briefcase, she reminded me that it was illegal for anyone to be out on the streets without police or FBI permission.

She glared a warning at Angus, then me. "Angus can get away with it, Samantha, but you'll end up warming a cell if you try."

Not if Angus made me invisible first.

Her stare morphed into a disapproving frown. Damn, she was starting to know me too well. With an air of innocence, I assured her I wouldn't dream of leaving. As soon as the door closed shut behind her, Angus and I dissolved in giggles.

An hour later, I waited alone in the house, while Angus went off to arrange for our trip. Only after he left did I wonder precisely how we were going to travel to Italy. I mean, the airport was closed—I'd seen that on the news. However he planned to transport me, I was going, no matter what. Still, the questionable transit mode did make me feel queasy.

With nausea in mind, it occurred to me that I never saw Billy leave. Was he *still* in the powder room? I crept to the door, relieved to see it wide open. I feared what I might find in there if indeed he had been sick. I peered through the doorway. Not only was the room empty, it was sparkling clean. The almond pedestal sink looked so shiny, it might have been wet. There was absolutely no sign that anyone had been ill in that room.

What a relief. I didn't relish the idea of cleaning up after Billy, and I didn't know how to summon the brownie. What had Billy been doing in there? And how had I missed seeing him leave?

I needed a vacation, all right. Bored with waiting for it to start, I threw myself on the sofa and flipped on the TV with the remote. Thoroughly fed up with the bad news, I tuned into one of the Molly Claire movie marathons several cable networks were running.

Too jumpy to concentrate on any one film, I actually found switching from one to another, as if they were scenes run in sequence, pretty entertaining. Besides, it was all predictable stuff. Molly wrinkling her nose sweetly for some gorgeous French hunk, Molly begging for her life in some slime-ridden cellar, Molly winning over the adorable children of the widower she was meant to end up with.

Seeing those scenes flash now, I had to admit she was believable in every one of them. Molly Claire was a better actress than I'd ever given her credit for. Maybe she could even have played the strong parts she'd longed for. Only now we'd never know. Though I could swear I'd never seen those films before, one of those scenes felt awfully familiar.

I lost that train of thought when the phone rang. I looked around for it. Despite her penchant for neatness, Haggerty was always leaving her cordless someplace different. That electronic buzzer kept piercing the silence with its annoying whine, as I ran from room-to-room.

I finally spotted it on the living room coffee table. When I heard Lisa's voice, I was sorry I'd answered it. While listening to her, more or less, I wandered to the front window, glancing out cautiously, always afraid of what I'd see out there. Of course, I meant gangsters, looters—people to fear. I hadn't expected to see something that just made me feel weird.

The gnome was back. Standing now, not in the flower border, where I'd seen him first, but propped up next to one of the apple trees. It—not him. How the hell...?

"Samantha, did you hear me?" Lisa's exasperated voice snapped into the phone.

"No, sorry. Something caught my eye." Did that gnome just move? My attention started wandering again.

She jerked it back. "Annabelle never showed up here. She and Jake got separated along the way by a military caravan, but he didn't worry until she didn't arrive. He's out searching for her now."

"Maybe she's—"

"Samantha, the police just found her car, abandoned by the side of the road. Agent Rusler wanted you to know that she's missing."

As stunned as I felt, as scared for myself, for Haggerty—I could swear that before she hung up, Lisa had stifled a laugh.

CHAPTER TWENTY-EIGHT

Lisa's announcement floored me. Shocking me most was the sense of loss I felt. How could that exasperating, tight-assed goddess have come to mean so much to me? I didn't engage in denial, though. I'd seen how the bad guys had treated Molly, and then me. I knew Haggerty didn't have much time.

I glanced out the window, at one of her beloved apple trees. The garden gnome was gone now. The second surprise in as few minutes hardly had an impact.

Suddenly, Angus just appeared at my side. Startling surprise number three. Once again, Haggerty's disappearance overshadowed it.

Excitement had brightened my lover's blue-and-silver eyes to such an extent, they looked sprinkled with glitter. "It's all set, my girl. Me mate in Venice has turned over a whole wing of his *palazzo* to us. And he's hosting a ball in our honor, so bring along some of your pretty frocks."

When I didn't budge, he went to the guestroom without me, talking animatedly the whole time. After a moment, I followed along and found him standing beside the bed, where my open suitcase sat, while my gowns just floated into the suitcase.

"Angus, wait. Haggerty—Annabelle, I mean. Annabelle is missing." I told him about the cops finding her car.

While Angus comforted me in his strong arms, his words had the opposite effect. "It's for the best, Samantha, my girl. It's past time our Annie came home. She's grasped none of what we wanted her to learn during her time here. She's still as rigid and stubborn as she was as a toddler. Nobody in the family can understand her ridiculous devotion to that job."

I pulled away. "Too bad for them. She deserves the chance to keep doing it, if she wants to." I couldn't believe what I was about to say. "I can't go with you, Angus. I have to find her."

He just stared at me in disbelief. My tummy began to hurt, worse than when I ate too many of Loco Pepe's burritos. This felt like the biggest mistake in my whole sorry life. Still, I had to do it.

Angus took my hands. "The fuzz will look for her, Sammy. Besides, you can't leave this cottage without them tossing you in the hoosegow."

Someday I needed to work on his understanding of present day idioms. Assuming we had a someday. "I could leave with your help, Angus. With all your powers, there has to be a way I could go out undetected."

He tossed my hands away in anger, storming back to the living room. "And why should I help? I am the god of youth and love and laughter. No mere mortal can refuse me."

I'd joked to myself about his mother hurling thunderbolts. Now that his footsteps shook the house like a 5.0 temblor, I was less flippant about the actions of angry gods.

"What's happened to you, Samantha? Why did you have to go all sincere on me?"

On me, too. And wasn't that a shock? Yet I couldn't help it. "I can't leave her, Angus. I owe her." It was more than that, but I wouldn't admit it to him. I could hardly admit it to myself. Haggerty and me, we were...connected somehow.

"Then I'm going alone," Angus said. He turned, and like every mortal man I'd ever known, walked out the door, slamming it behind him.

My sense of loss became a bottomless pit. I'd been left by the only man I ever really loved. For a woman who didn't even like me. The worst of it was Angus was right. There was nothing I could do to help her. It wouldn't do Haggerty any good if I left the house only to be picked up by the first passing patrol. And with my luck, that was how it would go. The cops might not be able to contain the looters, but they would contain me.

Frustration built to the breaking point. I roamed from window to window, peering out almost as if I were searching for a concrete solution out there. Only I was so worried, I couldn't really focus on anything at all—until I looked out the back window into the rear yard. The stupid mobile gnome was there now, plopped amidst a large flowerbed filled with lush purple-and-peach pansies. And the little bastard winked at me again.

That was too much. In my world, movie stars didn't get pummeled to death, cheerful fake psychics didn't get strung up over bowls of liquid metal, and goddesses didn't leave perfectly wonderful Hondas by the side of the road. I stormed out the back door. I slowed when I hit the yard, meandering around the flowerbed as if I hadn't seen the gnome. But once I moved around it, I tackled the little statue and held it in my grip.

To my surprise, it didn't feel as hard as a ceramic figure should. Before I could identify what it did feel like, the form began to move. Naturally, I assumed it was trying to get away, so I tightened my grip. But it wasn't trying to wiggle free, it was *expanding*. Wider and wider and wider. The force of that rapid growth threw my arms off of it and tossed me backwards onto the flowers.

I gave only the slightest thought to the flower fairies I was sitting on, probably poised to bite me on the ass at that moment. With my neck bent back, I stared up at a form that had bloated many, many times the size of that little statue. And completely changed its appearance.

Standing fully formed in the flowers before me was—Special Agent Billy Finkner.

CHAPTER TWENTY-NINE

"So, Samantha," Billy asked when I brought him into the house. "Am I your first shape-shifter?"

His pudgy cheeks glowed with such pleasure, you'd think he'd been my first in another way. He plopped himself down on the family room sofa. Despite his size, his body scarcely made a dent in the couch's cushions.

"Where—" My mouth felt too dry to speak. I swallowed hard. "Where are you from?"

Billy patted his big belly. "Tarzana." A town a short distance away in the San Fernando Valley. "Local boy."

"I meant...your home world."

"Home world? Kid, you gotta wean off the Sci-Fi Channel. It's warping your judgment." He wiggled bushy gray-and-brown eyebrows at me. "But I get your meaning. My parents were both born in Jersey City. Nasty air there."

"You mean you're like this because...?"

With a shrug, Billy said, "That's the family's theory. It's not so bad. Some of the neighborhood kids were born with gills."

Too much information again. If I weren't already on sensory overload, I'd scream.

I sat before him on the floor, clutching the pint of vanilla Häagen-Daz I'd had the presence of mind to snatch from the freezer on our way in. I yanked the cover off and discovered Haggerty had removed exactly one small scoop from it. That's the kind of person she was, someone who not only favored plain vanilla, but who could be content with what nutritionists insisted was a single serving. Me, I knew I'd eat all the way to the bottom of the carton and would resent the loss of that scoop.

I asked Billy why he kept coming here, disguised as the gnome.

"I've been watching you," Billy said. "Given the accuracy of your visions, you've gotten someone really worried, and he pays me to keep an eye on you. Doing it as a gnome was just me having some fun."

It occurred to me that I hadn't told him yet about Haggerty's disappearance and my earlier abduction, so I did that now. When he didn't react, I tossed the ice cream container aside and threw myself on him, grabbing hold of his lapels. "Billy, tell me who you're working for. Don't you see, whoever hired you to watch me has to be the same person who abducted Annabelle. He has to be the one who strung me up, the one behind all this crime and chaos."

He pushed me away. "Get off of me, Samantha. Do you have any idea how your elbows feel pressing into a shape-shifter?"

Didn't know, didn't want to, and they could keep the T-shirt.

"I can't help you, kid. I'm sorry about Annabelle. She's always treated me right, not like some of those shits at the Bureau. My freelance jobs come through an agency that finds work for lots of shape-shifters. And I doubt the agency knows any more than I do. This guy is too smart to give himself away. Look at how he tried to take you out." Billy absently smoothed his saggy jacket over his big belly, which jiggled.

Stymied by his refusal, I struck out with nastiness, drawing a wide arc over his huge stomach in the air. "Lemme see if I understand this, Billy. You could take any shape and you took—this?"

Billy glanced at me across his wide middle. "You should talk. Glass houses, Samantha, glass houses. Besides, what's wrong with this form? It reflects the inner me."

I swallowed a big gulp of ice cream and said, "You're full of it."

"Strictly speaking, kid, if you understood the principles involved, you'd know I'm full of nothing."

I sat there, glaring at him. Then I remembered something, and it occurred to me that pissing him off might not be the wisest choice. "Shape-shifter? Lots of people regard that term as synonymous with *werewolf.*" Please don't let him shift right here and rip my face off.

Billy shook his big, round head. "That's strictly fantasy lit crap."

I sighed with relief. "I knew they couldn't be real."

"Oh, they're real, all right. They're just not shape-shifters, even if they do get a little hairy occasionally. We call 'em by another name."

"Really? What do you call them?"

"Werewolves. Get with it, Samantha."

Yeah, what was wrong with me? I smacked the ice cream carton against the coffee table. "You gotta help me, Billy. Can't you, at least…you know…tune into Annabelle? Read her thoughts. Figure out what—"

"Whoa," Billy said, holding up small hands with sausage fingers. "I'm not a psychic, nor a telepath, nor clairvoyant. I'm not like Annabelle."

That was supposed to be my song. "You knew about…how she is?"

"Oh, sure. When people are, you know…different—we get a sense of each other sometimes. Not always, mind you. Naturally, we erect barriers to keep each other out. But Annabelle's good. She's gotten around mine a few times."

He had let his barrier slip this morning, I guessed, when he was in her bathroom. That's what she sensed at breakfast and nearly revealed.

"We can all deceive each other on that level, too," Billy went on. "So even if I could pick up her thoughts, it didn't mean they'd be true." He waved a hand at me. "You should know all this Samantha. Your barriers are titanium."

"Me? No, you're wrong, Billy. I'm a total sham."

He gave me a shrug that said, *Suit yourself.*

Me, the real thing? *Way* too much information. Information I planned to discard instantly, rather than allow it to upset my delicate charlatan equilibrium more than it already had. And wouldn't you know? Angus picked that moment to return, by walking *through* the front door.

"Sammy, me love, can you ever forgive me?" he shouted.

I tossed the ice cream container aside and ran to him, melting faster than the Häagen-Daz.

"You're the best thing that's happened to me in centuries, my girl. I'm not letting you go. If it's important to you to help Annabelle, it's important to me."

"What about the ball your friend in Venice is hosting for us?" I asked.

He rolled his sparkling eyes. "You don't know me mate's

fêtes. It'll still be going strong when we're finished. Now, where do we start?"

CHAPTER THIRTY

"You'll help, too, won't you, Billy?" I asked, once Angus pledged his support.

Billy pursed his lips pensively. "Depends on how much you're paying."

I stared at him, aghast.

"Don't go all judgmental on me, Samantha. You know you're no different. I said I like Annabelle, but I need the bucks."

"Don't they pay you at the Bureau?" I asked.

"Lowest possible scale and no promotions—they've seen to that. All they want there are empty suits that know how to play the game. That's not me."

"But they do pay you. And you've got your freelance work. What do you do with your money?" I demanded.

He fidgeted uncomfortably. "Well...I got a thing for the ponies. You see, I thought I'd be onto a certainty if I shaped myself into something innocuous in the jockey locker room. Scope 'em out, you know, figure out which one had the strongest urge to win. Only it's not that easy to tell. Along the way, I got addicted to the rush of the race."

His eyes, which were brown again now, became dreamy. I snapped my fingers to bring him back. "Billy, I'm so poor, you should make me your favorite charity." I looked to Angus.

He held out empty hands. "I've never had any money. I didn't even take any at the clubs I played in. I wouldn't know what to do with it."

Wish I could say that.

His face brightened with an idea. "I can give you one golden apple." He turned my way. "Me mum only allows me to make one at a time, though, without her permission."

Don't tell me I did it again—picked another mama's boy.

Billy squinted at me. "Can he really do that? I mean, I knew he was, you know, different—well, who wouldn't know after he walked through the door?"

"Show him, Angus," I said.

Angus grabbed an apple from one of Haggerty's bowls. He wrapped his hands around it. Only moments later, resting on his palm was a golden apple that glistened as brightly as the Egyptian treasures I'd seen at the museum. Billy reached for it.

Angus yanked the apple away. "Uh-uh. I know mortals too well. You say you'll work for the carrot, but it takes the stick to keep you in line." While strolling around, Angus mused, "What if I give Samantha the power to turn you into something? What should it be, my girl?"

"A gnome." I glared at Billy. "For eternity."

"Why don't we say for as long as you like, Sammy? More flexible." Angus wrapped his hand over my shoulder. After a moment, he gave me a nod.

Funny, I didn't feel any different. I wanted to test it, but we didn't have time. "Okay, Angus, now give him the apple, and let's get to work."

We gathered around the kitchen table, where I alone ate a cheese sandwich. I remembered what Lisa had said about Billy not taking a lunch break. Didn't he need to eat? Had he really *chosen* to make himself look like that?

"The way I see it," I said, after a swallow, "either Rusler or Lisa has to be involved. Too many trails lead their way." I hadn't forgotten that snicker I thought I heard when Lisa told me Haggerty had disappeared.

"Rusler wouldn't have the balls," Billy said. "All he cares about is covering that crack in his behind. Look at the people he surrounds himself with—nobody who can show him up."

I thought as much myself. But I couldn't let it go that easily. "We need to be sure."

"I'll prove it to you." Billy bounded to his feet and rushed from the kitchen so fast, Angus and I had a tough time keeping up. He really was made of air. Lots and lots of it, though.

We found him kneeling before the VCR and satellite receiver in Haggerty's TV cart. "Good setup. Ideal for my purposes." He looked at the Timex Ironman watch strapped too tightly around his fat wrist; irony yet. "Rusler should be home now. Keep all the equipment on and I'll send you a live feed so you can see for yourself."

"I don't understand, Billy," I said. "You're going to question him on tape?"

He snorted. "You kidding? I never question anyone. I just become something in the background and wait around till they tell me what I need to know."

Did anyone in the Bureau work in the traditional way? Man, had the TV shows gotten it wrong.

"I'm going in to Rusler's place as a nanny cam with a transmitter." Billy adjusted Haggerty's equipment. "Watch for it now, Samantha." He loped toward the door, stuffing his golden apple in his saggy jacket pocket.

On the TV, the rerun of another Molly Claire talk show appearance played, different from the one I'd viewed on tape. I turned the volume down.

Excitement brought out the silver in Angus's eyes. "Detecting agrees with you, Sammy-girl. You look beautifully flushed. Do we have enough time to—" He gestured toward the guestroom.

No! This wasn't fair. After letting my impulse control grow hopelessly flabby, I couldn't exercise it now. Calling on every last ounce of my strength, I told him we didn't. Responsibility sucks.

I forced my thoughts back to the case. "Okay, we have Rusler covered, but Lisa bothers me more." Frustrated, I paced before the TV.

Too late I realized that could have been her handwriting on the message that she claimed had come from Angus. I'd seen her writing once, all frilly and girlish, like the note.

"And she could have arranged to have me strung up over that smelter. Her uncle owns that dump." Stymied, I ceased my pacing. "But she's never seen you, and whoever picked that thug who hit me over the head knew what you looked like."

Angus shrugged one of his muscular shoulders. "Rusler has, though. That night I came out for wine, he was here with Annie."

That explained Lisa's probing for what had happened when Rusler and Angus met. Obviously, Rusler had told her something about him. When she discounted Angus, she'd said something about his type.

"This just brings us full circle," I said, bummed. "Dead end."

"Not at all," Angus said. "Just as Billy can observe without being seen, so can I. I'll find this Lisa-girl, and I'll let you know what I see. Now quick, show me what she looks like. Visualize her really hard in your mind."

I did as he asked, holding Lisa's image strongly into my mind's eye, after clothing her in a really ugly dress. Angus slipped his fingers around my wrist.

I remembered something I had to ask him, but suddenly another possible connection hit me. Before I had time to think about it, I jumped in with, "Wait—Plotnik. You should know what he looks like, too." We repeated the Celtic god mind-meld.

Angus bounded away, but he stopped and turned to me. "Dowdy frock she was wearing, that Lisa. Nowhere near as nice as your special things."

Finally, someone who noticed.

With a broad grin, Angus just disappeared. Unfortunately, it was only after he popped off that I remembered what I wanted to ask him—how I was going to travel away from that house. I was sure he could have given me a way. Assuming his mom allowed that, I thought sourly. What did it matter now? I had to wait for Billy's images anyway.

I flopped on the couch and raised the TV volume with the remote. Molly was yammering on again about the new guy in her life. Then, before I was even ready, a grainy colored feed from Rusler's house began playing. I was shocked by how fast Billy pulled it off. I mean, I thought he'd drive there, and it would take time to get through the checkpoints. For all I knew, he made himself into a bird and flew. There was something to this shape-shifting, all right.

The transmitted image depicted a modest, '50s kitchen, right down to the avocado stove and fridge. Rusler sat on one side of a small Formica table, with his nose buried in a stack of reports. His wife sat across from him, stuffing her face with Pepperidge Farm Milanos.

His wife was a shocker. She looked so much like an older Haggerty, it floored me. Same milky white skin, same copper-colored hair and big, blue eyes. It was just that there was at least seventy-five pounds more of Mrs. Rusler. And she was like an automaton. Those wide eyes just stared out, while she stuffed one cookie after another into her trap.

When Rusler slammed his fist on his stack of reports, she slowly turned his way. "Something wrong, dear?"

Rusler's chiseled chin began to quiver. "I think I'm in trouble."

Ooh, boy—here we go. I inched forward on the couch.

"All these rotten gang members I've secured jobs for seem to be setting me up," Rusler said in a voice thick with emotion. "Someone has been planning this revolt for a long time, and he took advantage of my ability to place people in key positions."

"Bingo," I said softly. I learned something pretty important there, which probably cleared Rusler, assuming he was telling her the truth.

Then the big loser started sniffling. "Mommy," he wailed. "Baby's scared."

Ewwww! Kinky.

Mrs. Rusler came and pressed her husband's head to her cantaloupe breasts. "Hush, now. You're such a smart boy, Kale. I know you'll work it out."

Gradually, his sniffling stopped. Her stroking of his hair slowed, and it started looking way less maternal and more erotic. "Kale, darling, I want you so badly that—"

Rusler jerked away, his tears suddenly dried. *"Now, Elizabeth? Don't you think I have worries enough?"*

What was it with these guys and their Madonna-harlot complexes?

"I have to go," he snapped, moving out of Billy's camera range.

After a fleeting rat-tat-tat of his distinctive walk, a door could be heard slamming. Mrs. Rusler flexed her lips pensively, before stuffing two whole Milanos into her mouth.

Just as fast, Billy's feed ended, and the talk show once again filled the TV screen.

Molly simpered girlishly to some chic African-American woman I'd probably know if I watched daytime TV. Still talking about her man, apparently.

Molly gushed, "He's so smart. Like an Egyptologist, sorta."

Whoa! I knew it. I snapped off the TV to process that thought in silence. I had sensed that the convergence of *The Power of the Pyramid*, with Molly's kidnapping, and Haggerty's goddess-ship, and my coming into the picture—was too coincidental not to be connected. And nobody believed me.

A sudden thought choked me. With me factored in there, that would mean all that had happened really was my fate. I felt scared all over again at what might await me out there, not just today, but in the years ahead. I gave my wild curly hair a toss to dispel the thought. No time to think of it now, I reminded myself. And if I had any sense, I'd never revisit it at all.

I turned instead to what Molly had said. How does someone become an Egyptologist—*sorta?*

CHAPTER THIRTY-ONE
Haggerty

With growing consciousness, Haggerty became aware of a dull throbbing behind her forehead. It wasn't one of her usual vision headaches, though. Her mouth felt so dry, it was hard to swallow. And she sensed a peculiar metallic taste in her mouth. Had she been drugged? She couldn't remember anything.

Her eyes were still closed; her lids felt too heavy to lift. As sensation returned to her body, she discovered she was lying on something hard. She found the strength to move the fingertips of one hand. It felt like a wooden floor below her.

She opened her eyes and raised herself up on one elbow. She was on the floor in the Museum of the Antiquities. How had she come to be there? She wasn't alone, either. Stretched out around her were the bodies of cops and museum employees. Dead? she thought, with a catch in her throat. No. She could see the slow rise and fall of their chests. Those people were deeply under. Some of them still clutched beverage containers or the remains of fast food in their hands. Their drinks, spilled when they fainted, pooled in brown puddles on the floor.

Just as the surprise of seeing all those bodies faded, another shock hit her. The museum's display cases were virtually empty. A few items remained, but most of those cases had been cleaned out. Samantha was right about the Egyptian connection. Who'd have thought?

Haggerty's purse was on the floor near to her foot. She started to reach for it, to see if her abductors had been careless enough to leave her Bureau-issued 9 mm. But she heard voices and the sound of someone's approach, so she sank back to the floor, feigning unconsciousness. Through narrowed eye slits, she watched a young Asian man come into view. Baggy jeans rested low on his narrow hips. He was naked from the waist up, and gang body-art covered every inch of his torso. He went to the last of the exhibit treasures, which he carelessly tossed into a box.

After he left, she heard another set of footsteps. A distinctive pattern this time, followed by a voice that she knew too well.

CHAPTER THIRTY-TWO
Samantha

The Egyptian connection continued to gnaw at me until I flashed on how I might learn the identity of Molly's man. In addition to videotapes, there were photos in that box her manager had provided. Behind-the-scenes shots. If Molly had spent any time on the set in his company, he might have been caught in those pictures.

I leaped to the box. A bee, which obviously viewed it as his territory, buzzed my head. Screw Haggerty's bug sanctuary—I swatted it away. I began hurling tapes to the floor. The phone rang before I could make it down to the photos beneath.

"Yeah?" I growled to the caller.

"And hello to you, too," Billy said just as sourly. "Did you catch it, Samantha? My feed from the Rusler's. See what I meant?"

I admitted that he had been right about Rusler being nothing more than an incompetent dupe. A creepy one at that. "Okay, let's forget about Rusler. Now I need you to check out the Museum of the Antiquities. There's a chance Haggerty could be there." She would disagree with the direction I was taking things, I knew, but I was in charge now.

Someone should have told that to Billy. "Hey, babe, this was a one-shot deal." he said. "I cleared Rusler for you in exchange for the apple. Now we're quits."

That bloated excuse for an FBI agent was really pissing me off. "Billy, how'd you like to be a gnome forever?" Okay, I'll admit it—I was itching to test the little gift Angus had given me. Good thing I wasn't really a Celtic goddess. I'd be forever drunk with power.

Billy must have believed I'd do it, since he began back-pedaling. "Maybe later, huh, Samantha? You know I'd help you if I could, but—"

"I know how fast you move between places, Billy. Do it—the museum. Now." Then remembering the carrot-and-stick theory Angus put forth, I softened my stance with, "Maybe Angus will give you another apple." Hell, *I* could give him one. I didn't say a *golden* apple.

That pushed him over. "Okay, I'll check it out. But that's it, Samantha. Don't you go asking for anything more."

Yeah, yeah, I thought, hanging up. Like I kept my word any better than he did.

I dove back into the carton. Only the phone rang again. The world was falling apart, but everyone had time to call? I grabbed the cordless, expecting it to be Billy, back with new arguments why he couldn't do as I asked. To my surprise, it was Angus.

"Samantha, is that you?" he shouted, as if to the profoundly deaf. "I followed that Lisa-girl from the FBI to a café near the museum. She's there now, constantly checking her watch and looking around, like she's waiting for someone."

The shock of Angus having telephoned drove his news about Lisa from my mind. After a few more eardrum-splitting responses, I discovered he was calling from a payphone across the street from the restaurant where Lisa waited.

"Angus, how did you get money for the phone?" He hadn't called collect. I doubted he would have known how. He obviously didn't have a clue about the volume required.

"It's absolutely brilliant. There's a drawer full of it right here in this phone. I told it to open for me, and it did," Angus explained. "There's lots more money here, Sammy. Want some?"

I hesitated. No, I couldn't let him do that. But impulse control was getting harder with practice, not easier. I told Angus to stay on Lisa because Rusler was probably in the clear. He promised to send me a message if he encountered anything interesting there.

Finally, I remembered my movement predicament. "Angus, wait. I might have to go somewhere. Can you give me the power to move around undetected?"

"Someone's coming, my girl. Got to be off. Why don't you talk to the flower fairies? Sounds like this would be right up their alley." With that, he hung up.

The flower fairies? Crap. I glanced at the vase of cut flowers. I should have been nicer to them, huh? Too late now. I considered trying to make amends, but I couldn't grovel before those stupid fairy bugs. Instead, I attacked Molly's carton again.

Only the phone rang for the third time. Sheesh! Maybe I

should just stand there, waiting for it to ring. This time I didn't vent my anger to the caller, however. I was secretly grateful for anything that put off my begging forgiveness from gnats I could barely see.

It was Billy once more. "Samantha, you're not gonna believe this," he said, his voice shaky.

Uh-oh. It must have taken a lot to rattle that old cynic. I wasn't sure I wanted to know what could do that.

"Annabelle is not here now, but she was. I found her purse on the floor. And...uh," he stammered and gulped. "Cops—unconscious, everywhere. And the joint has been cleaned out—all the artifacts are gone. The doors were left wide open. No alarm going, no nothing."

Having my own suspicions confirmed gave me the heebie-jeebies. Too stunned to process it, I yanked the stack of photos out and absently began pawing through them. Further distracting myself, I changed the subject with Billy. "Are you calling from your cell phone?" Maybe he was just discovering payphones, too.

His sigh at my stupidity came through loud and clear. "I'm not *using* a cell phone, Samantha, I've *become* one."

No question, shape-shifting was the way to go. Why had I ever thought being a Celtic goddess could beat that?

While continuing to flip through photos, I said, "Now, Billy, what I need is for you to come back here and get me."

"No dice, kid. I said I'd go to the museum, and I have. This time we're through."

"Gnome, Billy," I said.

I said it only half-heartedly. Because while I spoke, I flipped a photo over—and that next shot captured my attention. It was taken on the set of the movie "Cairo Caper." That was the film in which Molly initially locked horns with the American police detective who tracked her to Egypt, believing her to be an antiquities smuggler, before making him fall in love with her—unlike all her other pictures in which she locked horns with men in other professions, before making them fall in love with her. The photographer had caught Molly hanging over the occupant of a canvas movie set chair, on which the word "consultant" had been stenciled, though the consultant himself was turned away from the camera. Next to Molly stood a slight blonde woman a few years younger than the star. The younger woman bore such a striking resemblance to Molly, she might have been her sister.

Molly's stand-in. I'd seen another photo of her in Molly's condo. Only Molly wasn't her sister—I realized now that I'd seen the stand-in's true sibling on the news. The one who worried that her sister could be a target, since she looked so much like Molly.

I flipped that photo over. The next picture in the stack must have been taken just an instant later. Everyone was in the same position, apart from the man in the consultant's chair, who had turned toward the camera. I gasped aloud when I saw who it was sitting in that expert's chair. So shocked was I by that photo, I dropped the whole stack to the floor. Suddenly, a lecture I'd dismissed earlier made a whole lot more sense.

Without warning, yet another connection fell into place. I grasped the significance of one of the scenes I'd witnessed when flipping through those movie marathons with the remote control. How could I have been so stupid? How could Haggerty?

The repeated blows of so many revelations just wasted me. Vaguely, I heard Billy mutter something about putting himself out of "gnome-zapping range," along with his plans to melt down his apple, but I was powerless to react before he hung up.

It was only afterwards that the words, *melt down,* came back and hit me with a wallop.

CHAPTER THIRTY-THREE

The tidal wave of information that had come my way absolutely floored me. Yet I still couldn't bring myself to beg the bugs for help. I mean, I had my pride, right?

Instead, I went to Haggerty's home office. She had done a nice job of making the small room off her bedroom into an office. Covering one wall was a bookcase crammed with a variety of books, while a small rosewood desk had been placed below a window. A laptop computer and a telephone and answering machine rested on the desk.

Since I wasn't dorky enough to get into computers, I ignored the laptop and started yanking the desk drawers open. I found an address book in the second one I checked. What passed for an address book in my life was a stack of business cards and pieces of paper bound together by a rubber band. But I trusted Haggerty's highly developed sense of order, and she hadn't let me down. When I flipped to the "R" section, I found Rusler's home and cell phone numbers neatly printed.

With a sigh, I pulled the telephone toward me and dialed his cell. He answered with brusque identification.

"Hey there, Mr. Rusler," I said brightly. "It's me— Samantha."

The bastard didn't bother to disguise his groan.

"I think I know where Annabelle is," I said, rushing on. "So you can rescue her."

"And why would I want to do that?" the smarmy louse asked.

"But she—"

"Agent Haggerty has made her choices. Let her live with them," he snapped.

Pretty snotty for a guy who blubbered to his wife.

"I've had all I can take of you, too, Samantha. I'm ordering a patrol car to pass Agent Haggerty's house. If you set foot from it, I'll see you do hard time, you annoying fraud."

There were frauds, and there were frauds. The one that posed as an FBI Special Agent in Charge hung up on me then.

I went back to the guestroom for my own messy address-recording system. As I sorted through all those cards and scraps of paper, I had to admit there might be some advantage to Haggerty's organizational method. Next life, maybe.

Even though most of my friends, and even my clients, were lowlifes, there had to be someone in that stack who could help me. I flipped through the cards until I came across the most ideal person. So perfect I wondered why I hadn't thought of her before. Thoughtfully, I tapped my pink polished nail against the costly ivory business card and embossed purple ink that spelled out—Dodi Drake.

Ooh, problem alert! With all the excitement, I had forgotten my last appointment with Dodi. My best client, and I blew her off. Would she be the type to hold a grudge? You bet your ass she would. I started back toward the telephone, but changed my mind. It's too easy to hang up on someone you don't want to talk to. Rusler proved that.

Somehow I had to see her in person, appeal to her good graces. Which meant I really had no choice about dealing with the flower fairies. I trudged to the entry of the house, where I first encountered them in the planters.

I felt like a fool, but I said, "Hey, maybe we got off to a bad start. No question—my fault."

I waited for some response. Nothing. Could they speak? I went on then, spilling out the whole story. After a while, it felt pretty good, kinda like therapy must. Not that I'd ever know, with my income.

"And that's why I have to get to the *Bonne Chance,*" I concluded. "Only official vehicles can be out on the roads. But Dodi is a former vice presidential spouse—for her, getting permission should be a snap. She's Haggerty's last hope. What do you say?"

I waited again. Still nothing. I was about to shout at them once more, only then I began to feel myself shrinking. I jerked, clutching my own body with my hands. But I kept getting smaller. Smaller, smaller, smaller. Until I was thousand-of-angels-on-the-head-of-a-pin-sized. Well, maybe not that small, but I was pretty tiny.

There were always problems, it seemed. Granted, I could now move from the house without being noticed. Given the current length of my legs, it would take me a lifetime just to reach the sidewalk out front, not to mention going across town.

Only then a bee began to circle around me. Did they mean…?

"No!" I shouted. "Not the bee. *Please,* not the bee."

I couldn't do it. I couldn't ride that bee. I mean, what if it stung me? After a moment, it flew away. I waited. And waited. Nothing came to replace the bee. Had I blown it?

Just when I thought I'd have to grovel again before those stupid, vindictive teeny fairies, they came through. Sorta. A dragonfly, one of the ones that buzzed across the bowls of water Haggerty put out for them, came to rest beside me, swooping in for such a delicate landing, it moved with the grace of a glider.

A dragonfly. Bigger than the bee, of course. And they didn't sting. But it was still a bug.

I waited. It quivered, in anticipation perhaps, or annoyance because I didn't do anything. Oh, what the hell. I wanted a life filled with adventures, right? I climbed onto the dragonfly's back and held on. It lifted off as gracefully as it had landed. It swooped around the room, before flying toward the bathroom window, the only one I had left cracked a couple of inches, and simply whisked me away.

CHAPTER THIRTY-FOUR
Haggerty

Someone slapped Haggerty's face. "Come on, honey. Time to wake up," a vaguely familiar female voice said.

Haggerty had been feigning unconsciousness since she came to in the museum. It had worked, too. The two men who grabbed her by her ankles and arms and carried her to a truck filled with the stolen treasures hadn't suspected she was awake. She remained in that state even after they carried her from the truck at their destination, wherever that was; she hadn't risked even a peek when she arrived.

The woman slapped her again. And her voice grew sharper when she shouted, "Didn't you hear me? I said, *wake up.*"

Haggerty slowly fluttered her eyelids and found herself staring into a face she never expected to see. "Aren't you dead?" she asked.

Molly Claire laughed. "What's the point of having a stand-in if you can't make use of her when it counts?"

Haggerty supposed she followed that logic, even if she didn't know precisely how it had been pulled off. "You fooled us all into believing that body was yours."

Molly straightened and pulled Haggerty's own gun from her pocket, which she aimed at its owner. "Thanks to my sweetie, who encouraged one of his boys to take a job as my dentist's records clerk. After that it was a simple matter to convince my stand-in to use the same dentist so our x-rays could be switched."

It *was* simple. But that wasn't the extent of it, Haggerty guessed. They also had to bribe or coerce the medical examiner to limit his identification of the body believed to be Molly's to the dental x-rays. Haggerty remembered how he'd anxiously shredded the paper towel he held. In hindsight, it was so obvious. What was the point of having magical powers at her disposal, if she was so reluctant to use them? No matter how she wished it, she really wasn't an ordinary mortal being, after all.

195

Haggerty pulled herself into a sitting position and looked around. She was back in the foundry, which wasn't empty anymore. All the treasures from *The Power of the Pyramid* had been moved there. Pallet upon pallet, box stacked on box—objects revered for centuries, piled up to the high ceiling. The smelter had been fired up again. And some of the young men who had carried out the city's reign of terror were now retooling the equipment there. She had no doubts that the foundry would soon be turning out gold bricks.

Haggerty looked back at Molly, who still stood before her near the foundry door. "What about Molly's Clowns? Were they legit?" she asked.

Molly shrugged. "Actors. Wannabes, so desperate for the limelight they would risk prosecution. One of our crew was supposed to finish them all off, but Plotnik survived. Didn't matter, because he was so open to a deal, he didn't mind being put into a coma for a while."

That didn't explain how Plotnik's coma was brought about, or how he'd come out of it, but Haggerty was pretty sure she understood that now. She felt like such a fool. She kept insisting that the gang siege, with its inexplicable twists, was nothing but a smokescreen. But she never figured out what all that smoke had been screening. They turned the city on its ear, so that no one would realize the object was to raid the museum. Samantha had insisted that from the start. Which of them was the goddess?

Molly leaned over Haggerty again. "It was you I sent those images to, not that girl, Samantha. Right?" Molly asked. "Nobody believed me when I said I had paranormal abilities, so I knew nobody would suspect. But I'm crushed that you didn't recognize that I sent you images from movies I made earlier in my career."

Movie images? Haggerty had suffered blinding headaches so Molly Claire could flash movie scenes in her mind?

"You all underestimated me," Molly said, drawing away.

Haggerty knew she had. Molly looked cleaner now than in the bank robbery videos, but she wasn't dressed glamorously. She wore tight black knit pants and a dark top. Her wavy blonde hair had been shampooed and left to dry on its own, and her pretty face was devoid of makeup. But there was a glow about Molly, a magnetism that radiated from her, which told Haggerty this woman really was someone special. Yet she'd betrayed those gifts, as well as the people who'd once cherished her.

Molly strolled around the spot where Haggerty sat, gesturing with the gun. "Don't you want to know why?" Molly didn't wait for an answer before going on. "I'm Cleopatra. That is, I was in an earlier life. I'm just reclaiming my things."

Why did they always believe they were someone important in a prior life? Haggerty wondered. Were they never scullery maids? She rose to her feet, careful not to threaten Molly. Molly didn't seem to care about anything beyond securing Haggerty's praise.

Haggerty waited till she stood level with Molly, before laughing in her face. "Hah! I know Cleopatra, and she's nothing like you. History didn't record her accurately." How would this spoiled woman feel, if she were to learn Cleopatra was now a happy mother of three living in a Cairo suburb? As she always wished she could have been in the first part of her life. It was Cleopatra who had served her koushry, an Egyptian dish that Haggerty now kicked herself for not remembering.

"If you were Cleopatra, you wouldn't allow your family's treasures to be melted down," Haggerty snapped.

Doubt shadowed Molly's eyes. "It's just the smaller pieces we're melting down. The ones not worth transporting."

A Latino gang member passed close by, flashing a glance Molly's way that held amused contempt. If Haggerty had any doubts, that look would have negated them.

"You've been used to make someone else rich," Haggerty said.

Molly tightened her lips. "You're wrong. I'll prove it, too." She looked to the clubhouse doorway at the side of the foundry. "Darling, would you come out here?"

Haggerty heard the sound of that distinctive walk again. The scuffing that she once thought would peel away the finish on her living room floor. The sound that still had the power to tear her heart apart. The man behind the crime wave stepped into the doorway. The man Haggerty once entertained dreams of a future with.

Jake Azar.

He was dressed nearly the same as Molly, in black pants and a knit shirt. To his version of the look, he'd added the tan shoulder holster holding his gun. His dark eyes swept over Haggerty before moving on to Molly. If they reflected any triumph, or even regret, it passed too quickly for her to notice. Haggerty saw now that he had stopped restraining his aura. It was pitch black, while the melody that came off him sounded like a violin screaming.

Molly stomped her small sneaker-clad foot. "Jake, tell her she's wrong. Tell her we're not melting down the important pieces, that they're being returned intact to me."

For the first time, a smile played around the edges of Jake's lips. "No can do, Miss Molly. She's right as rain."

Molly opened her mouth to object. Before any sound could come out, Jake pulled the gun from his holster and fired at her. Molly's body fell to the floor.

When the sound of gunfire faded away, Jake looked at Haggerty and said with marked indifference, "This time, Miss Molly really has left the building for good."

CHAPTER THIRTY-FIVE
Samantha

The ride to the *Bonne Chance* tower on the back of the dragonfly gave me another reminder to be careful what I wished for. Sure, it wasn't as bad as riding a bee would have been. But did you know that urban dragonflies regard every swimming pool as another pond to be buzzed and claimed? Do you know how many pools fill the landscape between Haggerty's house and the *Bonne Chance?* When the dragonfly finally blew in for a landing in the luxury condo's driveway, I was soaked. Worst still, I felt I had to mutter thanks to my bug transport when I climbed off, just in case I needed it again. With a little luck, I wouldn't need it, however. And, man, was I due for some luck.

Like every other place in the city, the *Bonne Chance* was locked up tight. No valet today, naturally, and security gates closed off the garage. I still didn't know how this would all work; I trusted the flower bugs to know what they were doing.

The dragonfly had set down on the driveway just outside the garage gates. With a three-inch clearance under the gate, I had no trouble making my way into the garage, naturally, since I was only a couple of inches high. Just when my nerves began to settle, however, I suddenly began expanding. As rapidly as Billy Finkner had when I tackled him in his gnome state.

Thirty seconds later, I was back to full size. And I did mean full. Rats! I was hoping to come back smaller. Well, thinner. What can I say? Even if Angus did love my body, like every other pudgy female from this century, there was a thin Samantha inside me screaming to get out. Fortunately, if I fed her enough chocolate, she kept her mouth shut.

Uncertain of what would be expected of me today, I'd worn pants and a T-shirt, which were now sopping wet. Amazingly, my clothes had contracted and expanded along with my body. Checking again to make sure I had my purloined *Bonne Chance* keycard where I placed it in my pocket, I loped across the garage toward the elevator.

A woman's voice, from somewhere within that car tomb, stopped me. "Hey, you. You, fortune-teller-lady. Wait up."

Fortune-teller-lady? The check-in chick from the front desk came toward me. Not running exactly, but walking just as fast as possible when someone carried her change-purse in her butt. I expected her to try to throw me out, and I was prepared to deck her. But she surprised me.

She gave her eyelids a few rapid blinks, and glanced at my wet things. "Is it raining?"

"Depends how you define 'rain.' What do you want?"

"I was hoping I'd see you again before I left here. You were right about this place. They accused me of stealing keycards. Can you believe it?"

Cards—plural? She really wasn't much of a guard if she kept letting people make off with them.

"They've forced me to stay down here in my car until Marshall Law is lifted. They won't even let me into the valet break room, where I could lie down or use the bathroom." She sniffed, nearly in tears by the end of her pity party.

What the hell. I was responsible, after all. I showed her my keycard. "Where is it? I'll let you in." When her eyes narrowed on me in suspicion, I added, "Dodi gave it to me."

The check-in girl snorted. "Oh, yeah—Mrs. Drake. She gave me strict orders that Madame Samantha wasn't to grace her door again. Apparently, you did something unforgivable."

I was afraid Dodi would hold a grudge.

The girl gave her straight hair a decisive swing. "You're lucky that card still works. There's a service call in for the technician to reprogram all the cards, but he can't get here now. I'll tell you what—you let me in to the valet room, and I won't stop you from going up to Mrs. Drake's unit. I don't owe these bastards anything after the way they've treated me."

We hurried together to the door of the valet break room. One pass of my keycard and the door clicked open. I took a gander at it before leaving. Nice sofa, kitchenette, bath—I began to feel I'd done her a favor by getting her fired. Once I got Ms. Blinks settled, I rushed to the elevator.

Dodi's floor was as quiet as a morgue. All the doors were closed, and nobody even peeked into the hall. Chicken-shit rich people—I'd ridden a dragonfly to get there. I rapped hard on her door. When nobody answered, I pressed my eye to the peephole. Another eye peered back at me, and then went away. I expected to have to make a total pest of myself, which fortunately came easily to me. But Gus, her Secret Service agent, admitted me after a moment, and showed me into the living room.

Impeccably dressed, as always, in one of her pastel knit suits, with her purple highlighted hair, Dodi paced at the far end of room, glaring at me. "Did we forget something, Madame Samantha? Such as an appointment with an important client. Or even," she gestured at my clothes, "your special things."

Apart from her money, the only good thing I could say about Dodi was that she admired my taste in clothes.

"I know I screwed up, Mrs. Drake, but you're not going to believe what's happened this week. You can take it out on me, but not my friend. It's in your power to decide whether she lives or dies."

"Cut the drama, you—"

I broke in before she could get nasty. Keeping all the supernatural stuff out of it, I told her about Haggerty and where I thought she was being held. And then I begged for her help.

"Why should I?" she demanded.

"Because I know you're a good person, and you won't let an innocent woman die," I said, selling the lie with all my might.

"You were misinformed," she answered coldly. Then, to my shock, she suddenly relented. "I'll make a deal with you, Madame Samantha. You give me a reading now, at no cost, naturally. And I'll *consider* helping your friend."

She wouldn't, I knew. She was too angry and vindictive. I felt so mad at her, I decided to pay back her in kind.

We took our usual places on the sofa. I closed my eyes and did a quickie rendition of my swoon. "There's been a change of climate on the other side. Manfred is seething with jealously over Jason. He demands that you end it instantly."

"Really? Tell me more."

The sudden warmth in her voice caused my eyelids to fly open. Her cheeks were flushed with pleasure. Was *that* what she wanted to hear? What was wrong with me? I knew she was petty. I should've imagined that she'd want to stick it to the old man, even in the afterlife. *When* would I figure out what it took to be a good fake psychic?

Once I had a handle on the deal there, I really laid it on, describing all of Fred-man's outraged reactions in detail. I'd known enough buttheads in my time; it wasn't hard to make it sound realistic. To my complete surprise, when the reading wound down, Dodi went to her desk and pulled a fistful of cash out of a drawer, which she stuffed into my hand.

"Next time, Samantha, dress less ordinary," she insisted. "Now, how can I help your friend?"

I told her I needed her to call the Director of the FBI and get him to order Rusler to rescue Haggerty. She left to place the call from another room. When she returned, anger pinched her well-bred face.

"Apparently, being a former Vice Presidential widow doesn't carry as much weight as I thought. The Director wouldn't even take my call." She walked to the desk and picked up her small designer purse. "However, they are faxing me a pass that will allow me to take my car out. Gus and I will help you. Jason hasn't been coming around as often lately, so I need all the excitement I can get."

Gus shook his head. "Mrs. Drake, I can't allow you to leave here. It's too dangerous."

Dodi directed her steely gaze his way. "Gus, have I ever let you win that argument?" A phone rang in another room. "Now go get the fax, and let's be off. Your friend is in our hands, Samantha."

That was what I was afraid of. I felt more anxious now than when I rode the dragonfly.

CHAPTER THIRTY-SIX
Haggerty

"So, Jake, the whole thing was a setup right from the start," Haggerty said. "Molly's kidnapping, the Clowns—everything." As well as the gift of coffee and donuts at the museum, she realized, which lowered Lieutenant Nobel's guard enough to accept another round without question.

He nodded, while watching his men work. "Speed it up," Jake shouted to them. "I want it all in bars before nightfall."

That meant Haggerty had to work fast, too. She couldn't let him carry out his plans, although she didn't know how she would stop him. At her feet, Molly Claire's blood ran along the concrete floor, as she clung to life. With that blood loss, she couldn't have long.

Haggerty tried to draw Jake's attention to her, away from Molly. She asked how he came to implicate Rusler and Lisa. She'd never yet met a criminal who didn't love to brag.

He laughed. "If you only knew how many frames I had in place. Business leaders, like the guy who owns this foundry. Politicians, philanthropists. Men like Rusler, who twist arms to get these kids jobs. I didn't know I'd wind up working with the Bureau. But I had a lot in play, and it took so little to bend it this way or that. It was sheer chance that all our paths crossed as they did."

Was it, though? "All for the money, right, Jake? That's why you did it?" she asked.

Jake's face darkened with fury. "For *my* money, for what's been due me and mine for centuries. Unlike Molly who thought this should all be hers, I *knew* it. My ancestors guarded the Pharaohs, just as I guard the people of L.A. And what do I get out of it? When I heard the exhibit was coming here, I knew this was my chance to make things right."

A small gold cup had fallen on the floor next to Jake's foot. He gave it a vicious kick. So much for his legacy.

"And me—that was part of the setup, too. Right?"

Jake's dark eyes met hers. "Maybe at the beginning, but you and me, Annabelle, with all the magic we share, we could be so good together."

He took a step closer, leaning without regard over Molly's body. With his fingertip, he gently traced the outline of her lips. To her eternal regret, she felt her body responding to his touch.

Jake took a step back. "Of course, we both know you would never cross over to this side of life."

Haggerty laughed in his face. Not her usual laugh, the ordinary sound that she used before mortals, but the musical, tinkling laugh that all of the gods shared. "I might join you, if I thought you were anything more than an ordinary man," she said, not meaning a word of it.

Jake thrust his gun closer to her chest. "How dare—"

She held her hand up, seemingly unconcerned by the weapon. "Trust me, I know a little about how powers get diluted over time." She shrugged. "Sure, you retain some remnant of your ancestors' gifts. You were able to contain your aura, and shelter your true thoughts and feelings. You even picked up on me, that I was the one receiving Molly's visions, not Samantha. That's why you kidnapped me. But that's only because I was careless occasionally, and let my guard down." Careless? Or had some part of her wanted to reveal the truth to him? Shame nearly gagged her.

"I'm warning you—"

Haggerty risked strolling away from Molly. As she'd hoped, Jake followed her. "Sure, you still possess the recipes for the potions the ancient Egyptians used. That's how you were able to put Plotnik in a coma and bring him out. But you did it by injecting the stuff into his IV with an ordinary syringe. That's not supernatural, Jake."

Something that looked like fear flickered through Jake's black eyes.

"What a busy boy you were that morning after we found Molly's stand-in's body. Injecting Plotnik's IV to bring him back to consciousness, so he could leave the hospital, then stringing Samantha up—how it must have pained you to be the one to rescue her."

Now such anger flared on his face that steam practically rose from his ears. He was out of control—precisely how Haggerty wanted him. She threw a quick glance around the foundry to confirm that the men working for him were too intent on their own tasks to pay attention to them. She didn't think she could take them all on.

"Lucky little bitch!" Jake snapped. "I had every intention of dropping her into that vat. It was just my bad luck that her necklace caught in my zipper."

"That wasn't bad luck, it was me—I made it happen. Unlike you, I have strong powers. But you, Jake, you're little more than an ordinary mortal man. Everything you did was carried out in such a mundane fashion. Such as when we searched all over town for gang members. Sure, you and Mrs. Terry and Jorge put on outstanding little performances for Samantha and me. But you passed instructions to them by writing codes on your business cards." When his jaw dropped, Haggerty laughed again. "Yes, I figured that out." Even if too late.

"How can you say that?" With a wave of his gun, Jake gestured to the men working in that foundry. "I united them. *Me*. Nobody else has ever succeeded in doing that. No one else has ever masterminded such a daring crime."

"You simply appealed to their greed better than anyone else." After a pause, Haggerty went on. "You have great charisma and personal power, and they've taken you far. But you're still just an ordinary *thug.*"

"But I've won, Annabelle. And you've lost."

A teenage boy working at the smelter called to Jake. "Looks like we're ready, boss."

With a smug grin, Jake nodded his approval. "Then let's roll."

No! She couldn't allow them to melt down all those treasures. She knew what she had to do. She'd devoted her life to defending what was right. She couldn't do less now, even though what she planned would probably be her last act on this plane that she loved so much.

She closed her eyes and prayed to her ancestors. Then drawing on all her powers, every bit of her energy, she gave a silent command, unsure whether she was a strong enough goddess to pull it off.

Within an instant, every single artifact, down to the kicked cup on the floor—just vanished.

Everyone froze in shocked silence. The men working there

began to scream, to cry out in fear. They looked at her seeming to sense that she made it happen. One by one they ran into the clubhouse in fright.

"What—" Jake sputtered. His eyes widened when he stared at Haggerty. Then he directed his stunned gaze to all the missing pallets and boxes that had once held those riches. "You bitch!" He jabbed the gun in her direction. "Bring them back, Annabelle. This minute, you hear? *Bring them back!*"

Haggerty couldn't hear him. Her basic senses scarcely operated anymore. Drained of all her energy, she began to sway, powerless now to save herself.

CHAPTER THIRTY-SEVEN
Samantha

My impatience just about killed me. Despite the lack of normal traffic, the trip to the foundry took forever, since we were stopped at every checkpoint, and each time Dodi had to impress upon the soldiers manning them how important she was.

All the while, I kept second-guessing myself. Was it really Jake who hung me up over that lava pool, who hired Billy to spy on me? Our Jake? But once I saw his face in that photo when he had served as a police advisor on one of Molly's movies, and noticed the way she nuzzled up to him, it all fell into place. I didn't get how he was "an Egyptologist, sorta." Unless that was what you call guys who intend to steal everything ancient Egypt produced. But still, how could I be sure I hadn't put things together wrong? Were they really at the foundry, ready to melt everything down? Was it already too late for Haggerty?

We finally made it there. When I saw the lot was filled with cars and trucks, that convinced me my theory was right. Even before Gus brought Dodi's limo to a stop, I threw the rear door open and jumped out. I ran to the foundry door, whose earlier bullet holes were now covered by duct tape, and pressed my ear against it.

"Bring it back, Annabelle, all of it—or you're dead. I swear," Jake screamed from behind the door.

Yes, I was right! With no time to spare, I ran back to Gus and Dodi, who were making their way from where Gus had left the limo in the street. I grabbed his hand and dragged him toward the door, explaining as we went that he would have to kick it in.

Dodi, I saw, took cover behind some pickup truck. So much for her spirit of adventure. Gus gave the door a hard kick. It flew open. While he moved to the side to protect himself, I pushed past him. I stopped just inside the door and took it all in at once: Molly Claire lying on the floor, Haggerty swaying into a faint, Jake taking aim at Haggerty. What I did not see was all the stolen stuff, which I'd felt certain would be there.

Suddenly, shocking me further still, Plotnik appeared in the room. Just appeared! Only he was caked in ice now, like some really ugly wedding reception sculpture. Angus said he would send me a message. It must have been Plotnik who met with Lisa. A meeting that Angus, in his own special way, had just broken up.

The sight of his frozen cohort incensed Jake to his limit. As if in slow motion, I saw his trigger finger begin to flex. With no thought in my head, I just threw myself at Haggerty, knocking her to the floor.

I felt the bullet pass through my hair.

Almost instantly, I heard another shot. When I risked lifting my eyes, I saw Gus had returned fire, hitting Jake right in the chest.

CHAPTER THIRTY-EIGHT

Jake died before they could get him to the hospital. Later, Haggerty told me how she'd taunted him with being much more of an ordinary man than a supernatural being. He sure died like one. Maybe his story would serve as a lesson for future woo-woo bad guys: Use a gnome, go to the morgue.

Amazingly, Molly survived. Too bad for her the court-appointed shrink determined she wasn't sane enough to stand trial. I mean, thinking she's Cleopatra, believing a cop could put people into comas, not to mention gods and goddesses—where did she get this stuff? You might think she was getting off easy, but Molly would've loved a trial. She'd grandstand start to finish, just as Plotnik had, and get off. For her, being put away without an audience was the worst possible punishment.

Of course, nobody really wanted a trial, given all the things that couldn't be explained. Such as why all the items stolen from the museum were found floating on a diving platform that had broken loose from its mooring, off the Malibu coast, where it was being pushed out to sea by a pod of dolphins. And why the icy shell around Plotnik refused to melt.

The days that followed passed in a blur. Though the mopping up was expected to last for months, it didn't take long to restore order. Without Jake to lead them, the gang members who'd united behind him surrendered in droves. Many of the cops who questioned them remarked on how docile they'd become. If those cops knew what some of those guys had seen happen in the foundry, which Haggerty related to me in detail, they might not find it so strange.

And hey, I finally achieved my objective. As the one heroine to emerge from the whole sorry saga, I attained instant notoriety. One reporter after another described my participation in the caper with the words, "Celebrity psychic, Samantha Brennan, saved the day." I was downplaying the Celtic goddess part for the masses. They might make me Molly's roommate.

And man, were the bucks rolling in. I had more clients now

than I could handle. People flew in from other parts of the country, just to pay for my mumbo-jumbo. Sadly, I hadn't put much money aside for my move to Sedona yet. What can I say? My favorite vintage shop got in a shipment of duds from some Shakespearean acting troupe. You don't want to know how much I dropped there.

Next to me, Lisa came out the best. She received a commendation for tracking Plotnik down before he...you know, got iced. The funny thing was I was right that day at the hospital when I thought she was getting awfully sneaky in order to outshine everyone else on the taskforce. How weird that I would get such a strong sense of something that proved to be true. It wasn't like I was psychic or anything. Hell, it wasn't like I was even a good judge of people.

With that commendation, Lisa decided she'd achieved all she needed in law enforcement. She quit the Bureau and moved on to the next phase of her life. Not teaching, as I'd predicted. She joined some biker gang and was writing articles about their adventures. Go figure. She really didn't have the wardrobe for it.

I hadn't seen Haggerty since that day, when we were both rushed to the hospital. Me, they released almost immediately. Finding her suffering from extreme exhaustion, they kept her there for two days. She might have recovered quicker if I hadn't kept pumping her for everything I missed in the foundry. But I'd invested too much time and effort into our caper to miss a thing.

I'd learned from Dodi that Haggerty wasn't working for Rusler anymore. Dodi didn't take being ignored lightly, even if it was in the midst of a wave of civil unrest. She eventually got through to the Bureau Director. After chewing him out for the really important matter of not taking her call, she also told him how Rusler refused to come to the aid of one of his subordinates because she'd rebuffed his sexual advances. He's on suspension now, pending an investigation. And if you can believe it, they've put Billy in charge of the L.A. Field Office. I think he'd be a pretty cool guy, uh, shape-shifter, to work for. I wondered how Haggerty felt reporting to one of her own, so to speak.

She called me a few months later. It seemed I was entitled to a portion of a reward someone put up during the worst of the siege. Yay! More great dresses. We agreed to meet for coffee so she could hand over my check.

I almost didn't recognize her when she walked through the

door. She still wore a suit, but a less tailored one than she used to. Her hair also waved loosely to her shoulders. And her face looked brighter somehow. I expected to see the effect of Jake's betrayal, but if she was still suffering, it didn't show. Who knows? Maybe when you perform a miracle like she did, at great risk to your own life, sorrow just can't measure up.

She directed a jerky smile at me, then quickly looked away while she waited in line for coffee. Even after she took the seat across the small table from me, she seemed uncomfortable. Adjusting her skirt, sipping her coffee, studying the posters on the walls too determinedly.

Finally, with a heavy sigh, her eyes met mine. "You saved my life, Samantha. How can I—" She broke off when her throat required unexpected clearing.

I got it—she felt embarrassed. As a goddess, she was unaccustomed to feeling beholden.

With a straight face, I said, "In some cultures that would mean I'm responsible for you now. Fortunately, this isn't one of them." I broke into a giggle. *"Really* fortunate for you."

Haggerty finally joined me in a natural laugh.

Theoretically, since we had both saved each other, our debts should have cancelled out. Yet somehow, they felt stronger than ever.

Taking refuge in small talk, Haggerty said, "I hear you and Angus are still together."

In addition to being my lover, Angus had also become my mischief mentor. Haggerty obviously hadn't heard rumors of some of the stunts we, and a few other gods, had pulled. She'd probably say the last thing I needed in my life was a bad influence, but as far as I was concerned, you can never have too much mischief.

She lifted her coffee container to me in a salute.

I flushed. "I know it can't last. He'll never grow any older, while I'm..." I gulped. "Twenty-nine and counting."

She shrugged. "Never know. You might join the family yet."

Wouldn't that be something? I'd always wanted to be some family's black sheep, and in mine, I didn't even qualify as a finalist.

When we ran out of things to say, Haggerty rose and gathered her things to leave. Of course, she told me to stay in touch, and of course, I said I would. But that wasn't gonna happen. Not like girlfriends or anything.

Yet Haggerty and me, we were bound together in a different way. I had a feeling our paths would cross again because that was my...fate. There I said it. Nothing else could explain what had happened to me since that clown car came my way. I still didn't know how much of life was scripted, and I wasn't gonna get all philosophical or anything. But sometimes I found myself thinking about a question Haggerty had posed: Why are we here? Haggerty felt certain it was to learn something. I figured it was so when we arrived at this time and place, we'd each be there to watch the other's back. That was good enough for me.

Haggerty had nearly reached the door when she turned back with another thought. "Samantha, you might want to explore your own special—" She seemed to remember where she was then, because she looked around at the other inhabitants of that coffee house. She went on to conclude with, "Your own special gifts. You do seem to have some, you know." After leaving me with that thought, she walked away.

Me, the real thing? No way. I could maybe handle Celtic deity in-law. If it happened, I mean. Otherwise, I was a total sham all the way, and that's the way I wanted it.

Still, I couldn't live in complete denial anymore. Not with all I'd seen. Who would have thought that I, Samantha Brennan, the most devout skeptic in the Western world, would someday—woo-woo?

But that was my destiny. What a concept, huh? I could hardly wait for my next adventure. Wouldn't it be a hoot if I actually made it to Sedona? Or went in search of aliens or UFOs. I never believed in aliens, but I never believed in gods, either, and look at how that turned out. Or, now that I was a celebrity, maybe I'd cozy up to rock stars, become a real A-list person. Or... Hah! As if. What a goof I was.

Guess I'd just have to wait and see what fate had in store for me.

Acknowledgments

The idea for the first short story in which Samantha and Annabelle appeared came to me on a trip to Sedona, before I moved here. I credit the red rocks and their powerful energy for inspiring and sustaining these characters and their ongoing adventures.

Special thanks also go to:

- Jo Grossman, for her suggestions and support of this book;
- Jack Trimarco, who told me about the workings of the F.B.I., although I added a strong supernatural streak to my version;
- Susan Budavari and Suzanne Flaig, publishers of Red Coyote Press, for giving Samantha and Annabelle a home, first when they included my short story, "Hocus Pocus on Friday the 13th," in their *Medium of Murder* anthology, and now with this novel;
- Sedona's readers and writers, to whom this book is dedicated — I cherish your presence in my life;
- And especially, my husband, Joe, my eternal cheerleader, for his unfailing support and encouragement.

Kris Neri is the author of the Agatha, Anthony and Macavity Award-nominated Tracy Eaton mysteries, *Revenge of the Gypsy Queen, Dem Bones' Revenge* and the forthcoming *Revenge for Old Times' Sake*. Her other books include *Never Say Die* and *The Rose in the Snow*. She has published sixty short stories and is a two-time Derringer Award-winner and a two-time Pushcart Prize-nominee for her short mystery fiction. With her husband, she owns The Well Red Coyote bookstore in Sedona, Arizona. Kris is hard at work on the next title in this series, *Magical Alienation*. Readers can reach her through her website, www.krisneri.com.